Saral Sarkar

From Kamrabad to Cologne. Wanderer Between Two Worlds

Autobiography of a Modestly Known Indian

To Biggi and Jakob (Brigitta and Jakob Perings),

without whose multifarious help in
leading my everyday old-age life, with Maria and alone,
writing this autobiography would not have been possible at all.

From Kamrabad to Cologne

Wanderer Between Two Worlds

Autobiography of a Modestly Known Indian

Druck: Libri Plureos GmbH, Friedensallee 273, 22763 Hamburg

Bibliografische Information der Deutschen Nationalbibliothek: Die Deutsche Nationalbibliothek verzeichnet diese Publikation in der Deutschen Nationalbibliografie; detail-
lierte bibliografische Daten sind im Internet über dnb.dnb.de abrufbar.

Kontakt: saralsarkar@t-online.de, ernst.schriefl@chello.at

Buchsatz und Covergestaltung: Ernst Schriefl

Bildnachweis: Alle in diesem Buch verwendeten Photos (inkl. Cover) stammen aus dem
Privatarchiv von Saral Sarkar.

Verlag: BoD · Books on Demand GmbH, In de Tarpen 42, 22848 Norderstedt, bod@bod.de

ISBN: 978-3-7597-8817-7

Table of contents

Preface

Now that I have finished my last serious book[*], but am still living, some of my friends have been telling me that I should now write my memoirs or my autobiography, whatever I would like to call it. I have been hesitating, because I am now 88 years old, and my health is fragile. I do not know how long I would still live, nor how much time I still have to write about my modestly eventful life. Nor do I know whether my life-story would interest anybody. These friends say it would, because I am, as they express it, a rare person who has spent half of his 88 years long life in India – in spite of all economic development, still a poor and backward country – and half in Germany, one of the richest and most modern countries of the world. I have experienced, have had intimate knowledge of, life in the East and the West, in the North and the South. I have taken part in political and social movements in both, thought, studied and written about these. One of the friends said, history should better be written by people who lived it.

I have now acceded to their pleadings, started writing this life story. I have nothing else to do, so why not. I cannot possibly commit suicide out of boredom. But, in my mind, the doubt remains: Will it be regarded as just a pastime of an old man? I remember Nirod Chaudhury, a Bengali intellectual, much more known in his active days in his native West Bengal than I am today in Germany or even Cologne. Chaudhury wrote his autobiography – at which age I do not remember – and called it "Autobiography of an unknown Indian". Maybe he was too modest or only pretended to be modest. But the title encourages me. I think I have also many interesting political matters to narrate about.

I have given much space to my childhood, because it lies now so far back in time, more than 80 years. It is as if I am describing a journey to an almost different, till now unknown country. Moreover, my nephews

____

[*] Sarkar, Saral (2024): Factors of Conflict and Conditions of Peace. An Essay, Books on Demand

and nieces and their children ask me often about my childhood days. They are eager to know about their heritage.

But I have not neglected to describe the thorny road I have had to traverse to reach my present life and my present thoughts and conclusions. I hope, apart from being interesting, it would also be useful for all young and old political activists.

Finally, I want to remind the readers that an autobiography is not an history of the particular decades. It is the story of the decades as perceived by the author. It is mainly centered around his life-story. The quality of the story depends entirely on the quality of the perceptions of the author.

And just another word, with age, my memory has also blurred a lot. Many details, which could have been interesting, are missing. I hope the sympathetic reader will excuse me for this shortcoming of the text.

Last but not least, I want to take this opportunity to express my heartfelt thanks to my Viennese friend Ernst Schriefl, who has edited and typeset this text, not only this text, but all my other writings that have seen the light of day since August 2023.

Chapter 1:
Childhood, Fatherland, Motherland, Family Background

My early childhood was not so interesting. I was born as the fifth child of my parents. I cannot say whether I was a desired child, because my parents already had two sons and two daughters. Nowadays, we would think, already the fifth child is going to be a burden. In Germany, in the recent past, I have often heard, having a child is a "poverty factor" ("Armutsfaktor") – in Germany, one of the richest countries of the world. A few years ago, I read a report on 10 young German women who wanted to have a child, but could not find a suitable young man as a willing partner. But I do not know how people thought in those days – be it in India, be it in Germany. Apparently, in India as well as in Germany, children were regarded as products of God's wish. They had therefore to be welcomed, gladly or grumpily.

When I studied German and later married Maria, my German fiancé, I came to know more about the situation in Germany in those days. Maria, born in 1931, was the seventh child in a small peasant family of 12 children. I, in contrast, also a product of the 30s of the 20th century, belonged to a six children family.

In my childhood, our family consisted of six children and the two parents. That was the average family size around us. When I was eight years old, I came to know families that consisted of as many as ten children, two parents, and one or two grandparents. And, moreover, some relatives, near or distant, used to live as members of the family. In our family too.

In an average family, children used to be brought up carelessly, and often sons were treated very badly, they were even beaten by the fathers, sometimes even by the mother, for allegedly bad behavior. I cannot say, probably my eldest brother and my eldest sister were treated lovingly.

After all, they must have been well desired children. But I do not remember having ever been taken on my parents' arms or cuddled by some of my parents and elder siblings.

Father's Land

My father came from a family that originally lived in what is since 1971 called Bangladesh. They were administrators by tradition; his father was employed in the administration of a tax-collecting landlord (*Zamindar*) of East Bengal. The village where they lived was situated roughly at the confluence of two great rivers – the *Padma*, which is the name of the main arm of the Ganges when it passes through East Bengal, and *Yamuna*, which is the name of the other big river which comes from the North-East, i.e., Brahmaputra.

River scene in Bangladesh. Photo credit: Saral Sarkar

Together, they transport the whole rain- and snowmelt on both sides of the Himalayas and Northern India to the Bay of Bengal. In the dry summer months, they are fed by the Himalayan glaciers. Try to imagine a village in such a location in East Bengal in the year 1900, when my father was born. There were no dikes on the banks of the two great rivers. That meant, every year, in the rainy season, as a matter of routine, the village and all the surrounding areas were flooded by the waters of the two rivers. My father told us how they went to school (just primary school, of course) wading through flooded village roads/pathways. The mud-hut buildings, [clay-built] big or small, in which they lived, of course, were built on raised platforms, also built of mud [clay], so that they were not flooded. Children who went to school, before they came down on the flooded village pathways, had to take off their clothes and hold them on the head, so that they would not get wet.

My father also told us, that peasants in their region planted a special species of rice that grew in height simultaneously, when the water level on the fields rose, so that the ears of corn always remained above water. The corn generally ripened before the water had receded from the fields. And the peasants had to do the harvesting in knee-deep water.

Before I could see with my own eyes one of these two mighty rivers of my home country (Desh, Pitribhumi, in Bangla; Heimat, Vaterland, in German), I had the opportunity to see the two "mighty" rivers of Western Europe: the Rhine and the Danube. I saw the Rhine already as a student in Germany in the 1960s. And now I am living in Cologne for the last 42 years. Impressive, of course. But then, sometime in the 1990s (I have forgotten, in which year exactly), Maria and I had an invitation from a best female friend of hers, a native of Bangladesh (Farida Akhtar), to visit her and her NGO establishment in Dhaka and the adjacent rural areas, where their development projects were located. I expressed the wish to see one of the two mighty rivers of my fatherland ("Desh"). They fulfilled this wish of mine on our way back from one of their projects. I stood on the east bank of the river Yamuna. On the west bank was my "*desh*" (fatherland), the region where my father came from. It was afternoon of a clear sunny day in late August. Yet I could not see the west bank. There was nothing but the river in front of me, a vast expanse of water. It was as if I was standing on the shore of a peaceful sea. It was almost the end of the rainy season. Our hosts told us, when the water level goes down at the end of the rainy season, one can see some large uninhabited sand-banks (called "*Char*" in Bangla) in the middle of the river. These Chars were probably not just useless sandbanks. They must have been useful for something, maybe for cultivating melons. For I heard from one of our young "uncles" (a relative of father, who came to live with us) that big landlords used to try to occupy Char-lands when they emerged. Often their respective "armed" groups fought it out.

From the unsystematic and rare narrations of my father, some relayed to me by my eldest sister in later years of my life, I could gather that life at the confluence of the two large rivers had another problem, namely, the two rivers used to gnaw away land at the banks. Oftentimes, whole villages (or parts thereof) were eroded away by the currents of the two mighty rivers, and the residents of the destroyed villages had to move further away from the banks and build new houses. Sometime in my childhood, I heard a song on this phenomenon – composed, however, by a city-dwelling poet. The first two lines of the song read: "The river breaks this bank and builds up the other. That is the game of the river." From the narrations of my father, I could further gather that the family lived in three different villages in that region: Kurhigram, Bagmara, and Sonapadma. The reason, I guess, was this phenomenon of erosion. Once he also spoke of a huge fire that destroyed their house. No wonder, in those days, the houses in Bengal villages were mostly thatched with rice straw.

Father did not tell us (or I did not get it) in which of these three villa-ges he went to his first school. But one story I vividly remember. It was surely about going to the secondary school. His elder brother was already in secondary school in the town nearby. I cannot say exactly in which town that school was. Maybe it was called Rangpur or Berhampur. Both are situated in North Bengal. My grandfather had to send money to the elder son for his school, boarding, and lodging expenses. He once asked my father, the younger of the two sons, to bring the cash to his elder brother in the town where this school was. My father resented that only the elder son was sent to the secondary school and not he too. After reaching the town (let me suppose it was Rangpur), he said the money was for both the brothers to go to school. Father did not go back home after that, stayed back in the town and went to the same school.

There, father used to tell us very proudly, Kalidas Roy, who later became somewhat famous as a poet, was one of their teachers. I remember having read a poem by this poet as a part of our reading material on Bangla literature. Many years later, when father had retired from service and we had settled down in Calcutta, he heard that also poet Kalidas Roy, had left East Bengal and was living then as an old man in Calcutta. Father took up contact with his former teacher. He also invited poet Roy to the party he gave on the occasion of the marriage of his eldest son, my eldest brother.

I did not get it directly and clearly, but somehow, mostly by asking my eldest sister, who knew more, that after finishing high school, father went to college in the town of Berhampur. He did his intermediate arts (a certificate after 12 years of school) there. After that he emigrated to Calcutta, like his elder brother before him.

I do not know exactly whether he did a B.A. degree course. If yes, it was at a short-lived National "University" which was founded by the leaders of our independence movement. But I do not have any clue as to whether he could also complete that course and get his degree. I guess not. Anyway, such a B.A. degree would not have been recognized by anybody.

My uncle, father's elder brother, did indeed get his B.A. degree from the University of Calcutta and became a school teacher. He had a very interesting episode in his career, which I heard from my mother: In the far west of India, in the province of Punjab, there was a shortage of graduate teachers for the schools that were being newly founded there. So, a delegation came from the town of Hissar to Bengal to recruit a headmaster for a school there. My uncle, who was an ordinary teacher, accepted the offer, and went to Hissar. That must have been in the 20s of the 20th century. In the distant Hissar, my uncle and his wife must have felt very lonely among the Punjabi population. So they invited his brother, i.e. my parents, to visit them. I did not hear much from my mother about these holidays in Hissar, except that it was an adventure and everything was at the beginning so strange. My uncle apparently did not relish that job as a headmaster and came back to Bengal to again become (I guess) an ordinary teacher.

My father's career also had been interesting. As a young man, he had to start doing something. His first profession was teacher of spinning and weaving. He had joined the independence movement as a volunteer. Under the leadership of Gandhiji and in the wake of the Non-Cooperation Movement, people were to be inspired and taught how to spin yarn from cottonwool and to weave cloth that could be made into self-made "*swadeshi*" clothes. I did not get to know whether it was a paid job, nor, if paid, who paid his wages. In pursuance of this vocation, he had to go to several villages. And in one of these, called *Dakshin Barasat*, he saw my mother, then a 15 – 16 years old girl, with whose eldest brother he became friends.

The Non-Cooperation Movement did not result in India winning independence from British rule. What happened then is part of India's history, but what I want to tell here is what happened to my father. He went back to Calcutta. What he did then I did not get to know. One thing I heard from father himself was that he was working as some sort of a salesman or sales agent. Of which company and for which products, I did not get to know. Many years later, when, as a boy, I was rummaging in an old trunk containing useless things, I found pieces of skins of leguaans. Father was probably an agent for an exporter of such things.

The next thing I heard about his efforts to make a livelihood was that he found a job as a cashier in a company called *Indo-Swiss*. This job gave him, it seems, a little stability and security in life, and he started thinking of marrying. Then, the next thing I heard was that he met mother's eldest brother who had become a friend. He told this man, Kalidas Chaudhury, that he wanted to marry his sister, whom he had seen in their Village (Dakshin Barasat).

Mother's Land Dakshin Barasat. Her Family Backgrounds

I had the opportunity to see my mother's home village, *Dakshin Barasat*, for the first time when I was nearly 8 years old, and several times later on. It was (is) connected to Calcutta by railway. It took in 1944 about one hour train travel from Calcutta to reach that village. In the first trip to the village, it was already late afternoon when we reached it. On the way to our mother's ancestral home, I had the first glimpse of the village. It was a foot march on narrow pathways between ponds – a pond on the right and a pond on the left. Later I came to know that all villages in southern Bengal were villages of many ponds. I would understand later why it had to be so. Southern Bengal was the huge low-altitude delta area formed by the silt content of the waters of all the rivers of northern India that flowed into the Bay of Bengal. In this area, whenever one wanted to build a house, one had first to dig out earth from a place, use the same for building a raised platform and then building one's house. The byproduct of the exercise, a large hole, was soon filled up with ground water and rainwater in the rainy season.

The ancestral house of my mother was a solid two-story burnt-brick house. One of our maternal uncles was living in one part of it, with some other relatives who were living in their own households in other clearly designated parts thereof. On arrival, we children were very tired. After having our evening meal, we soon fell asleep. Waking up next morning, the first thing I heard was that Dilip, my brother, who was only two years older than I, had sighted a snake that was lying across a step of the stairs and prevented him from going to the ground floor. Somehow, the snake was made to give way.

Next day we started learning about life in a southern Bengal village. That was necessary, because in the nearly eight years that I had till then lived in this world, I, also my siblings, had always lived in towns of north-western India, where my father had been working as a government employee. The learning was especially necessary, because a week or so later, we had been scheduled to go to another southern Bengal village, called *Kamrabad*, to live there permanently in our own house.

Let me here close the gap in the narrative that has opened up, because I am not following a strictly chronological order in it: After marrying, my father worked for some more time in the same company, Indo-Swiss. But then his in-laws thought that this job in a small private company was not good enough and did not give any job-security, which was and still is very important for a married man in India.

How he got it I do not know, but his next job was some sort of an accounts clerk in the military accounts department of the central government. It offered job security and prospects of rising up in the hierarchy, but it had the disadvantage that the employee could be transferred to an office of the same department anywhere in India. For this reason, father, and along with him his whole family, never in our early youth had a really settled life anywhere. In the course of the first eight years, I remember and heard, I lived in six different towns: Meerat, Jhansi, Ramgarh, Danapur, Patna, and then in the village Kamrabad – the first three in Uttar Pradesh, the next two in Bihar, and the last one in southern Bengal.

The first lesson came the next morning. My brother Dilip told me that there was no toilet in the house, that people had to go to the bamboos forest near the house to empty their bowels. He further said, while doing his shitting, he was visited by a fox. He was afraid, but succeeded in shooing it away. I was surprised, and afraid too. But I also had to go to the bamboos forest. All the houses, in which I had lived till then, had an old-style pit toilet in the farthest corner of the inner courtyard. We were used to that system. But that was all in towns, some in cantonment towns, no foxes, but many swine from the poor people's quarters. But Dakshin Barasat was a village in southern Bengal, in the midst of thick lush greenery. For years thereafter, this trouble was the main reason for my reluctance to go to the maternal uncle's house. Later, however, I was told that grown-up women of the house did not have to go to the bamboos forest. For them there was a separate arrangement in the house, which I too would be allowed to use.

The second lesson I learnt there was that one takes a bath in a pond and not in a bathroom. The villagers had selected two or three ponds with relatively clean water for that purpose – one for men and children, and another for grown-up women. One or two deep-dug wells were also there in rich people's houses. Water from them were used as drinking water. It was common tradition that owners of such wells allowed their neighbors to draw drinking water from them. One was not fussy about neighbors entering the courtyard and have a free view of the inner parts of the house.

It may be in this first week of my life in southern Bengal that I learnt basic swimming. But it may also have been in Kamrabad, where we subsequently went to live in our own house, which father had bought.

But let me first finish the story of my mother's family backgrounds. She was born in a quite educated family. The railway connection and the location in the vicinity of Calcutta – in those days still the Capital of the British Indian Empire – made it possible for her father and the uncles to get modern western higher education. Her father graduated as an engineer from the most renowned engineering college of those days (Shibpur Engineering College). One uncle became a chemist, and another a school teacher, whom we often saw when he, as a very old man, visited his niece, my mother.

My grandfather, the engineer, was sent to the *Shal*[*] forests of southwest Bengal to work in the project to build a railway line there that would connect that region with Calcutta. He went there with his family and lived somewhere near what is known as Jhargram. My eldest uncle from mother's side (her eldest brother) told us that his father, being the engineer-in-charge of the Jhargram section of the project, got from the railway company an elephant as means of transportation along with a driver (the *mahut*). He also remembered that his father often took his son along on elephant's back when he went to the work site. He was very proud that in the railway station building of Jhargram, a portrait of his father still hung as the builder. Mother's chemist uncle used to make talcum powder for the women of the house.

The good luck of the family ended however with the sudden death of the father. The widowed mother returned with the children to Dakshin Barasat. There they managed to survive. How? – I could not get to know that. Maybe they just became part of the extended joint family, as was (still is) the traditional social security system of India. My mother was sent to her maternal uncle's house in south Calcutta (Ritchi Road, Ballygunge) to grow up there with the children of the family. There she went to school to get some primary literacy education. Her three brothers did not get any high school education, or they could not finish it. I do not know why. All three learnt a technical trade – the older two became

---

[*] *Shal*: a species of high-growing hard-wood trees, good building material.

electricians, the youngest became a radio mechanic. Such qualifications must have been in great demand in those days, when application of these technologies was spreading in Calcutta. And, as I wrote above, Dakshin Barasat lay in the vicinity of Calcutta. These maternal uncles took charge of all the electrical work in our house, when father bought a half-finished house in south Calcutta (Ballygunge) and shifted home from Kamrabad to Calcutta.

I must here also narrate the story of my maternal aunts. My mother had good luck. It was my father who proposed to marry her. But her two sisters, being daughters of a penniless family dependent on relatives, were not so lucky. My eldest aunt, mother's elder sister was married to a widower, who already had a daughter from his first wife. But for mother's younger sister, although she was a very beautiful woman, her relatives could not find a suitable match. My father, the son-in-law of the family, was also trying. And it was he who found, believe it or not, a "prince" who was willing to marry her. It was a "prince" of "Shovabazar." His father was actually a very big rent-collecting landlord (zamindar), who had command over the land of several villages, but who lived in *Shovabazar*, a locality of old Calcutta. Such landlords used to be given the title "raja" (king) by the British, whose king in London was the Emperor of India.

This prince had in his youth lived as an ascetic monk. That meant only that he did not marry, but he was rich and carried on with his high life-style in a villa in Dehra Dun (on the foothills of the Himalayas). But later he did want to marry and start a family-life – at what age, I did not come to know, nor did I ever ask. The couple did not get a child. My eldest sister told us that, as a child, she had spent 3 to 4 months in the house of this couple. From mother I heard that they wanted to adopt her as their child. But my parents did not agree. What remained from this sojourn in the mind of my sister were happy memories and a life-long penchant for a beautiful life-style, which she later always missed in our ordinary middle-class household.

This prince-uncle of ours died relatively early. So our aunt became a widow. She left Dehradun and came back to West Bengal and thereafter lived in Howrah, the twin city of Calcutta, where a brother of hers also lived. She must have been a rich widow, having inherited her deceased husband's property. But I did not come to know how rich. We visited her once or twice, and she showed us two very thick albums of postage stamps of many different countries and a collection of coins of different countries. She often visited us in Kamrabad. And even I, still a child, could see that she put on airs.

My father had no sisters, or they may have died very early. But we came to know a cousin sister of his. Her fate was also mixed. She too was bestowed in marriage to a relatively rich land-owning widower in a village of West Bengal. This man already had 6 children from his first wife, and he fathered six more with this second. I heard from father that he had two brothers. About his elder brother I have written above. But a younger brother died in his boyhood. He had climbed a tree to pluck some fruits. And he got bitten by a red ant of a vicious type, whereupon he lost his grip, fell to the ground, got severely injured and died.

Generally speaking, in those days in India, in the absence of modern medicine, people used to die early. Octogenarians were quite rare, I think.

Kamrabad

Before we shifted to Calcutta, we lived about three and a half years in Kamrabad. These years gradually formed my consciousness. I started noting things and happenings around me more intensively. I became aware of many things, also became politically aware, and developed political sympathies and antipathies. Unknowingly, I also became worried about the ecological predicament of mankind. But I shall come to these points a little later.

Kamrabad was not a poor village. Because of job and small-business opportunities in Calcutta, there were (or had been) quite a few well-to-do families there. That could be seen in the numerous well-built burned brick houses (although many were somewhat dilapidated). Two houses were very big. One was, however, shared by many families. But higher education was a rare commodity.

My father was a respected person because of his professional status of a higher-level central government officer. There was, in those days, just another college-educated person in that village, who was very proud of being a graduate.

My mother too was a respected person, but for other things: for her tailoring and sewing skills, which were totally lacking in the village. She also did some social work in that she offered to the local girls to teach them sewing. I remember them meeting on the roof terrace of our house for the purpose. I do not remember whether she already had her hand-driven sewing machine in Kamrabad or got it in Calcutta. But I remember some poor neighbors occasionally coming to her and requesting her to do some tailoring work for them.

In such a village, relations between neighbors could not but be very informal. Our house, like all other neighboring houses, was an open-access one. That is, the compound doors of the houses were never closed to visitors except in the night. Anybody, immediate neighbor or not, could enter the house compound and come up close to the veranda, where they always met somebody or the other from the usually large families. Or else, they would simply call out for the chief of the household.

Our house was particularly open in this sense. It was situated in the middle of the locality where we lived. And the pathway from one corner of that locality to the diagonally opposite corner was around a few houses and a big pond, making it somewhat longer than the diagonal distance between the two corners. Since our house had two compound doors – one at the front and one at the backside of the compound, and both were open from morning to evening – people who wanted to go from one corner to the other made a shortcut through our house compound. Sometimes, even strangers made use of it. We, having earlier lived in towns of Western India, were not used to so much openness. I remember I told mother of this unusual thing. But she had learnt about this a few days earlier and told me we have to tolerate that. This was a traditional right of all people including strangers.

Like all south Bengal villages, Kamrabad too was full of ponds. We also owned a pond with foul water, but only half of it. The other half belonged to another house. This pond was full of two-three special kinds of fish that apparently thrived in foul water. Here I discovered (by observing other boys) the technique of angling, which I at first did not understand. I made a fishing rod with a bamboos twig and some thread from mother's sewing box. Then I tied a small and thin piece of wood at the far end of the thread. When I first used this self-made fishing rod and hoped that some fish would remain hanging on it, nothing happened at all. Again, it was my mentor Dilip who explained the technique to me. Later on, we both became "expert" anglers.

My brother Dilip (left) and I. Photo credit: Saral Sarkar

Apropos of foul ponds of the village, they of course belonged to some house, but it seemed to me that they too were open-access things. Once a poor man came to our house with some foul-water fish (maybe caught from our pond) and requested mother to "buy" them in exchange for some rice. Otherwise, he said, he would have to grow hungry that day. Mother had to "buy" them.

My father developed our living standard a little, because it was embarrassing for mother to use our pit toilet in the outhouse situated at a distance of some 15 meters from our house. He let a sanitary closet built attached to our house. He also let a borewell dug on our courtyard so that we could always have clean drinking water. This latter action had the side-effect of increasing the number of neighbors who visited our compound.

Like our uncles' house in Dakshin Barasat, our house in Kamrabad too had a house snake. When I first saw it, I had already learnt that not all snakes were dangerous. Our house snake was a nonvenomous one. But it had the bad habit of lying straight across the doorway on the backside of our compound. We were not afraid of it, but we did not dare disturb its sleep. So we had to jump over it when we wanted to go to our garden. Actually, snakes were ubiquitous in south Bengal villages. My father told us, once a snake even crawled through the kitchen of his in-law's house in Dakshin Barasat, when he was taking dinner there sitting on the floor. The snake was apparently chasing a mouse. That was of course in the 1920s or 1930s.

In Kamrabd, under a big banyan tree, there was a small temple of goddess *Sitala*. She was worshipped regularly on particular days. It was said that she guaranteed protection for the devotees against small pox, which was in those days a deadly epidemical disease. The vaccine against the disease was already there. But some people did not have faith in it. For protection against it, they relied more on consecrated water from the Sitala temple.

During our residence in Kamrabad, we became witness to a tragic failure of goddess Sitala. A neighbor who had absolute faith in the efficacy of the consecrated water from the temple, had always refused to get his family vaccinated. But this time, the water failed him. The two eldest children of the family died of the disease. A third child, a teenage daughter, survived, but was left with a face full of pockmarks. Most people in the village had however got themselves vaccinated. Nothing happened to them, but that did not mean that they ceased going to the Sitala temple. There was no harm in having oneself doubly protected.

In Kamrabad, I also witnessed a case of practice of magic. Somebody in the village had lost something valuable. He thought it had been stolen and suspected that the thief lived in the village. He requested some magic practitioners to find out the thief. When I heard of the event and rushed to the courtyard where it was taking place, it was already in progress. Two grown-up men were playing (so it seemed to me) with two ca. 4-metres-long pliable pieces of bamboo (which were made by longitudinally splitting a bamboo into 4 equal parts). One of them was holding in his hands one end each of the two long bamboo pieces, the other man the other two ends of the two bamboo pieces on the opposite site. Both men were forcefully pushing the bamboo pieces toward the other side, as a result of which the bamboo pieces were bending and twisting and making otherwise funny movements. When after sometime this "play" came to an end, one of the two "players" said with a grave face that he knew now who the thief was or rather the house from where the thief came, but that he could not say that, because the family was known to many. The whole thing appeared to me to be a damp squib.

Scene from rural India. *Photo credit: Saral Sarkar*

An attraction of Kamrabad was a snack stall in a thatched-roof mud hut. It used to be opened only on Sunday mornings. Its proprietor was an old emaciated man. He was called *Bhonda Ghosh*. He must have had a proper first name, but hardly anybody knew it. *Ghosh* was his family name, but Bhonda meant in Bangla unsmart, unintelligent man. Whether he deserved this epithet, I could not know. But his only item of snack, "Beguni"* was famous in the village. Many grown-up Kamrabadi men gathered there for a chat and to enjoy *Bhonda Ghosh's Beguni*. The especially articulate men among them (yes, only men!), who were fond of discussions and debates indulged in their hobby there. The graduate Kamrabadi I have mentioned above was especially articulate. He appeared to know a lot, and he also spoke a lot. And if anybody doubted the solidity of what he said, he used to reply with the sentence: "I am a graduate and my father was an officer." My father didn't go there. Often, I used to be sent there to fetch some Begunis for the family.

There was a small family-owned grocery shop in the village. But the range of goods offered there was small. For most necessary goods, fish and fresh vegetables, and services, like e.g., haircutting saloon and tailoring shop, we had to go to the market, which was situated in Sonarpur, already then a small town. A badly asphalted road, on which a sort of a share taxi or small bus plied, connected the town with Rajpur, its twin small town. I had my first experience of a ride on a motor vehicle on this road and with this share taxi. It was probably the only motor vehicle in this region, and it was in a very bad shape. I heard from an acquaintance that once, when he was travelling with this vehicle, suddenly it sagged on one side and stopped moving. He could see that one of the wheels, which had separated itself from the vehicle, continued to role on forward.

Sonarpur was (is) also the railway station for Kamrabad. We could reach the station in 10 minutes by walk. There we learnt a special kind of walk: walking on the wooden sleepers of the railway track, which were placed at uneven distances from each other. This kind of walk was necessary, because the railway track was the shortest way from Kamrabad to the railway station. One could of course take a proper pathway to the

---

* *Beguni*: a tasty snack, made out of slices of Brinjal dipped in batter and then fried.

station, but that was much longer, and moreover muddy in the rainy season. I never saw this pathway.

In the towns in which we had lived till then, most people used their feet for going from A to B. We too. But later, maybe it was in Jhansi, father bought bicycles for my elder siblings. When we came to Kamrabad, they were hardly used, because it was a small village, and every place we needed to reach, was within a short radius. But there was one exception. My eldest sister, then 14 years old, needed to go to a girls' school in Rajpur, because it had higher classes, which the Kamrabad school did not have. For her ride to her school, she used her bicycle. My parents may not have had any thoughts about it. But, I remember, it was a subject of talk in the village. A teenage girl wearing skirts and riding a bike. The only other time I saw someone riding a bicycle there, it was a grown-up man, very corpulent. And I thought, the thin tires would burst, but they did not.

Another thing was striking for me there. In the towns where we had lived before, horse carriages were the means of transport for people of importance and people with money. I had seen some of them. In Bengal, however, I never saw one. Not in Kamrabad, not even in South Calcutta, when we were going there to school. I saw there buses and trams, but no horse carriages. I heard of bullock carts in Kamrabad, but never saw one until many years later. The first time I had a bullock cart ride, was when I travelled to a rural area in North Bengal to bring father's old widowed aunt to her daughter's house. The latter was the wife of a wealthy landowner. This son-in-law, who lived in a village, quite far away from the railway station, sent a bullock cart to pick up his old mother in-law. It was rainy season. The unmetalled roads for such travel were just muddy tracks full of potholes between rice fields. It was a difficult ride, an experience.

The most pleasant and enjoyable spot in Kamrabad was the *Jhil*, the largest of all ponds in the village. Its water was not foul, because there was no tree on its banks, from which leaves would fall in it and rot. It was popular among the villagers of all age groups – for taking bath and for swimming for enjoyment. On one side of the Jhil, almost hugging it so to speak, ran the railway track. On the other side – between the Jhil and the next pond was an open level space, just large enough for children and teenagers to play "football" on it. I use here inverted commas, for the ball we played with our feet was not at all of the usual size. It was actually a used and discarded tennis ball. That was all the village youth could afford to buy. A real football, the usual size, was too dear for them.

After each game of such football, particularly in the football season – the summer and the rainy season – the players used to sweat. After the game it was such a pleasure to take a dip in the Jhil and wash away the sweat. Some of my playmates straight away jumped into the waters, some took off their shorts and jumped naked into it. In the late afternoon many elderly people came there just to enjoy the fresh breeze. For their benefit, the owner of the big house that stood close to the Jhil, had built a cement-paved platform (ca.5m x 4m) and two cement-built longish benches.

One peculiarity of the Jhil was its shape. Unlike all the other ponds of South Bengal, it was not roughly round-shaped. From a child's perspective, it was exceptionally long and comparatively short in width. It was the ambition of many children to be able to swim the whole length. I did that once, and was very proud of my achievement. I later fathomed the reason for its longish shape. The Jhil was dug to get earth for raising the ground level of the railway track. This explained for me the formation of all the ponds on the two banks of the railway track.

Education

Before coming to Kamrabad, my elder siblings had gone to school, where Hindi, naturally, was the medium of instruction. I did not go to school in those towns. I was a child, not yet a boy, and kindergartens were an unknown entity in those days. I stayed at home and played with our neighbors' children, all the while speaking Hindi. But I learnt my ABC at home. I was fortunate to have a private teacher, a young man, who had come to Jhansi in order to search for a job, and was staying in our house as guest. Father was to help him get a job. He gave me the first lessons in English and arithmetic. I cannot say how old I was then, maybe somewhere between 6 and 7.

I do not know how I learned to read Bangla. But I remember that my father, when he went to Calcutta for some office work, brought for us

Bangla children's books. And I could read the story books presented to me. I read it them loudly to show the others that I could read Bangla.

In 1944, Kamrabad had a rural kind of primary school: Two big tiled halls, each divided by means of moveable cardboard partition walls into four class rooms. One housed the boys' school, the other the girls' school. There were plain long benches for the pupils, but no tables. There were teachers for each class.

Kamrabad was located very close to Calcutta. Just half an hour's train journey was needed to reach this political, business, educational and cultural hub of entire eastern India. So life in the village was very much influenced by everything that was and that happened in Calcutta. People went there to work, to high school, to do business etc. So, it was no wonder that there was even a girl's primary school in Kamrabad. When we came to live in this village – in April 1944 – new rooms were being built to house the middle school.

I started school here, in class four. It was in April 1944; I was not yet 8. But my father thought I had learnt enough at home to skip the preliminary classes. It was a catastrophe for me. I did not know at all what school meant, how it functioned, what were the rules of the game, what were the duties of a pupil, and what the roles of teachers. Actually, nothing about the whole thing. And nobody cared to me anything. My parents just sent me there. Somebody must have brought me there in the beginning. Maybe it was my second sister, four years older than I, who also went to school there, namely in the girls' school, also in class four.

On the very first day in school, I got a hard slap on the cheek, from the very first school teacher in my life, from a full-grown man. The school year had begun in January, I came in April. The teacher had given the pupils a home task. They were supposed to have learnt certain things at home for the next class on the subject, and answer the questions of the teacher correctly. Those who could not, were punished. The next pupil who could answer correctly, had to come to those who had failed to do so and give them each a slap on the cheek. That was the rule, which I did not know. I failed to answer the very first question put to me by the teacher. The boy who could answer it correctly came to me and wanted to give me a slap. But I resisted vehemently. The teacher, maybe he was called Mr. Shoiombar, became very angry and gave me a hard slap on the cheek. He rebuked me with words like: "Do you think it is your aunt's house?"

It is not possible here to narrate such stories in detail. A class-mate, who later became my friend, was instructed by the teacher Mr. Shoiombor to always tell me what the home task was for the next class. I do not know any more whether this helped me. In short, I was a complete failure in that first school. But I impressed everybody there by my ability to read English. Otherwise, I did not speak at all, with nobody, so that I got the nickname "speechless pupil", in Bangla "*Nirbak Chhatra*".

Dilip, my immediate elder brother, was much smarter. I had told him the story of the painful slap on the cheek. He later found out more about Mr. Shoiombor He informed me that Mr. Shoiombor was a member of a music group, where he played the "*dhole*" – a drum that was played by slapping with bare hands the two tightly leathered sides of the same. This made the skin of Mr. Shoiombor's palms like hard leather, and that was why his slap had caused me much pain.

It was complete dereliction of duty on the part of my father to have sent me to school so totally unprepared for it. My mother did not come in question, she was uneducated. But also my eldest siblings did not think of it. It was another catastrophe, when it turned out that in the arithmetic class, I did not understand what was being written on the board. In Kamrabad, maybe in the whole rural Bengal, they used special symbols to write monetary-arithmetical figures. For instance, they wrote "I." to write four *annas* of the old monetary/currency system.

To make some amends for his failings, what father did was to appoint the same Mr. Shoimbor as my private teacher. He must have told father that I did not know anything. I remember I learnt from him the rural Bengal system of writing monetary figures. But I do not remember what or how much more I learnt from him.

One vital thing, which father could not have made amends for by any means, was that I was the youngest boy in that class, actually still a child., and short in stature. And there were several fully grown young men in the class. They may have been sons of farmers from outlying farmlands, who were simply late beginners in their alphabetization process. All in all, the circumstances were fearful for a barely eight years old child.

Actually, it did not surprise me too much. Even before being sent to this school, I had rarely experienced loving or gentle grown-up people, neither father nor mother were gentle and loving to me. The two eldest siblings were aloof, busy with their own hobbies and affairs. The others of the younger group were just playmates. Dilip was close to me, but he was a sort of mentor who himself needed mentoring. Particularly father was a very fearful man. I remember one incident in Ramgarh, when I was perhaps just five to six years old. Father came back from office in the late afternoon and immediately started searching for something that was important, and he could not find it. He made a terrible ballyhoo out of it. He started shouting, and throwing aside things which he suspected to be covering up the particular important thing. In the process he also threw a beloved toy of mine against the wall. The toy broke apart. Such scenes I also experienced many years later in Calcutta. That may have been a common character trait of fathers in those days. Only much later did I experience my father as a loving man, i.e., when he had become a grandfather. He was very loving to his grandchildren: Unfortunately, I never experienced a grandfather's love, nor the love of a grandmother.

The third catastrophe in that early year of my life came when one day, I heard from my second sister that we both had to take an exam and for that we had go to another village, rather a small town, called Baruipur, which too had a railway station. I did not know what examination meant, nor what this particular one was for. But I went, along with my sister, the second one, who was in the girls' primary school, and all my "fellow pupils" from class four. The purpose of the exam, I learnt later, was to select a few good pupils of the region whose further education the government wanted to promote. I failed in the exam, naturally. When I was told about that, a month or two later, I had already forgotten it. But I learnt what an exam was.

It was not only I, who had difficulty with the school system. Also Dilip had difficulty, though of another kind. He had some earlier acquaintance with the Indian school system at one or two earlier stations of my father's service carrier. He appeared not to like school. In Ramgarh, he was sent to a Christian boys' school managed by "brothers" of the church. I heard later that he often skipped that school and, instead, spent the school hours observing the many animals in the garden of Mr. Habbot. In Kamrabad, he had another problem. He was put in class 5 of the local school. How he fared in his exam, I could not care to know. But I heard later that while answering the questions, he of course began answering them in Bangla, but ended up writing Hindi. His teachers and others were amused.

I doubt the teachers of the primary school of Kamrabad were paid a regular salary. Most probably they were paid a small honorarium. Dilip had found out, some teachers were actually farmers, who disappeared in the busy seasons of ploughing, sowing and harvesting. He had actually seen one teacher coming back with the rice harvest loaded on his bullock cart.

Many years later, I heard from Maria, my wife, how her early school years in the late 1930s in her village primary school were. They apparently had a school in every village, but only one large classroom and only one teacher for all the kids of the village (6 to 14 years old). The different age-groups sat in different corners of the classroom. The teacher gave them different tasks and they learnt in the school itself. One pupil or another from the older age groups assisted the teacher and helped the younger ones learn their lessons. In regard to the building and number of teachers, our Kamrabad primary school fared comparatively better. But in Germany in the late 1930s, the primary teachers had some teachers' training, whereas in Kamrabad, our teachers had none. They probably did not even have a school-leaving qualification. They probably were just reasonably self-educated farmers.

And, what in my judgement weighed more, the German teachers – mostly women – appeared to have been loving teachers, and not brutal men as in strictly gender-separated India. Moreover, German kids learnt from these loving teachers in the school itself.

Back to my biography: I think, nobody took this early failure of mine seriously, neither mother nor father. Father was convinced that I was an intelligent boy and had learnt a lot for my age. So next year, in January 1945, I was sent to another school, a high school, and put in class 5. My brother Dilip was also put in class 5 in the same school. It was in Calcutta (Ballygunge), was called *Jagadbandhu Institution*. I remember, when I was brought to the teacher in charge of new admissions – accompanied by my eldest brother –, the teacher asked me, then just a little over eight-and-a-half years old, in a doubtful tone whether I thought I could do it. I still remember I had replied: "Of course, I could, if I try." I do not know what my eldest brother had told that teacher. I also do not remember whether I had given this reply spontaneously and knew its implications, or whether I had been taught beforehand to say that. To make the narrative short, from then onwards, I passed all my school exams, but without any distinction. For most of the time, however, Dilip and I also had a private teacher.

Generally speaking, our whole education system was very bad. Even in Calcutta, in the late 1940s and early 1950s there were no nurseries and Kindergartens. Our country was simply not developed enough. Our school buildings were well built, and teachers in Calcutta were graduates, some even M.A. degree holders, but few had any teacher's training. Moreover, they were very poorly paid, and so lacking in motivation. One of them even had a small book-selling business in the school itself. Giving private tuition against cash was widespread among teachers. Sometimes they themselves organized smaller groups of pupils whom they taught privately.

I do not remember having learnt anything in school itself. Going to school was for me only a routine daily activity that made going out and meeting classmates possible. Whatever I learnt, I learnt myself at home or from private teachers. Almost every pupil needed private tuition to learn anything.

But I must also say, a part of the explanation why I hardly learnt anything in school itself, was that I was, so far as character was concerned, unsmart, dreamy and easily intimidated by grown-up big people. I, e.g., did not ever tell the teachers that I did not understand something.

Upbringing

One cannot imagine today how bad children's upbringing was in those days, the 1940s, in Bengal. We belonged to the educated middle middle-class. In this class, fathers were more or less educated, but most mothers not, though they were not illiterate. Children were many; on average six per family. There were families with ten children. Most parents had no idea about a good upbringing of children. They also did not care much, they appeared to leave it to their and their children's fate. Children grew up somehow, like in nature, but in the urban milieu. That is why often there were wayward sons in educated middle middle class families. I know the case of a university professor who had two sons. One was OK. But another, the older one, became a street rowdy of the locality. That was in South Calcutta, in our locality (Ballygunge). So, much depended particularly on the character and quality of the parents and the teachers. The most important thing they cared about was the marksheet of the children after the annual exam.

Otherwise, generally (at least in Bengal), fathers were stern and severe. Punishing, even thrashing sons for "bad" behavior and disobedience was usual. Loving fathers, as a rule, were very rare. Mothers were loving to their babies and small children, but to their boys and girls at best indulgent. From the boys they expected old age security. I repeatedly heard my mother saying: "I have three life-insurance policies." She meant us, her three sons.

In our family, father was mostly absent. Since he was a central government employee and an auditor for the British-Indian Army, he was frequently transferred from place to place. He was also sent to different places for short auditing tours. All the while, we were under the care of mother, who managed the family after a fashion, with the help of relatives and family friends. Father soon realized that this kind of nomadic life was bad for the education of the children. So he decided to settle us down in Bengal in the vicinity of Calcutta, and carry on with his professional fate of being transferred from city to city and town to town. That was the background of our coming to Kamrabad.

I cannot really say, whether it was good or bad luck for us. He was, it appears to me in retrospect, unhappy with his nomadic career that made him live further at different stations – Calcutta (i.e., Kamrabad), Shillong, Dibrugarh, Allahabad, Lukhnow, Secunderabad, and again Calcutta. We children, I believe, were at least not unhappy about the absence of father.

He was a typical stern and severe father, frequently scolding angrily for the slightest thing he happened to dislike, be it our behavior, be it the food he was served. In his early youth, I have heard, he even beat my eldest brother.

Of course, he earned an above-average salary (he had got promotions in his job), kept us well-fed and well-clothed. But he, when he was at home, hardly contributed anything directly to our upbringing, our learning good manners and behavior or to our formal education. Only once, I remember, he tried to inspire me and Dilip to learn well, when he said: "If you learn well, I will send one of you to Cambridge, and the other to Oxford." I do not really think he earned that well, but the question did not arise. We were simply not good in formal learning.

My father's earnings and savings may not have sufficed to send us to Oxford and Cambridge. But it sufficed to buy a house in Calcutta. That was in 1947. Ever since, we lived in that megapolis. After retirement from service in the late 1950s, father could permanently live with us, his family.

In Calcutta, we could imbibe some urban middle class Bengali culture, but not much and not all of us. So far as formal education was concerned, our performance did not become better. After all, such things are determined partly also by the genes we inherit and by the milieu of one's broader family and friends.

Becoming Aware of Identity / Political Awakening

It was in Kamrabad, that I really became aware of and understood my ethno-cultural identity. I became aware that we were Bengalis, a people among several peoples that constituted the people of India, the Indian nation. In the towns where we had lived before (Meerat, Jhansi, Ramgarh, Danapur, Patna), people spoke Hindi. We too spoke Hindi, at home perhaps a hodgepodge of Hindi and Bangla. After all, Bangla was our mother tongue.

In Kamrabad, I also became really aware that we were Hindus, and not Muslims, and that there was a conflict between the two religious groups. Previously, when we were living in the northern Indian towns, I had known that there were also Muslims in our town. Among our playmates and friends in the neighborhood there were also Muslims. I still remember the name of one: Taher. Once I observed from our terrace a big ballyhoo in the house opposite to ours us. Many people had assembled there and a lot of sweets were being distributed to the guests. I felt greedy for the sweets and wondered why we had not been invited. I learnt the reason later: It was because they were Muslims and we were not. They were celebrating the circumcision of a boy of the family.

I learnt that it was the British who ruled over India. I remember, in Jhansi, a cantonment town, I had often seen white people. I knew that they were different. But that they were the rulers of the country, this fact was beyond the knowledge and comprehension of a child that I was then (maybe 6).

In 1946, at a turbulent time in the history of India's independence movement, I came to hear that they, the Muslims, were our enemies. Why, I did not know then, but learnt rapidly in the course of subsequent events. On a late afternoon, a rumor reached Kamrabad, which was a Hindu village, that an armed mob of Muslims from a neighboring village were going to attack the Hindus of Kamrabad and kill them. I saw the young men of our village prepare for the fight and observed their show of bravado. However, nothing happened that time. But some days later, a young man from Kamrabad, who had gone to Calcutta to his regular job, was killed there. He was from the neighboring house. When his dead body was brought back next day, we even saw the wound on the back of his neck inflicted through a machete strike.

This was, incidentally, my first encounter with the phenomenon of death. I saw the widow weeping. But why she was weeping, and the other grown-ups not, I did not understand. I knew through observation that children cried and wept when they suffered some pain, but elders not. So why was the grown-up woman weeping? I had to wait many years to understand the difference between physical pain and mental pangs.

My political awakening began early in life, also in Kamrabad. Already as a child, sometime in 1944, I had indirectly heard of the Second World War. It was perhaps in Jhansi (around 1944) that I heard that father would have to go to the war. What war was, I did not really understand, but I understood that it was something bad, because mother started worrying.

I understood later that father had to go to Cox's Bazaar as an auditor of military accounts. That was the time when it was feared that the Japanese army, that had conquered Burma, would also invade India in Chittagong district. So the British had amassed their armed forces there to defend their colony India.

Father came back home after three months, unscathed, and everybody heaved a sigh of relief. The next time I heard of the Second World War was when I was admitted to school in Calcutta in the *Jagadbandhu Institution* (1945). There I saw that the large Windows of our classrooms in the ground floor were protected by big walls. When I asked somebody about them, I got the reply that they had been built to protect the school boys from Japanese bombs. I read much later that the Japanese had indeed bombed the Calcutta port three times.

The next thing I heard about the war was from my eldest brother. He said that a bomb the size of an egg had destroyed a whole city in Japan. That was of course Hiroshima in August 1945, and it was of course the atom bomb. But it was not the size of an egg, as I learned later.

Kamrabad was also the place where I first came in contact with political ideology. It was 1945, just two years before India became independent. One day, some young men of the place came to meet father and wanted him to buy a newspaper. They were the local communists and it was the daily newspaper of the communists of Bengal called *Swadhinata* in Bangla (*Independence*). They could persuade father to subscribe to the paper, and thereafter I often saw these young men in our house, one of whom was later to become a brother-in-law of ours.

In 1945, the Communist Party of India was already 20 years old. Therefore, it was no wonder that there were some communists also in and around Kamrabad. But they were disliked, even hated, by many, who were supposed to be members or followers of the *Congress Party*, that was spearheading the independence movement. Not only were the communists, in principle, propagating some kind of revolution instead of just transfer of power in the hands of the Indian bourgeoisie, they were also trying to "instigate" sharecroppers (tenant farmers) to demand a higher share of the crops at the cost of the share of the landowners. They even succeeded in starting a radical peasants' movement in 1946 (called in

Bangla *Tebhaga Andolan*). We were no landowners, nor were we share-croppers. So, we were not required to take sides.

But strangely, and unknowingly, at that age (I was nine or ten), I became worried about the ecological predicament of mankind. Once Dilip and I were standing at the *Jhil*. There was nobody else there. I expressed my worry roughly in these words: Look, at the beginning father and mother were two persons. Then we came. Now our family has eight people. How can it go on like this? Dilip, my de facto mentor, replied very wisely. He said: you are stupid. Look at the Jhil, every rainy season millions of drops of rain fall in it. The water level goes up.Then, in 6 months, the water level goes down again. What happens? Nothing.

I was not really happy with his reply. But I could not say anything at the moment. Many years later I came to understand the problem. Whereas, in reality, I was worried about a growing economy, Dilip was talking about a steady-state economy.

In Kamrabad, there were rivalries between the two political groups. When the communists built up their cultural organization, they called it Peace Association (*Shanti Sansad*). Their specialty were cultural events, and a hand-written and well-bound literary journal decorated by local artists. They made only one copy of each number, and it was lent out from one family to the next.

I do not know what their rivals and opponents, the group closer to the *Congress Party*, offered, except that they had a small military-music-band. My parents somehow stood closer to the Shanti Sansad people. And we, the children, generally took part in the activities of Shanti Sansad. But that did not mean that our parents and/or we, the children, had anything against the other group. For example, Dilip, joined the other group, because he was musically gifted and the music-band was a strong attraction for him.

Chapter 2:
Growing Up,
Coming of Age

The Eventful Years of the 1940s. Learning the Complexities of Life

In 1946, I was already going to school in Calcutta, to a school called *Jagadbandhu Institution*. The big city did not anymore fill me with fear and awe, as it did at the beginning, i.e., in 1945, and I became acquainted with at least South Calcutta where our school was situated. I did not become a good pupil, but I understood how a school in the big city functioned. That was some progress. I was then in class 6. Dilip and I went to two different sections of the class, so I was left alone to find my way in the school and the class. There were of course the two-three bullies in the class, who were much bigger than I in stature, but I learned how to avoid them.

1946 was important for my development, especially political development. Apart from the Hindu-Muslim riots, which I mentioned in the previous chapter, I was also confronted with knowledge of India's independence movement. I was even touched by everything that was going on in Calcutta, which I could not see with my own eyes. I heard of the anti-British demonstrations on the streets, in which even some pupils of our school took part. During one such demonstration, which probably had become violent, police used live bullets against the demonstrators. I heard that two pupils from our school, both from class 10, were killed in this incident.

The other pupils were of course proud of their two martyrs. I too. Some came up with the idea that there should be a memorial monument for them on our school compound. They went to the headmaster and told him about their idea. But he said the school could not spend any money for such a thing, and, he added, that they were our martyrs, and so we should raise money from our pockets to build the monument. He could convince the initiators of the idea. After a year or so, the small monument was built.

Even at that early age, as a ten years old boy, I was confronted with some complexities of this world. Firstly, when I heard of Netaji Subhash Chandra Bose and his Indian National Army, he and his soldiers were, of course, our heroes. But then I did not understand why these soldiers, who wanted to fight for India's independence from British rule, had in the first place been fighting for the British and against the Japanese. And why later they collaborated with the Japanese, who were equally imperialistic. At that time, I did not know anything about the debate in India on the question as to whether Netaji Bose was a fascist.

Secondly, I did not understand why my father, who was in his youth a volunteer in the Non-Cooperation Movement for India's independence, later decided to work for the British rule in a government office. In 1946, he was still working in an office of the British government, but he also showed his nationalistic fervor by introducing the technique of spinning yarn in our family – not of course with a spinning wheel (charkha) as one sees in pictures of Gandhiji, but with a simple spindle.

These and many other such questions accompanied me for many years, until, late in life, I came to some sort of conclusions, which may also turn out to be provisional.

Let me finish the story of this eventful year 1946 with an amusing anecdote. It was also the year in which I had the good fortune of seeing Gandhiji. In a public prayer meeting, of course, and from a distance; even so, it was the great Mahatma Gandhi. A group of our family friends had organized a train journey from Kamrabad to Sodepur, where the prayer meeting took place. Mother went with them. Father was probably out of station. They had to take the children along. Decades later, in a political discussion in Germany, I referred to Gandhiji. A young man, very much younger than I, asked me whether I knew Gandhi. I said yes. Without asking me anything more, the man exclaimed: "What, you knew him? Shook hands with him and said Hallo, Mr. Gandhi?" I laughed, of course, but I was not sure whether he was joking.

India became independent in August 1947, the year I became 11. I was by then ripe enough to understand that it was not the same India, the glory, beauty and unity of which poets like Rabindranath Tagore had sung about in their poems and songs. It was a truncated India. There was no celebration in school. Nobody organized any such thing; we only had a holiday. Overall, a sad, somber mood prevailed. Of course, there was also a little joy, but it was quite attenuated. Only in our immediate small locality, there was a little flag-hoisting ceremony organized by the local youth.

I guess, in Pakistan, they rejoiced at independence, especially because it was perceived as a full victory in their struggle for getting rid of Hindu dominance in the independence struggle. I remember having heard or read that their "battle slogan" during the riots of 1946 was "We will get Pakistan by fighting."

I read many years later about the *"two-nations theory"* of Mohammed Ali Jinnah, the father of Pakistan. According to him, India was not a nation, never had been one. India was, according to Jinnah, rather only a union of several South Asian nations. He defined the collective identity of Pakistanis in terms of religion. He said, in the Indian subcontinent, the Muslims formed a nation.

Unfortunately, the Muslims of India were not living concentrated in those provinces of the subcontinent which later became Pakistan. Substantial numbers of Muslims lived in almost all provinces of India. Similarly, in the Pakistani provinces of Western Punjab, Sind and East Pakistan, large numbers of Hindus lived since long. In Jinnah's conception, the Muslims, who would, after 1947, continue to live in the other provinces of India, should receive rights to live there in peace and as a large minority, and he was ready to grant minority rights to the Hindus, who would continue to live in Punjab, Sind and other parts of Pakistan.

But that was only the pious wish and logical conclusion of a political leader. So far as the people were concerned, they could not care less. They were not moved by piety, nor by too much sense of logic. They were raw people, uneducated masses, brutal and steeped in hatred for the other religious community, who stood against their heart's desire. So, just after the partition, there were orgies of vengeance in both newly independent countries: orgies of killings, displacements, forced migration, and maybe also of spontaneous and hurried exodus. At that time, and also later, killings provoked retaliatory killings.

I heard of these things from grown-up people, but at that time I could not imagine the dimension of the killings and displacements. There was no TV in those days, and I, still a child, rarely had interest in reading the newspapers that were available. But later on, in Germany, when I had access to TV, I often saw such old documentary reports, or perhaps they were enacted scenes for a film on India's independence struggle. I saw pictures of these forced migrations and spontaneous exodus in both directions. But in 1947, a month or two after Independence Day, I saw something. One day, we heard from a passerby that there were several dead bodies lying on the Ballygunge railway station. We rushed to the station to see the matter. These people, most probably Muslims, were traveling by train and they were murdered in the train. When the train had stopped for a short while at Ballygunge railway station, the dead bodies were thrown out of the train, and they were lying on the platform.

In Independent New India

As a child, I had thought that the British must have been very bad rulers. Otherwise, why would all Indians be against them. But even one year after August 1947, I did not see anything different happening or anything being changed. School remained the same uninviting place, the teachers as disinterested in teaching and parents as fearful and disciplining as before.

Of course, I had not been aware of things beyond my immediate surroundings. So I, and I guess most others among my classmates and in my age-group, were harboring vague illusions about good things happening after Independence. That it was merely a transfer of power from British hands to Indian hands, was beyond my comprehension.

I think at the age of 12, I started reading the headlines of the daily newspaper that father had subscribed to. There I read about the small intervention of the Indian armed forces in the then princely state of Hyderabad in the northern part of South India. The Muslim rulers of this state, the vast majority of the population of which were Hindus, refused to join the Indian Union. And the leadership of the newly created independent state of India was not prepared to tolerate this. It was while reading such news that I, incidentally, also came to know that in the same state, an armed communist-led rebellion was going on in the rural districts of *Telangana* region. Maybe they had been inspired and encouraged by the rapid success of the Chinese communist Red Army, about which I had been reading in the newspaper.

The history of this rebellion can be read elsewhere. Here I want to narrate only how it was received in my mind. My brother-in-law, Mr. Mukherjee, who was a communist, and who was by that time accepted in our large family circle, and I, then a 12- or 13-years old boy curious to know everything, had become friends. I told him that I thought it was bad that the communists were disturbing progress in India. Mr. Mukherjee said that I was only repeating the views of the ruling class. I told him I read these things in our newspaper, not heard from some ruling class men. Mr. Mukherjee said, "but how do you know that the newspapers are telling the truth." This was another lesson. Before, I could never think that even printed words could be lies. Five or six years later I would experience that not only printed Indian daily newspapers could lie, but even printed and well-bound books written by apparently respectable people from America and the Soviet Union could lie. I shall come back to this theme again.

As for the *Telangana Rebellion*, it had to be ended under the oppressive rule of the military government installed by the Indian Army. Also, some concessions made by the government of India, led in those days by the first Prime Minister of India Jawaharlal Nehru, motivated many peasant-rebels to go back home half-satisfied. The Communists were allowed to take part in the first general election of free India held in 1951. Their leaders who had led the rebellion registered resounding success in the same and represented Telangana in the first Parliament of India. Many years later, in the late 1960s, by sheer chance, I came to personally know the most famous of those leaders, Mr. Ravi Narayan Reddy. I lived namely as a tenant of his house that he or his son got built for letting out.

A Marriage Ceremony in the Family

In 1949, for the first time in my life, I saw at closest possible quarters a big Indian Bengali-Hindu marriage ceremony. It was in our house, and the bride was my second sister, who was at that time only 16 to 17 years old and was still going to school. My eldest sister had been married at a marriage registrar's office. So, there was no ceremony on that occasion. The marriage of the second sister came very suddenly. It was what, in India, is called an arranged marriage. The two families, the boy's and the girl's, both look for a suitable match. When they find the right one, negotiations, and, in case of agreement, preparations begin. In the case of my sister, for both sides, it was a good match, except however for one thing: the age difference between the bride and the bridegroom was 17 to 18 years. My sister was still a girl, and the man was, at 33 or 34, not quite a young man. Otherwise, the bridegroom had a good secure job in state service. And my father and the maternal uncle of the bridegroom were friends from their student days. I do not know whether father had to pay a dowry, but I could see that quite a lot of gold ornaments had to be got made for my sister.

But the aspect that impressed me most was the big tam-tam and the huge number of people who had to be invited to attend the ceremony. Firstly, all members of both clans, father's and mother's, relatives all, had to be invited to attend with kith and kin, with children and children's children. And families were large in those days. For example, my father's cousin sister came from her village with 12 children – six her own and six from her husband's first diseased wife. The eldest son was, moreover, married, and he came with his wife and a child. Then there were father's friends and close ex-colleagues, our, i.e., our parents' six children's, friends, our neighbors living in the same street, people from Kamrabad, who had been our neighbors. Unlike in modern times, all were explicitly or implicitly invited to come with their whole family. In Bangla, the word used was: "*saparibare*", which said it explicitly. If anybody had not been invited, he/she was offended, felt sort of neglected. Some close relatives, who lived in some distant town, expected father even to pay their travel costs. Affordable hotels were very rare, and most relatives from distant places expected to be accommodated in our four-room house.

Of course, not all invitees could come. But those who could, invariably came. Nobody wanted to miss a chance to come to Calcutta and do sight-seeing. For some, the prospect of meeting distant relatives was attractive. For others (or rather for all) a delicious and rich festive dinner was the main attraction.

Someone from our close relatives estimated that, counted together with those who came along with the bridegroom, nearly 1000 people had to be fed on the marriage evening. Relatives, those who camped in our house, had to be given the usual 3 to 4 meals for 3 to 4 days. We could not provide a bed to everybody. Nobody also demanded one. All slept on the floor side by side, 7 or 8 in each room, without mosquito-nets.

One thing, however, I must not fail to mention, only because it was so disturbing for the big joyous ballyhoo. Particularly on the wedding evening, when we were dining hundreds of invitees with delicacies, we also had many uninvited guests – scores of beggars and poor people from the nearby slums. They waited patiently on the road until a batch of guests had finished eating. The leftovers on their plates were then collected by our servants and distributed among the waiting beggars. The process was accompanied by a lot of quarrels among these uninvited guests.

This ugly show was repeated every time a marriage ceremony was held in our family. Many years later, this show stopped taking place, because celebrating people started hiring closed spaces for their ceremonies.

Calcutta and Ballygunge

Calcutta was until 1911 the capital of British India. The central areas of old Calcutta, therefore, contained correspondingly imperial buildings. It developed into and continued, after 1911, to be the business, educational and cultural center of whole Eastern India. The residential houses of the local rich there were big, and partly majestic. The main roads were quite broadly laid. But in central Calcutta, where the middle class – lower, middle and upper – lived in those days, the houses were small and dark. The approaches to them were narrow streets, narrower lanes, and very narrow by-lanes.

As the population of India and Calcutta continued to grow, new suburban residential areas were built up (Bhowanipur e.g.). When we came there in 1947, our residential area, Ballygunge, was one of the latest and southern-most of the city. Most houses there were well-built, airy and allowed a lot of daylight in through big windows on all sides. Window casements were mostly without glass panes (lagging development of glass industry), but they were mostly kept open, summer or winter. Home builders were required to keep an unbuilt free space of ca. 3 meters between two houses (1.5 meters each) to allow monsoon winds to pass freely. Everything was good, but there was also a bad byproduct. Because windows were kept open in all seasons except in the winter nights, much that was expressed loudly, family-intern quarrels e.g., was audible in the neighboring houses. In one family with ten children and parents, they quarreled frequently, and we had to bear with that. In the same family, a young musically talented girl used to sing the Indian equivalent of the do-re-mi in the early morning to train her voice. That was loud, but at least pleasant.

Because it was a well-built modern area, Ballygunge attracted many well-to-do, well-educated and highly cultured middle and upper middle-class people. Many were reputed professors and intellectuals. Figures in Bangla novels and films were often shown to be living in Ballygunge. So, the area acquired a special kind of high reputation. Some years later, when I went to college in central Calcutta, some of my fellow students asked me where I live. When I told them I live in Ballygunge, they sort of exclaimed in respect: "Oh, Ballygunge!"

But, in fact, the particular corner of Ballygunge, where we lived, namely *Jamir Lane*, had not contributed anything to this reputation. There was a medium size iron and steel factory in the space between Jamir Lane and the railway track. The railway station and the Bus-Tram-Terminus were just five minutes away, which was of great advantage to us. A stone's throw away from our house, – in the middle of Jamir Lane, between two rows of middle-class houses – was situated an old Muslim graveyard, which was later occupied, I suppose illegally, by poor people, who built their huts there, and a slum arose. Jamir Lane was formerly known as Jamir Mistry's[*] Lane, signifying it was formerly a poor Muslim people's quarter.

Fortunately for us, also a milkman from Bihar province lived there with his family and 4 cows. Every morning, some of us went to the spot where he used to milk his cows and fetched fresh milk. This kind of milk supply system was common in Calcutta of those days. Milkmen (in Bangla called Gowala) were suppliers of an essential product. Although totally uneducated, they enjoyed some power and respect. In North Calcutta, there was even a lane named after one Kinu Gowala.

This system of milk supply existed in Calcutta up to about the mid-1950s. But it was also precarious to depend on individual milkmen for such a vitally important children's food. That is why in the wake of development, the government took up the task of supplying bottled milk to the residents of the big city. In the late forties and early fifties, it was also the government that guaranteed the supply of at least some important food items like rice, wheat and edible oil (later also kerosine) at a fair price. There was a rationing system in place; each family had ration cards for each one of its members. I remember, I often had to go to the ration shop with our bunch of ration cards.

In the context of general topography of southern Bengal, I have written in chapter 1 about the ubiquitous ponds, which had to be dug to raise the level of rice fields or swampland where a house was planned to be built. This could also be seen in our corner of Ballygunge. About a hundred meters to the West of Jamir Lane runs a parallel road, which is called *Cornfield Road*, obviously stating this was all rice field a few decades ago. And indeed, the piece of land on its side, that was still unbuilt was low-lying land. And also the larger part of our playground could only become dry ground through the excavation of a pond on adjacent land.

This pond too had a history of its own. In the beginning, it must have had clean water. But when we came to live in Jamir Lane, it had already become a pond for washermen to wash clothes in and hang them on lines on the open space at the banks. Later it became also a bathing place for

---

[*] The word "mistry" means in Bangla and Hindi mason and also a competent/trained craftsman/worker in any branch of industry.

all the buffaloes and cows of the surrounding areas. Moreover, it became a dumping ground for waste metal pieces of the iron and steel factory mentioned above. Years later, suddenly we saw workers recovering the same pieces of waste metal, then of course largely corroded, which had earlier been dumped in the pond as waste. I found the explanation sometime later. I heard that the Japanese iron and steel industry was buying such waste steel, obviously to smelt it to fresh steel.

The residents of this corner were almost all lower middle-class families. Only one businessman-family that owned a small garments factory, lived in our lane in a big house, half of which was rented away. At the beginning, no prominent person of Calcutta's cultural life lived there. But, some years later, a famous exponent of *Rabindrasangeet* (Tagore's songs), Ms. Suchitra Mitra, took up residence for some time in our Jamir lane. And later a professor of English too.

For us youngsters, there were still some open and unbuilt spaces – in Ballygunge as a whole and also in our corner, where we could play football and cricket. There was also a sporting and body-building club near our house. It was called *Broti Sangha*. The Bangla word *Broti* means devoted. Maybe the original purpose of founding the club had been to build up young people as devoted to the national cause or some such thing. We three brothers became members of the club. A boxing champion of India, who was selected to take part in the Helsinki Olympics (1952), trained in this club.

That was roughly the time, when I became a big cricket fan. I used to read reports in our newspaper on cricket matches between national teams. In those days there was a very famous Australian batsman, Don Bradman, who scored many centuries for his national team. What impressed me very much was that his picture appeared in the newspaper reports almost once every week. I was good in cricket, so I developed in my imagination the ambition to become a great cricket player like Don Bradman.

That was my undoing. I was intelligent enough to become a scientist or a college teacher in any branch of knowledge except perhaps mathematics. But I was not concentrating on learning anything seriously. I was dreaming most of the time. Of course, I regularly went to school. But as

I wrote above, I never really learnt anything in school and the teachers also did not care.

But I always learnt enough to pass my yearly final examinations for each class and was regularly promoted to the next higher class. In 1951, I finished school passing the central school-final examination[*] satisfactorily.

---

[*] All pupils who completed 10 years of schooling, i.e., passed the examination of the 10th class held by the school itself, had to take a few months later another such examination held by some department or board of secondary education of the provincial government. Passing this exam entitled the pupil to a certificate that was recognized everywhere in India. In our days the exam was called *"matriculation examination"*.

Chapter 3:
Going to College, Becoming Political

In the previous two chapters I have indicated that already as a child, I was exposed to and somewhat influenced by leftist thought. That was in Kamrabad, and later through my brother-in-law Mr. Mukherjee. In the tenth class in school, toward the end of 1950, I was also exposed to the question of war and peace, because the newspapers had been reporting about the enmity between the two nuclear power blocks, one led by the USA and the other by the Soviet Union. One day, a classmate, Sumanta Bannerjee, distributed copies of an appeal for world peace, nuclear disarmament etc. and requested us to sign it. I do not remember whether I understood everything that stood in the appeal, nor whether I signed it. I came to know much later that this kind of peace movement was also an initiative of the communists. But I did not have anything against a communist initiative. Moreover, even a 14-year-old child could understand that war was a bad thing, and peace was good.

After passing the matriculation examination satisfactorily (i.e., in second division), it was time to go to college. In those days, the additional two years of higher-level schooling (called the intermediate level) that had to be successfully completed to be eligible for a university degree course, used to be done in a college that offered B.A. and B.Sc. courses in various disciplines.

Because in our family circle there was a lack of good advisors on educational matters, it was by default left to my eldest brother to choose the college and also play the role of my guardian. He chose the *Bangabasi College*, to which he too had gone. It was a bad institution, having the reputation of being a mass college. Its main advantage was that it was situated very close to the main railway station of Calcutta (called *Sealda*), because of which it attracted many students from the rural and suburban areas, from where people could easily commute to the college. There was another such mass college in the same locality. In our college, there were two or perhaps three sections for the intermediate level in the natural sciences (ISc.). In each of them about 150 students were registered. Although the intermediate course was deemed to be for higher level schooling, the teachers were not called "teachers", but "lecturers", and the taught were not called "pupils" but "students", as if they were already university students.

At the age of 15, when I started college, I was simply not prepared for the 45-minutes long lectures by our lecturers. Consequently, I did not learn anything in college; everything I learnt was from reading the text books. And I skipped everything that I did not understand. Moreover, I had taken mathematics as one of my subjects – a bone-dry, abstract and boring thing. Unlike physics and chemistry, the sciences that at least helped us, teen-agers, understand some phenomena of the real world, I did not understand what mathematics that was being taught at that level was all about. I also never understood how some people of my age could be so interested in learning this kind of mathematics – Binomial theorem, Sard's lemma and all that – if it was not just for getting a high grade in the exam, that was easier to get if one was good in mathematics.

I really found it great that a law of physics explained to me why we often literally made a belly-landing on the street when we tried to get out of a running bus, or how it could explain the orbital motion of the Earth around the Sun through the interaction of centripetal and centrifugal forces. I was also fascinated by chemistry, when I learned that common salt was actually sodium chloride. But mathematics at the intermediate level did not explain to me anything about the world around me.

School-level mathematics was another thing. When I learnt, in geometry, that any two sides of a triangle are together greater than the third side, I immediately understood that any one side of a triangle is less than the sum of any two sides of the same. This explained to me why all grown-up people always preferred to take a diagonal path from A to B, if there was one. This also explained to me why in Kamrabad so many people used to pass through our courtyard.

In our close family circle, I remember, for some, I was the unsmart one. It was perhaps also because I often asked "why". For things that others learnt intuitively or automatically through observation and emulation, or accepted without asking why, I needed an explanation. I often insisted on clear instruction, when others proceeded on the basis of random guess. My eldest sister once told us that, as a child, I asked why birds can fly but not we; why we always eat with the right hand and not sometimes with the left. This kind of differences between characters of individuals is perhaps a matter of chance. I was the product of one of the innumerable ways genetic determination and cultural influences mix. I simply developed like that by chance.

I was told that the kinds of mathematics I was asked to learn would be needed if I later wanted to study engineering. But I never wanted to become an engineer. I wanted/liked to understand the world around me, both the physical world and the human society. I was glad that I learnt some elementary physics and chemistry. I could have, should have learnt some biology too. But intermediate level mathematics did not interest me at all. It was a mistake that I was registered in college also for mathematics. It was my eldest brother who decided for me.

But it was also my fault that I did not learn much at this level. It was not my ambition to learn everything that stood in the textbooks. I still wanted to be a famous cricket player like Don Bradman. That was my ambition. (I later thought, perhaps it was just a baseless dream.) At that age, I never thought about my future profession, my future career. In those days, particularly in India, it was not possible to become a professional in any branch of sports, neither in football, nor in cricket, not even in Hockey, in which India was world champion. All prominent players had to have a job for their livelihood. They were only given sufficient free time to practice their branch of sport. In any case, I reported to the tests and got selected for the college cricket team. I was not particularly successful in the first match I played for the college team. In the second match, my batting skill was not tried, because those batsmen who were sent to the pitch before me, played out successfully the whole time allotted to us. And then came the hammer. My participation in the third match, for which too I was selected, was thwarted by my mother.

I was not at home, when the messenger from my college came to tell me that I should come for the match. He gave the message to my mother. But when I came back home, mother withheld the message from me. So,

I could not appear for the match. My brother Dilip, who knew about the message, also did not dare tell me anything. He told me about it only later, when the date was gone. I was very sad about the missed opportunity and furious with mother. For a few days, I did not speak a word with her and stopped even going to our local playing space. That was the end of my dreaming about becoming a famous cricket player. Some years later, when I looked back on this incident, I was no longer angry with mother, for my said ambition had ended.

Again, I learned just enough to pass the Intermediate Science exam satisfactorily, i.e., in the second division.

In Pursuit of a Bachelor's Degree

I knew that for any halfway decent job I had to have a bachelor's degree, no matter in which area of studies. I did not have much interest in pursuing further the natural sciences, not the least because I was not interested in higher level mathematics. As indicated above, I was more interested in understanding the world of humans and human societies and cultures. So, I changed course. This time I decided myself to pursue the social sciences and humanities.

I chose economics, i.e., political economy, and history. In addition to such subjects, every student of the Bachelor of Arts (B.A.) course had to take English literature as a third major subject, and Bengali literature, a little of that, was compulsory for all such students. I was satisfied with this selection, because, firstly, I wanted to understand how the economies of the human societies functioned, and political science, which was a part or even half of the whole subject of political economy, would give me, I thought, the possibility of understanding how states and human societies and their policies developed. I was not particularly interested in reading English literature, but I thought anybody who wanted to have a good command of English needed to read some English literature.

Hotbed of Leftist Politics

Bangabasi College, where I continued to study for my bachelor's degree, was a hotbed of leftist politics. The students' union was since long in the hands of leftists, and its leaders were members of the Communist Party.

Ordinary students like me, who were generally sympathetic to the Left, were persuaded to become members of the All-India Students' Federation (AISF), a front-organization of the CPI. They had no tasks and no duties, and also had no say in the affairs of AISF. Only, they had to pay a few cents to symbolize their membership of the organization. It was said that the student leaders were specifically sent by their party, the CPI, to such colleges to take over the students' union.

They did not have to try much. The whole atmosphere in Calcutta, particularly among the educated middle class, was sympathetic toward the communists. It was actually so since the second half of the 1940s. During the first half of this decade, there was a lot of ill will toward them because they refused to join the anti-British movement – with the argument that the Soviet Union was in danger and the British and the Soviets were allies. After the glorious victory of the Red Army in Stalingrad (1943) and then after the fall of Berlin (1945), the Soviet Union became immensely popular, in spite of all the preceding negative reports from the 1930s. All over the world, as we know from history, Marxist communists started to be treated with more respect, in the urban centers of India too.

In our college, in the mid-1950s, when I was doing my B.A., there were some highly respected Marxist intellectuals who were working as ordinary lecturers. One of them, Prof. Niren Roy, was teaching us Shakespeare. Younger lecturers — would-be intellectuals – could be seen discussing with him some intricate issues of Marxism. Prof. Roy was a leading light of a group of Marxist intellectuals of Calcutta, who regularly published a highbrow Bangla journal called *Parichay*. It became fashionable, also among young students like us, to read some Marxist literature or at least to pretend to have read some. Often, it was only showing off. After all, it was not so easy to understand Marxist literature, particularly to understand the original texts of Marx and Engels and Lenin and Stalin. For this reason, we were mostly satisfied with having read some Bangla literature, poetry and prose, written by some Marxist belletristic writers. Thus, I read a book by Gopal Haldar on the subject of, and also titled, *transformation of cultures*. Haldar was also a novelist. He became famous, at least among left-leaning readers, for a novel-trilogy, the hero of which, while being taken to the prison, said to himself: "You are not only a student of history, but also one of its weapons."

But it was very easy and cheap to buy the famous works of Marx and Engels and other famous Marxists. They were published in the Soviet Union, beautifully bound and sold for a pittance. They were so cheap that I could buy many of them from the pocket money I got from mother. I remember, I bought even the eleven volumes of Stalin's collected works. Not that I had the time to read them. There were many other more important things to read. But I thought I would later have time, and they were damn cheap.

Not only our college, the metropolis Calcutta itself was a hotbed of leftist politics. Apart from the Moscow-oriented Communist Party of India (CPI), there was also a Revolutionary Communist Party of India (RCPI) and a Revolutionary Socialist Party (RSP). The RCPI was created by the Indian Trotzkists when Trotzki and Stalin fell out with each other in Moscow. To what extent they were revolutionary and in which sense, I could not know, because I was then still not so interested in such finer points. I only knew that their leader, Soumendranath Tagore, a very fine Bengali intellectual, was a nephew of our great poet Rabindranath Tagore and he lived in the same very big house in Jorasanko area, in which Rabindranath had lived until his death.

RSP was perhaps the party of those radical socialists who were dissatisfied with the moderate leadership of the Socialist Party, which was actually a group within the umbrella party Indian National Congress, which had been formed by all those whose main purpose had been to fight for India's independence from British rule, and nothing else.

All these left parties and groups had their own weekly, fortnightly and/or monthly news-magazines and journals in Bangla and English. They offered a feast of news and views and highbrow analytical articles on Indian and global political and cultural affairs. An interested left-leaning young man like me could not control the temptation of reading them. I bought and read many, but to read all was impossible.

These parties often also organized meetings and rallies to propagate their own politics. The big rallies were a specialty of the CPI. They could easily mobilize a few thousand supporters who demonstrated for some demands or against some bad policy proposal of the provincial or central government. Also the large trade-unions, all under communist influence or even led by CPI cadre, held large rallies at the beginning or at the end of a demonstration-march through the streets. Very big rallies were held on a huge open space called the *Maidan*, at the foot of a tall monument, which had been built by the British after one of their military victories.

Failure due to Over-Ambition

All such books and magazines, meetings and rallies were not only highly interesting. They also constituted a strong long-term distraction, particularly for me. For my bachelor's degree, I had taken the honors course in political economy, for which students were required to read (and learn) much more than the general B.A. course. Just for example: for the political part of *political economy* the student was required to read Aristotle's *"Politics"*, and John Stuart Mill's *"Considerations on Representative Government"*. And recommended reading was also Harold Lasky's *"Grammar of Politics"*. And all this over and above the usual text book of political science and Government and a book on constitutions of various countries. The student was required to absolve a similar quantity of reading and learning also for the economy part of political economy.

It was expected from the students that they absolved this unrealistic amount of reading and learning, in addition to all the other things, in two years. As indicated above, our college mostly attracted students of average merit from lower and middle middle-class averagely educated and averagely-cultured families. They lived in their family home, where they also had to do some household duties. It was much the same in my case. So, no wonder that very few went for the honors course in political economy. And those who took it, did not succeed.

As indicated above, I was by character an ambitious, but dreaming young man, actually overambitious. When I passionately played cricket, I wanted to become the best cricket player of the world. When I took the intellectual path, I wanted to read everything interesting. And I was interested in many different subjects. Moreover, there were the various meetings and lectures that I wanted to go to.

I neglected reading the boring books that were prescribed for our honors course in political economy, i.e., I read only a small fraction of them. Instead, I was reading Marxist/leftist literature and texts pertaining to theory, history and philosophy and so on and so forth. For example, I read several popular books written by a leading Marxist professor of Calcutta, Debiprosad Chattopaddhyaya, on the history of human society. I became an admirer of his, and when, in 1956, his 500-page long magnum opus *Lokayata*[*], a deep study of ancient Indian materialist philosophy, first appeared in Bangla, I immediately bought it and started reading. The content of the book was so fascinating and it was written in such an accessible style, that for about three to four months, if I was reading anything, I was only reading this book. This way, naturally, I could not prepare myself for the degree examination.

It was usual for honors-students to take a year more for appearing in the exam. But even after three years, I was not sufficiently prepared. I started getting nervous and experienced frequent mental breakdowns. This experience of failure finally brought me down to earth. It was this that cured me of my high-flown dreams, of my overambitious character. It was then that I decided to give up the ambition of getting an honors degree and be satisfied with a usual B.A. degree. And I gave myself sufficient time that removed the feeling of learning under pressure. I appeared for the usual B.A. degree exam in 1958 and passed.

Many years later, I often looked back on those years in the mid-1950s and tried to understand my character, my failure and my nervous breakdowns, without of course any knowledge of psychology. Was I a unique character? Or was it typical of youth? It may be that young people who come in contact with a great idea (or ideal) are easily enthused by it. The great idea may be becoming a great cricket player, a great artist, writer, singer or scientist. Or to take part in a great movement for nothing less than changing the world. After all, already in my school days I several times heard from my elders the dictum of "plain living and high thinking". Of course, there was no knowing who meant what by this dictum. The people around me, including the teachers, all lived their mundane

---

[*] Chattopadhyaya, Debiprasad (1992): Lokayata – A Study in Ancient Indian Materialism, People's Publishing House

lives. The only exceptions were the revolutionaries, those who fought for making India free and in that endeavor sacrificed their life, or the communist revolutionaries who pursued the ideal of freeing human society from capitalism. But I could only read about them.

Chapter 4:
The Great Disillusionment

In the previous chapter, I have written about the mental crisis I suffered from due to my repeated failures in preparing for the BA Honours examination. That was in the mid-1950s. That was also the time, to be exact, 1956, when I suffered a great disillusionment in regard to socialism, a concrete embodiment of which, in the view prevailing in those days, was the socialist society of the Soviet Union.

In 1953, Stalin died suddenly after a short illness. He used to be idolized as, after Lenin, the second great leader of the Russian socialist revolution of 1917, as the generalissimo who led the Red Army of the Soviet Union to victory over Nazi Germany, and as the chief architect of the first socialist society in the world. I still remember having read in more than one newspaper of those days and also in magazines published by the CPI-communists, how his death was mourned over by all kinds of people everywhere in the world. I remember a photo that showed leaders of the CPI carrying symbolically a coffin on their shoulders and marching through the streets of Calcutta.

But just three years later, in 1956, this highly venerated leader Stalin was divested of his place on the high pedestal through the "secret" speech of Khrushchev at the 20th Congress of the Communist Party of the Soviet Union. This speech was in reality not at all secret, for it was released to the US-American media and was published in the US-American press. When I read about it, I first thought it must be another American lie about the socialist Soviet Union. But no denial came from Moscow, not the next day, not the next day after. It did not come at all. Then it was confirmed by Moscow. Khrushchev had indeed given such a speech. In the opinion of the then leadership, Stalin was a scoundrel of a leader, a criminal, who had got all those Soviet leaders eliminated, who disagreed with him and so, constituted a threat to his own absolute power as the undisputed supreme leader.

Those young people of today who consider themselves to be leftists, socialists or communists without having read the history of the Russian Revolution, that of the Soviet Union, and that of the global communist movement, cannot imagine the feelings of devotion and unquestioned adoration that communists of those days used to display toward Stalin. They therefore cannot, I guess, imagine the depth of disillusionment, indeed of depression, that communists of those days were afflicted with due to these revelations on Stalin's crimes. Not only that, in our mind (at least in my mind), the whole image of the Soviet Union as a socialist state, a sort of earthly paradise in the making, crumbled. At a different level, also the *whole theory of socialism* and the *conception of a socialist society* that was directly and indirectly communicated to us through books, lectures and conversations, became questionable, at least for me.

Hard on the heels of de-Stalinization came the uprising in the "socialist" state of Hungary in October-November 1956, which was suppressed by the Red Army. I did not know in those days, nor do I know to this day the truth about this uprising. It was depicted to us by our comrades as the unfortunate result of the efforts of the enemies of socialism to discredit our ideology. Whatever might have been the truth, that it had to be brutally suppressed by the Red Army caused a great disillusionment in my mind. For quite a few years, there was no ideal anymore for me to cherish. These happenings in the year 1956, in fact, deepened my mental crisis of those days.

A strong literary expression of this disillusionment came from Howard Fast, an US-American author, who wrote about this in his book "The Naked God". I think it appeared just a year later, which explains its emotionality. Analysis of such a huge failure of an all-comprehensive ideology, of a whole system and a state, and their consequence for personal feelings and course of life of their adherents take time. I have done my analysis. I have already written about it[*] and will write more about it at a different place.

---

[*] See in this connection my (1) *Eco-Socialism or Eco-Capitalism?* Zed Books, London, 1999 (Sarkar 1999). And (2) the essay entitled *From Marxist Socialism to Eco-Socialism – Turning Points of A Personal Journey Through a Theory of Socialism*. In my Collected Writings, Vol. 1 (Sarkar 2023b).

I think a year earlier, I happened to have a conversation with a fellow student in the same college. He appeared to be much older than I. And he was already then (in 1955 or so) very knowledgeable. He was critical of the Soviet regime. He told me about the Moscow Trials of 1937. He then condemned Stalin for being a ruthless dictator, for ruining the reputation of the Soviet Union and thereby also harming the ideal of socialism. I had already started reading the history of the Communist Party of the Soviet Union (Bolsheviks), [CPSU (B)], but had not yet come to the year 1937. I was very surprised to hear all that. I could not at first believe him. I thought that was just anti-socialist propaganda, and the fellow student was surely a Trotskyist, a member of the RCPI. But all that he had said was a year or so later confirmed by the General Secretary of the CPSU (B) Khrushchev himself. Only I had been an ignorant and stupid fool.

In the previous chapter, I have referred to my mental crisis in the mid-1950s. That was due to other reasons, which too I have written about there. The effect of this great disillusionment on me was to deepen and intensify that crisis. I could not think any more of continuing my academic studies. That is, I gave up the idea of going for an M.A. degree in any of the social sciences or humanities.

1958 was also the year in which my father retired from government service. He was getting a pension. In usual cases, when the father retired, the grown-up sons had already started their professional career. That was also the case with my two elder brothers. My eldest brother had founded a family and was living and working in a different province. My second elder brother, Dilip, the artist, had got a school teacher's job teaching arts and crafts. His salary was too low to found a family and live independently. And I, the third grown-up son, 22 years old, had no job yet and was living with my parents as a dependent son. That was not a respectable situation for me. My two elder sisters had already been married. I guessed father's savings had been strongly depleted through the three marriages and buying the house in Calcutta. So I did not even dare ask him whether he would be able to finance my living costs and further studies. I started searching for a job. And with the help of moderately influential family friends, I found one in 1959.

Life as a Bank Clerk – Forced Down into the Real World

It was a bank clerk's job in a big bank called Punjab National Bank (PNB). I was first posted in the branch office at Howrah (Liluah), the tween city of Calcutta on the west bank of the river Ganges. Small pay, but it was secure and offered a modest career, in which one could end up as a branch manager. My whole family was glad that I got this job. What more can a son of a Bengali middle class family wish for, they all seemed to think, particularly one who had failed to shine academically.

I did not make myself independent by, e.g., renting a small one-room housing facility in Howrah. I continued to live in father's house, where I had free accommodation apart from the company of my family. And that was also to my parents' liking, because that way, more than half of my monthly salary could be contributed to the joint family budget. So, I started commuting daily to my work-place – from Ballygung in south-east Calcutta, where our family home was situated, to Liluah, a north-western suburb of Howrah where our PNB-branch was situated.

It was a grueling daily commute, six days a week. Someone, who has grown up in, e.g., Cologne, cannot imagine how grueling it was. Some Chief Minister of West Bengal, of which Calcutta was the capital, had added prestige to the metropolitan city by introducing double-decker buses, freshly imported from England. There was a bus-route from Ballygunge to Howrah, which was served by such buses. On my way to work in the morning, I took such a bus, where I usually got a seat; those who came a bit later, were not so lucky. They had to be satisfied with a standing space. In order to reach Howrah across the river, the bus had to pass almost through the whole central city region. In Howrah Rly. Station bus terminus, I had to take another bus to reach Liluah. The whole journey took about one and a half hours; in the evening rush hour, on my way back home, often even two hours, a long time even for conditions of those days. It was mostly because the bulky double-decker buses simply could not move fast through the congested streets of central Calcutta, but also because if it did, it would risk toppling at the slightest maneuvering attempt. In contrast, the small primitive buses that plied between Howrah Rly. station and Liluah could move fast, though fully loaded with standing passengers. For this stretch, I mostly got a standing space. In rush hours, some passengers used to hang at the open entrance door.

In the public transport system of Calcutta, there was also a tram service on the main roads. There was a tram route from Ballygunge to Howrah. But such a ride took a much longer time to reach Howrah. For trams could only move on rails, so that any obstacle, such as a stray cow, could block its movement. Including the commuting time, I had in all ten-and-a-half hours working day.

The bank clerk's job in itself was a comfortable one. I, like all clerks, did not have any manual work to do. We all had a seat, a chair and a table, or a chair at the counter. But the work proper was so easy that we self-deridingly called it "posting, stamping, filing": I.e., writing some words and a figure on a particular piece of preprinted paper, thus creating a voucher, and then writing the figure on a particular page of a ledger, which was called posting. Then put a rubber stamp on the voucher, thus stamping it. And then, at the end of the day, sorting out the papers and putting them in the proper files or folders, which was called filing. The average clerk was happy with this job. But there were some ambitious people among them, who wanted to make an effort to rise higher in the ranks of bank employees. They studied at home more about the business and work of banking. Their aim was to pass a two-part all-India exam to get a title called *Certified Associate of the Indian Institute of Bankers*. There was a small immediate pay-rise after passing each part of the exam. And it generally led to quicker promotions in the hierarchy of bank employees.

The next higher rank among the clerks was that of so-called "officers" (actually supervisors), whose job was to distribute the every-day, routine bank duties among the clerks and, if necessary, to check and correct the work done by the clerks – the just mentioned "posting, stamping, filing". But checking was hardly necessary, the work being so silly and damn easy. That means, the officers had generally only to look at the figures on the vouchers and put a tick mark beside it. For this actually simpler work than that of the clerks, the officers were paid a little more than that of the latter. And finally, each branch office had an accountant, one rank higher than the officers, the de-facto manager when the real one was absent for a day or two.

In the underdeveloped India of those years, the 1950s and 1960s, in our branch office, we did not even have a hand-driven adding machine. We had to add long vertical columns of figures in ledgers, all with only the head of the clerk as "instrument". Even the type-writer, the only machine in the office, was not an electrically operated one. Overall, it was a soul-destroying job.

The only exception was that of the branch manager, who had the responsibility of getting business for the bank. He had to evaluate the credit-worthiness of the clients, and examine, recommend or reject their credit applications. So, he had to have some above-average intelligence and knowledge of the world of business. It was the ambition of the more intelligent bank clerks to end their bank career as a branch manager.

Fortunately for me, our branch manager was a Bachelor of Arts (B.A.) degree holder. And his command of English was very good, which was a rare qualification in Bengal in those days. The others who had a bachelor's degree, the accountant and two or three clerks had a B.Com., i.e., they had studied a course in commerce (*Betriebswirtschaft* in German). Since in those days in India, all official work was done in English, it was necessary to write all official letters, including letters written by banks to their clients, in English. Now, this was something that not many people in the banking sector could do well. In our branch, it was the branch manager who could write very good English, and after him, I was the only person who could write English well. Even my colleagues noticed that and they started valuing me merely for this extra ability. The manager also finally noticed that. Thereafter, he started giving me the task, when it was necessary to write a draft of an important letter. I must admit, this little appreciation did me a lot of good. It gave me some self-confidence and self-esteem. Later, they also came to know that I was very well-read, at least compared to them.

Another thing that did me good was that I was often sent to the small and medium-size factories in the industrial neighborhood. There I had to check whether clients of the bank who had applied for a credit had enough raw materials or finished or half-finished products in stock in their warehouse, against which they had applied to get a credit. This particular task was unpopular, even disliked, among bank workers in general – I was no exception –, because this required them to leave the comfortable and clean workplace with a ventilator above their head, and go to the dirty and noisy factories and warehouses to do simple counting.

With the wisdom of hindsight, I can say that this simple and soul-destroying job in the bank pulled me down from my dream worlds to the real world of ordinary people, whose main concern was to make money – small money or big profit – by means of hard work or crooked methods of business. They did not bother about changing the world for the better, nor about becoming a famous cricket player, nor about understanding the world. If they at all wanted to know something, it was how, in the given circumstances, they could earn more money, be it a higher wage/salary, be it a higher profit. For most people in this poor world, there was only plain living, no high thinking.

I had to acquiesce in this real world, had to comply with its rules. Nothing else in my life up to then had come to fruition, no dream, no real half-effort. Not knowing what else to do in the evenings and the Sundays, I started privately studying banking, i.e., a specialization of commerce, with the goal of passing the CAIIB examination. This time, to my pleasant surprise, I could concentrate on learning the necessary things: basic accountancy, commercial law etc. After a year or so, I passed the Part 1 of the CAIIB exam, and immediately got a small pay rise as reward.

Travel to the Andamans, Bay of Bengal

The grueling daily commute, the soul-destroying daily work in the bank and its whole drudgery soon prompted me to think of some leave. Not that I needed rest, but I needed to do something else, something that would allow me to evade the daily drudgery for a few days. Fortunately for me, it was then that my interest in reading literature stood me in good stead. A Bangla literary association, called *Banga Sahitya Sammelan* (in Bangla), that used to hold annual meetings of Bangla litterateurs, announced that their next meeting would soon take place in Port Blaire, the main town of the Andaman Islands situated in the middle of the Bay of Bengal. I asked them whether a person like me, who had not yet published anything, but had only read some literature, was also welcome to join.

They said such people too were welcome. Apparently, creative writers also needed the presence of their admirers, in front of whom they could deliver their addresses. So I took leave for some three weeks at the time of the said conference.

The Andaman Islands were originally a group of thinly populated jungle-covered wild islands which was simply taken over by the British rulers of India. Its original inhabitants were Negrito people – the Ongis, the Jarwas etc. The British later built in Port Blair a prison, where they incarcerated some of the leading Indian revolutionary freedom fighters. After India's independence, the government of India settled many Hindu refugees from East Pakistan on the main island. Such Bangla-speaking refugees got agricultural land and other financial aids to build up their new life there. In the wake of the refugees came administrators, teachers etc. and workers for the upcoming timber and transport industries. It was such Bangla-speaking people, who were interested in providing the organization for the conference of the litterateurs.

It was a wonderful experience, the four to five days long ship voyage across the Bay of Bengal. For ordinary participants like me, not the planned addresses of the famous litterateurs were the most interesting thing, but the ship voyage, the first for us all. Of course, the residents of the main Island were very glad to receive us as guests, also the non-writers, and treated us, under the given circumstances, very well. But unfortunately, I must say, some participants were not at all interested in the literature part of the conference.

For me, the other very interesting thing was the visit to the refugee settlements deep in the jungle. The last part of the visit was a foot march on a jungle path. For the return foot march in the evening darkness, the hosts provided petromax lighting.

Two other events were also remarkable: (1) the sightseeing tour of the Cellular Jail, where our revolutionary freedom fighters were incarcerated. The jail building was not remarkable in any sense. But for us Indians, it was a sort of pilgrimage. (2) The chance meeting of some of us, I among them, with four *Ongi* aboriginal men, the original inhabitants of the island. They were short-statured, snub-nosed and as dark colored as Africans of, say, central Congo. It confirmed for me the thesis of anthropologists that Homo Sapiens originated in Africa and then spread in all directions. But how they crossed the Bay of Bengal and, who knows, how many thousand years ago, and why their forefathers at all undertook to do that, that will always remain shrouded in mystery. The civilized man who had coaxed the four Ongi men to come close to our accommodation, told us that he met them at the market. They had come there in search of usable things. They were wearing shorts like ours, but nothing else. They could surely communicate their wishes to the marketeers in a few words. But how they paid for what they bought I could not come to know. Maybe they simply begged? I wanted to approach them and shake hands, but they refused. A photographer among us took some photos, which was no problem. But when he wanted the Ongis to take off the shorts so that he could take some nude photos, they refused with a smile. They obviously had some sense of shame.

When we were in the refugee colony in the middle of the jungle, our hosts told us to be very careful and not go to the edge of the jungle. Because they had seen *Jarwas* there. Jarwas were (still are) known to be hostile to people like us, and they had/have bows and poisoned stone-tipped arrows. Only a year or two ago (in the 2020s), there was a report in the German TV that the Jarwas had killed a young American tourist who had landed on a Jarwa island in disregard of the warnings. The TV report also said that Indian anthropologists have been trying since long to befriend the Jarwas by making gifts of useful things. But they have not succeeded yet.

When the conference was over, we took the same ship for our return journey via Nicober Islands, from where we sailed to Madras. The stopover there was necessary to take up many bags of coconut as cargo. It was done on open sea, because there were no port facilities there. The journey to Madras through the open Indian Ocean was quite rough because of strong winds. Most of us felt sea-sick due to the waves. This journey too took four to five days.

After arriving in Madras, we had to absolve another event: a meeting with some writers and other litterateurs of Tamil literature. It became a bit awkward for us when it came to introducing ourselves. After the real writers and prominent people of both sides had introduced themselves, it was our turn to say who we the non-writers were. I saved the day for many of us, when I stood up first and said in English, the language used for communication on that occasion, that we were readers of literature; that we too had written our first creative texts, but they had been rejected by our famous editors. The Bangla-Tamil assembly of writers, editors and literary critics found my self-introduction very amusing. They broke out in laughter. And nobody else was asked any more to introduce himself.

Excursion to the Sunderbans and Kakdwip

After these extraordinary holidays, I returned to my routine bank duties. But thereafter too, now and then, an opportunity came to undertake some adventure to break the drudgery. Once a group of people from Kamrabad, the village of my childhood, organized a boat trip through the Sunderbans, the tiger-infested big delta jungle area in South Bengal, through which all the river waters of North India flow to the Bay of Bengal. It was a middle-size motor boat jam-packed with tour members including some housewives and children. These middle-class people, me included, had heard so many exciting stories about the wood-cutters and honey-gatherers who dared into the jungle to earn their livelihood. We all had also heard or read some stories of getting killed by tigers and crocodiles. We boarded the boat very early in the morning, when it was still dark, in Canning, the last railway station of that line. At daybreak, we were already in the jungle.

The heavily laden boat meandered through the many broad and narrow waterways of the delta toward the confluence with the sea. On the way, we saw two crocodiles sunbathing on the bank of the waterways, also many exotic birds, some deers, but no tigers. Our "guide" told us in a dramatic tone, as if he knew it: "The king of the jungle is observing us; have no doubt about it. Only we cannot see him." On the way, only once at a clearing judged safe, where there was a small temple, we could land for a short time to stretch our legs.

We reached the sea at noon, proceeded a little further and parked at a sand bank. Most of us also took a bath in the sea. There was also picknick-food for lunch. But I cannot remember any more whether enterprising young people cooked the food on the spot on the sand bank. We spent a few hours roaming around on the sunny sandbank.

We embarked on the return journey late in the afternoon. It was already dusk when we were back in the jungle. I asked myself how the driver of the boat would find his way back when it would really become dark. But he had experience of driving on the route. And, after all he only needed to drive northward, and mind the depth of the water. But he also needed to return to Canning, our particular railway station. I saw he had an assistant who, at his order, measured the depth of the water with a long bamboo pole. And his boat had a search light, so that he could always keep to the middle of the waterway. Even so, sometime when it was really dark, word got around that the driver needed the map, that whoever had it, may please bring it back to him. In any case, we came back to Canning safely.

A trip to the sea had always been a weakness of mine. But it is so with many people. Soon, I had another such opportunity. This time it was to Kakdwip, a trading centre in the deep south of West Bengal, on the bank of the Bhagirathi River – one of he two major arms of the Ganges. This time it was a small group of three people: Mr. Mukhcrjcc, my brother-in-law, may have had some work in Kakdwip. He asked me whether I felt like coming. I was game for it. The other person was also a friend of his. Again, the trip started by train. This time the last railway station was Diamond Harbor, a town on the Bhagirathi. From there we took a bus ride to Kakdwip. Trading centre sounds like something important. But remember, it was in the late 1950s or early 1960s. And Kakdwip lay in underdeveloped rural Bengal. We took two cycle rickshaws and told the drivers to give us a "sightseeing" ride. Thereafter we drove straight to the seashore.

This shore was very different. It was not blue, but yellow. The Bhagirathi, which has been a yellow river already at Calcutta – in contrast to, say, the blue Brahmaputra (Yamuna) in Bangladesh – poured thousands of tons of yellow silt into the sea. We walked along the seashore, which was, on that day, completely silent. Nobody else was there other than we three, and even the sea was totally calm, completely waveless. And a big surprise: I saw my first sand dune on any seashore, a small hill made of silt.

Remnants of My Dream Worlds

Although I was pulled down into the real world, some aspects of my earlier dream worlds remained. Inter alia, my leftist convictions remained. So, I was approachable by the trade union leaders. And once, because no one among my senior colleagues in the Liluah branch wanted to go to the organizing committee meeting of the union, the leaders coopted me on the spot as a member of the same representing our branch.

Another thing that remained was my love for reading on many different subjects. So, although I had decided to take the CAIIB examination, I still made some time for reading other things of interest to me. For example, I had heard about the genes that determine not only our body and its functions, but also our character. So I decided to read some basic stuff on the subject. And my desire to read leftist literature, including history of socialist thought, remained great. I therefore also continued to read on this matter. Not of course the heavy stuff, the original works of Marx and Engels etc, but some simpler introductory literature. These are but some examples.

Sometimes I told my colleagues, with whom I had become friends, what I had read on this or that question. They were of course very surprised and impressed. Once a colleague requested me to contribute an article to their hand-written magazine. When I asked him whether they would like to take an article on a scientific topic, he said they would very gladly. So I wrote, on the basis of whatever I had read, an essay on genetic determination of living beings, in Bangla. And they indeed published it. That was my first publication at all.

Learning German

I would not call these small satisfactions described above petty. They, after all, gave me mental stability and some sort of peace of mind. But they did not give me a sense of fulfillment. I did not think that a bank job was my destiny. I thought I had more potentials in me. And I wanted to test that. I was about 25 years old when I started to think like that. I considered whether I should take an evening course in economics for an M.A. degree. But I also hesitated. I was afraid of failing again.

When I was in such a state of mind, I saw in the newspaper a short advertisement, which said "Learn German in six months". I was surprised that the advertiser claimed one can learn German in six months, German, a European language. The advertiser, Sarat Bose Academy, seemed to be a serious institution. After all, it was located in a renowned house, the house of the family of our liberation movement hero Netaji Subhash Chandra Bose. Sarat Chandra Bose was an elder brother of Subhas Chandra Bose and was also a stalwart, a leading man, in our independence movement.

I thought I was good in languages. My command of English was good, and I could write good Bengali. I thought, if I learned another European language, for example, German, the language of Marx and Engels, then I would have a sense of fulfillment. And moreover, I thought six months, that was not too much time. If I see I could not do it, then I would have lost only six months' time. I wanted to try it. I registered for the six months course. It was 1961.

I learnt that our teacher would be one Graf Keyserling. I remembered the name Keyserling from reading a biography of our great poet Rabindranath. Our teacher was a son of this philosopher Keyserling, who was a sort of a friend of Rabindranath. And later, I learnt that our German teacher Graf Keyserling was himself a philosopher. I wondered what he was doing in Calcutta, and why he was teaching just basic German to Indian young people.

At the time of registering for the course, the Institute, i.e., Sarat Bose Academy, sold us, in addition to our textbook, a thin book of Keyserling. They said that would be our book for learning German grammar. But it was not what it promised to be. It was an attempted philosophy, Keyserling's philosophy, of German grammar, useless for students of German. I doubt whether anybody interested in philosophy ever read it. And if anybody read it, whether he understood it. I read it and did not understand it.

Anyway, I was not discouraged by the disappointment, neither with the book on German grammar, nor with the second one, namely, Graf Keyserling was not a good teacher, though he was, as I observed later, a very friendly man. I knew how to help myself. I went to the College Street book market area, and bought three books: Teach Yourself German, Teach Yourself More German; and the one that was used in the University written by an Indian Dr. Haragopal Biswas, a chemist who had studied in Germany in the 1930s. These books helped me a lot. For whereas the textbook that came from the German Goethe Institute was written from the beginning to the end in German and thus compelled the student to attend a course, with the help of the Teach-Yourself books that explained German grammar in English and a good dictionary, the student could learn the language himself. In these books there was also a pronunciation guide.

So, with my old learning zeal and new-found ability to concentrate, I made rapid progress. I needed the institute, the class and the teacher only for encouragement and for confirmation that I was making rapid progress. In some problematic cases of pronunciation, I had to ask the teacher, but not for grammar, syntax and vocabulary.

One day, a fellow student surprised me by asking whether I already had a job. Of course, I had one, the bank job. But that was not what he meant. He asked me whether I already had a job in Germany, and when I was going. When I replied that I had none and was not trying to get one, he was surprised. He asked me why then I was learning German so zealously. It transpired that all other students in the class were some or other kind of technicians and industrial workers; one or two were also engineers. They were already writing applications to German companies offering their labor capacity, know-how and experience for employment there.

Around 1962-63, my colleagues in the bank knew that I was learning German. Often, one of them would come to me on behalf of a friend, relative or neighbor with a letter from Germany and request me to translate it. These were replies from German firms to unsolicited letters of application for a job sent by Indian young men. The firms mostly regretted that they had no need for the applicant's labor power. It was easy for me to translate the letters. But to spare everybody concerned the trouble, I told my colleagues that if they found in the letter the two words *"leider nicht"*, then they should know the reply was in the negative.

I think it was sometime in the early sixties – 1961 to 1963 – young people came to know of the German economic boom and that German companies were recruiting workers from other countries. That was of course within Europe – Italy, Spain, Portugal, Greece, Yugoslavia etc. But enterprising Indian young men with some technical know-how and experience, particularly from the Indian industrial areas, wanted to try their luck. In Germany, there was prospect of much higher wages and also of a much higher standard of living. Most attractive was of course the prospect of leaving behind the bitterly poor, underdeveloped, disease-stricken, and chaotic homeland India.

I would like to conclude this chapter with the story of an extreme case of such a desire to leave India. In our locality, there lived a family whose two sons were our playmates. The older of the two, Goltu, was recovering from a serious illness, when we came to live there. In our mild winter, we saw him, heavily attired, basking in the sun on the Veranda. When he took a bath, the bucketful of water had to be warmed up in the sunshine that fell on the Veranda. We could then see how weak his body had become. After full recovery, he resumed playing with us. But he always looked very emaciated. A few years later, when he started searching for a job, he could not find any. But then, a few more years later, we suddenly heard that Goltu had a job and that he was leaving India. He told us, he had a sailor's job and his first trip on a cargo ship would take him to America. We all envied him.

But how could such a weak and emaciated man get employed of all things as a sailor, we wondered. He told us how. The interview for the job was damn easy. He could answer all questions to the satisfaction of the interviewer. But after that came the difficult test, the health examination. For that, he had requested a stoutly built young man, also our neighbor, to accompany him. When, at the health center of the merchant navy department, Goltu's name was called out, it was not Goltu who went in, but his stoutly built friend. Goltu thus passed the health test, and started waiting for his first appointment as a sailor. In those days, the only personal identity card was the passport, which was needed only for travel abroad. For the passport, Goltu stood himself before the camera.

Chapter 5:
Going to Germany

I was not planning to go to Germany as a worker, nor was I willing to pursue a career in the banking sector. But what I was going to do in future I did not know clearly. I knew that I had to earn my livelihood and contribute something to the family budget. But was there something beyond that compulsion? For the time being, I was learning German and reading all sorts of books and journal articles on all areas under the sky. I was also going to musical soirées, theatre performances and exhibitions of modern art. But, after the great disillusionment, I had lost interest in going to political meetings and demonstrations.

In my pursuit of learning German, I was achieving one success after another. I finished Basic-1 course in German from the Sarat Bose Academy and went on to do the Basic-2 course at the Calcutta branch of the Goethe Institute of Germany, because I had learnt German grammar well. At the end of this course, I found myself able to speak some German. And that impressed my German teachers. Writing correct sentences in German was no problem at all for me. At the end of this course – finding no other more attractive alternative – I decided to continue with learning advanced German. But in Calcutta, there was no new course for the Advanced-1 level that the Goethe Institute offered. So I asked Mr. Pawlik, who was my teacher at the Basic-2 level, whether he would allow me to attend the Advanced-1 course that he was already giving since the previous year. Mr. Pawlik gladly agreed to allow me to do so.

I really did not need any more teaching. I could have read German books – simple and difficult – with the help of a good dictionary and thus improve my vocabulary. But it was necessary to have company of fellow students with whom I could speak in German and also hear German spoken by others. In that Advanced-1 group, however, there was actually no fellow student who could speak full sentences in German without previous preparation. They had difficulty in finding words and formulating full sentences. But there was Mr. Pawlik, our teacher, who was always speaking German to us, and only German. That was of benefit to me. Moreover, he organized a conversation club, which was also attended by people who had been to Germany and could already speak German.

On one rain-swept evening, I was the only student who had defied the rains and come to the class. Mr. Pawlik also came; after all he had a car. He was surprised to see me; he had not expected anybody to come. He said he could not teach anything when only one student was there. But he requested me to tell him why I was learning German with so much zeal. I of course did not tell him anything about my past failures. But I told him about my frustration in the job of a clerk in a bank. I told him I needed some solace for my intellect, which I got from learning German and advanced German. Mr. Pawlik asked me whether I would like to change my profession. It was a difficult question to answer. For, on the one hand, I disliked my bank job from the bottom of my heart, on the other hand, I liked it for the material security it gave me. Even in those days, in the first half of the 1960s, it must have been difficult for Germans to understand this ambivalence on the part of even educated middle-class Indians, because in Germany, since long, all people enjoyed a guaranteed minimum of social security. When I came to Germany in the mid-60s, I found German students taking it easy and not in any hurry to finish their studies.

On that particular rainy day, I replied to Mr. Pawlik (I remember it roughly): I would like to change my profession, if I had security in my prospective new job. I do not know how it is in India nowadays, but in those days, security was, in general, written large in the mind of middle-class Indians seeking a job/profession. Mr. Pawlik offered to recommend me for a German government scholarship for altogether two years of higher German studies – with the expectation that on successful completion, I would return home and take up a job as a lecturer in one of the several Goethe Institutes in India. There would not be any security in the job, for there was no guarantee that the German government would forever financially support the Goethe Institutes. Nor would there be any guarantee that I would get such a job, as there was no guarantee that I would successfully complete the projected studies.

The offer was very good, I was tempted to immediately say yes. But I asked Mr. Pawlik to give me some time to consider the matter seriously, to which he readily agreed.

Thoughts on Marriage, Founding a Family, and Security

In India, in those days, a young man had to marry if he wanted to come close to a young woman. He had to control his libido until he became "marriageable". Schools and colleges were gender-segregated, as it is said nowadays. He could not even freely talk to a young woman who was not a member of his own family. Going to a park with one like that just for a stroll was difficult if not impossible. In such rare cases, even in the later decades, there was always the tacit expectation on the part of the young woman and her parents that this would finally end in a marriage proposal. I knew it from a case or two in my own nephews' circle.

In my case, however, I needed a secure job, even one badly paid, primarily for my own mental stability, and secondarily for my contribution to the family budget toward my own living expenses. There was no thought in my mind of marrying or founding a family. I had even thought of not marrying at all, never. In my college days we had read and discussed about the curse of too many children being born in our poor country. I had played with the idea of finding a woman who would agree to marry me under the condition that she would not want to have a child, which was well-nigh impossible. How could one even imagine bringing a child into this miserable world, I had thought. So it was a little easier for me to decide in favor of the rather insecure enterprise that Mr. Pawlik proposed.

From a purely material point of view, it was a rather irrational decision. For in the rather soul-destroying but secure bank job, I could have made a career and risen up to at least the level of a branch manager and, who knows, still higher. In the Goethe Institute (GI), I knew already, there was no such opportunity. There, the "branch manager's" post (institute director's) was open only to Germans, even that of the deputy director's. But for me, the prospect of being able to leave the world of essentially only money-making, namely banking, and working in some kind of a "cultural" world was highly tempting. Tempting was also the prospect of seeing the world, i.e., Europe, that went with the scholarship – a small part of the world, of course, but that is where much of world history took place.

To Poona First

Before embarking upon the journey to Germany, however, I had to spend the first four months of the study program in Poona, India (October 1963 to February 1964). The higher-studies-in-German program, for which I got the scholarship, required that the scholar had utilized all the possibilities of studying higher German in his/her homeland and evidenced some aptitude for teaching. In my homeland, in India, the Goethe Institute had some years ago opened in Poona a residential facility for learning German rapidly through intensive two-months courses. There they also offered a very high-level course, called "Oberstufe" in German. In English, it could be called Advanced-3. The five Indians who had been provisionally chosen for the said scholarship, were asked to first go to Poona for four months and do the "Oberstufe" and two more months of still higher German. It was all the first part of the program and was also covered by the scholarship.

In Poona, we stayed in the Institute's own hostel, properly gender-segregated. But there was no segregation in the classes. We were three men and two women, plus two other men who had come for just learning more German. At this "Oberstufe" (Advanced-3+4) we had to read some classical German literature. I do not remember any more all the texts that we read. Only one I remember: it was Immanuel Kant's famous essay "Was ist Aufklärung" ("What is Enlightenment"), a demanding text. I mention it only as an example, to give an idea of the level. Apart from German literature, we also had to get acquainted with the outlines of German history, art history and geography of Germany. But I do not remember the details any more. And then each of us had to prepare and deliver a talk on a theme of our choice. I chose as my theme the philosophy of Hegel and his influence on the young Marx. It must be understandable to my readers given what I have narrated above about my life before I came to Poona for this course.

I must here mention a thing usually very much worth mentioning in all autobiographies: It was here in Poona, during this course, that I came to know my wife to be, Maria. She was then only one of our lecturers, Fräulein Maria Mies. There was no love affair between us in those four months. Maria later became very famous as a feminist theoretician and a leader of the leftist women's movement[*].

During these four months we also had to observe some Indian lecturers of the Institute teaching in their respective classes at the Basic-1 and Basic-2 levels. The advanced courses were all given by the Germans. The purpose of these so-called *"Hospitationen"* was to acquaint us with the teaching method used in the Goethe Institutes. We were expected to use this method when we would return home after finishing our higher German studies and start teaching German or some other foreign language, nobody knew where. I had doubts about the efficacy of this method – then, and also later when I myself started teaching German in India. But I was then only an observer (*"hospitant"*), not even a colleague of the lecturers. So I did not say anything.

At the end of these four months, sometime toward the end of February 1964, we had to take the exam for the first part of our scholarship-supported higher-studies program. I did well – to the satisfaction of all concerned, and was told to immediately start preparations for the journey to Germany. Two other fellow students (*"Kommilitonen"*) also succeeded and were selected for the scholarship. Two were not selected. I only knew why one of them did not succeed. He had become a good friend of mine. At the trial teaching of a Basic class, which was a part of the exam, he was so nervous that his hand trembled. That was judged as evidence of lacking aptitude for teaching.

I felt pity for this friend, for I had experienced similar nervousness before my B.A. Hons. Exams. And I too had experienced failures. I later visited him once in his home city Delhi. He came from a lower middle class educated family. He had done M.A. in psychology and was working as a laboratory assistant in the psychology department of the Delhi University – not a well-paying job. He lived with his family – wife, two children and old father in a two-room apartment in the old city. He too

---

[*] She also wrote her autobiography („Das Dorf und die Welt", Mies 2009).

must have dreamt of rising to the level of a lecturer in German. It was not too much ambition, and he was good in German.

Stuck in the Jungle of Indian Bureaucracy

At the time of writing these lines, 2024, we are hearing that the German economy is in the doldrums: One of the important reasons, why it has difficulty in coming out of this situation is, according to observers, the burden of widespread bureaucracy and too many rules and regulations. Even medical doctors in hospitals, school teachers and other such people in the public service sector are complaining about too much bureaucracy. And this in the age of computers and comprehensive digital communication. Imagine now how it was in 1964 in India. As soon as I got the official letter from the Goethe Institute in Munich saying that they are giving me the coveted scholarship and that I should come to join the course in April, I undertook all the work to get my passport. In those days, not all Indians could get a passport without sufficient valid reason. Of course, a scholarship was a good reason, but the passport officers in the Calcutta office of the Ministry of External Affairs could not issue the passport themselves. After I had met them several times, they told me that the matter had been sent to New Delhi. Why? Because, they said, my scholarship was related to higher education, the Ministry of Education of the central government also had to examine the case, to see whether it was awarded following due procedure.

While waiting for the passport, I already applied, without a passport, for a visa to go to Germany. The Germans in the Goethe Institute in Calcutta, my well-wishers and advisers, had told me that I needed one, because I would be staying there for more than three months. At the same time, I also applied for two years of unpaid leave from my job at the Liluah branch of the Punjab National Bank. There too, the branch manager could not decide on the matter. He sent my application to the head office of the PNB, also situated in New Delhi.

These were nerve-racking two months. The passport office in Calcutta told me that the Ministry of Education in New Delhi was asking why the scholarship was not advertised and the selection not made by a selection commission. Then I heard from the PNB, the Staff Manager had written that there was no such thing as unpaid study leave in the bank rules. That meant, I had to quit the job.

We Indians had been used to long waits before succeeding in getting something done in government offices. But I could not wait, for, in Germany, my course was going to begin sometime in late April. My Indian well-wishers, also elder relatives, advised me to go to New Delhi and to the various offices there to do some lobbying for myself. But that was too much trouble for me. I decided to rely more on my mastery of the art of letter writing.

Sometime later, Lufthansa's Calcutta office got wind of my travel plans and sent a sales agent. I was not at home, but his visit impressed my father and the rest of my family. They were clearly excited. And I got news from the Consulate of the Federal Republic of Germany that my visa had arrived and that I should now only come to them with the passport. But my passport was still not there.

In the meantime, I had written a strong and long letter to the Chairman of the Punjab National Bank (in those days, it was Mr. Ramnath Goenka, a big tycoon). I appealed to him to grant me the unpaid study leave, for, I lied a little, I very much wanted to make a career in the PNB. And I got a positive reply. The same Staff Manager, who had a month ago decided to reject my application, wrote now that he was pleased to inform me that I had been granted the two years unpaid study leave, and that I must now only tell him when it should begin.

The last day of April came and went. Nothing more happened. About ten days later, I was in the office of the Goethe Institute, the Deputy Director informed me that the GI in Munich had asked her to convey to me that it was now too late to join the course that had already begun in April, and that I should now try to come in September to join the next course that would begin on 1st October. I was not exactly heartbroken, but very disappointed. I took it stoically. I had indeed become a sort of a stoic after the experience of the previous two months.

After finishing that day's business (I do not remember what it was), I returned home at around 2 pm. My mother told me something had come by post for me. It was my passport.

Excitement in the Family

The arrival of the passport generated great excitement in my extended family. Until then, everybody knew I was learning German and was doing well in the subject. They knew I went to Poona for a higher course. They also knew that I had got a scholarship and that I was trying to go to Germany. But they also saw that after returning from Poona I was again living in our family house and regularly going to Liluah to work in the bank. Only a few of them also knew that I was having great difficulty in getting my papers. Only Dilip, my immediate elder brother, seemed to share my pains. Maybe because he was not yet encumbered with his own family matters.

But after the arrival of the passport, everybody understood that I was now definitely going to leave India and the family, that my departure from Calcutta was impending and that there was no knowing whether and, if at all, when I would come back to Calcutta again.

Actually, as described in the first chapter, ours was an average middle middle-class family. There was no tradition of higher education in our family circle. Only my maternal grandfather was a graduate engineer. And the only paternal uncle, father's elder brother had a B.A. degree. Moreover, in those days – up to the 1950s and early 1960s – simply poverty prevented most middle-class families from allowing, much less urging, even their brightest offspring to pursue higher studies. They had to start earning money soon after finishing their bachelor's studies. In some cases, where the family could afford to wait for a few more years, bright young people did an M.A. or M.Sc. degree. They usually became lecturers in colleges. Calcutta was full of high level scholars in various areas of knowledge, who only had an M.A. or M.Sc. degree. Research-facilities and -scholarships for doing Ph.D. were rare in India. And sending their most intelligent children abroad – to England or, say, Germany – was a privilege of only rich middle-class families with a tradition of pursuing higher studies. No wonder that such an act/event added some prestige to an average middle middle-class family. I guessed, my parents too felt proud of my going abroad for higher studies. Because of the prestige value of such events, there arose in those days, at least in Calcutta and surroundings, a funny practice of inserting a notice in the newspapers saying that Mr. so-and-so is going (has gone) abroad for higher studies – even when "higher studies" meant only a "technical training" followed by a job abroad. I prohibited my family from doing such a thing.

After it became known that I was soon going to Germany, some well-wishers came forward to give me good advices and help me prepare for the journey. An in-law of my paternal uncle, who was doing export-import business, and used to wear well-made suits, took me along to his special tailor and ordered on my behalf two sets of custom-made suits. A neighbor ("quasi elder brother"), who had been to Germany for a technical training, took me along shopping for life in Germany: "We" (i.e., he in my name) bought a good suitcase, a dressing gown and a winter coat. It was all very embarrassing for me, but I had to swallow everything; they were after all well-wishers.

Although everything went on smoothly thereafter, – I only had to wait until September – I was not spared some last few days of anxiety. Maybe a month before my departure, a light epidemic of dengue fever broke out in Calcutta. And a cousin of mine, who was living in our family, had it. For some time, in order to avoid the risk of getting infected, I thought of leaving our house, going to my eldest sister and spend the last few days with her. But I dropped the idea, stayed on in our house and waited stoically.

On the day of departure, I wore one of my newly made suits and a necktie (for the first time ever). Many of my colleagues in the bank came to the airport to bid me farewell. I had become a sort of a star for them. My parents, my brother Dilip and, I have forgotten who else, also came. My mother, strangely, looked glum and unhappy. Maybe she had wished that I stayed on in Calcutta and at the age of 58 retired as a branch manager in the Punjab National Bank.

Chapter 6:
Arrival In Germany

Although in 1964 there was no television in India, it was not as if Germany was terra incognita for me. Since I learnt German at the Goethe Institute (GI) of Calcutta, and since the Germans often showed in their premises German films – both feature films and documentary ones –, I was already acquainted with a lot of German landscape and knew a lot about German history as well as German society as it was in those days. But still, being there was a different experience. There I could also engage in conversations with Germans.

I arrived in Munich by the same plane as Ms. Kamakshi Mani, my compatriot, who too had received the scholarship that I had. Since we already spoke fluent German, we had no problem reaching by bus and taxi the office of the GI where we were being expected. From there we were taken to a restaurant for lunch, where we met several other foreigners, our would-be fellow students, and the director and staff members of the seminar, at which we would carry on our higher-studies.

I was asked there why I did not come in April. When I told them what the problems had been, they were surprised. They had thought, they said, in every state, any citizen had a right to a passport and could travel abroad any time. That was of course the case in West Germany. But we Indians did not yet enjoy the right to travel abroad. Firstly, we did not all have a right to get a passport, and, secondly, even those who got one, got it only for travel to a restricted number of countries. Moreover, we could not exchange at will our Indian Rupee for hard currencies at a free foreign exchange market.

I also told them about my long wait for a West German Visa. They were surprised to hear that. They said, there had been no need for me to apply for one. They told me, but too late, I could have come without one and the GI would then have done everything else. But nobody, no German adviser of mine, had said that to me in Calcutta. It would have saved me some unnecessary trouble.

When the reception with lunch was over, we foreign scholarship holders were told in the office where our first station would be. We of course already knew that it would not be in Munich, but not all of us knew the name, exact location and the logistics of travel to those small towns. Here I experienced my first case of the famous German perfection. All of us got a piece of paper, on which stood written not only the name and address of the GI, to which we had to go first, but also the details of the train connections to those places. We were told, somebody from the GI would be waiting there to receive us.

On this my first day in Germany, I also made my first experience of a pitfall of German perfection, of their famous punctuality. The first two-months' stay for me and three others was Grafing, a little over half an hour's train journey from Munich. Everything went according to plan, as noted down on the piece of paper we had received. We left Munich Hauptbahnhof (main rly. station) late afternoon by an express train. But because Grafing was a small place, and this train did not stop at all stations, we had to get down at a previous station and change over to a local train for commuter traffic (*Bummelzug*). For this action, we were given only two-three minutes time, which was usual and enough for commuter traffic. Now, all of us four, having arrived from foreign countries for a long stay in Germany, were travelling with heavy luggage, and for this change of train we had to go through a tunnel to another platform. We could not make it in the short time. The connecting train arrived punctually and also left punctually. We missed it. Unfortunately for us, this late afternoon local train was the last of the day for travelling to Grafing. We were stranded.

It was 1964. There was no mobile phone in those days. We could have found a call box if we had left the railway platform. But we did not have the private telephone number of the director of the GI in Grafing. It was a taxi driver who saved us that day. He scented business when he saw us stranded foreigners. He offered to take us all to Grafing plus all our luggage and started bargaining. I do not remember any more how much extra he demanded for his service. We had no alternative but to accept his demand. He brought us to the GI. Thereafter, the GI-employee who was waiting for us took over charge and arranged everything. I do not remember all the details. But at the end of the (for us) very long Autumn Day, in the semi-darkness of twilight, all of us landed in our respective rented rooms in private family homes.

This story of my journey from Calcutta to Grafing reminds me of another similar story from India of the mid-1950s, in which I was involved. My brother-in-law, husband of my second sister, who was an officer of the provincial government, had been ordered to go from Calcutta (in the south) to a higher post in the Himalayan town of Darjeeling in the far North of the province. We, his in-laws, had to help him arrange everything. He was travelling, as the Germans say, with "Kind und Kegel" – wife and three small children plus heavy luggage. We – our mother and we two brothers, Dilip and I – accompanied them, because we knew that they would need help at every step of the difficult ca. 24 hrs. long train journey.

In the middle of the journey, in the darkness of midnight, we had to disembark at Farakka, at a poorly lighted and poorly built provisional railway platform on the southern bank of the great river Padma, cross it by a ferry steamer, and then board on the river's northern bank another train that was waiting for us   again at a poorly built and poorly lighted provisional railway platform. All this hassle had become necessary because in those days after the partition of India, the Indian Railway was not allowed to use the old bridge across the river, which then was situated in East Pakistan. There was namely political and military tension between the two countries at the time. And, moreover, the Indian state was building a barrage across the river at Farakka.

We got down next day in the forenoon at Siliguri, the end station of that train on the plains, just at the foothills of the Himalayas. But our journey did not end there. At Siliguri, we were scheduled to take another train, a narrow-gauge mountain train, that would crawl through the foothills upward to Darjeeling.

In those days, punctuality was not written large in the Indian Railway system, nor in the mind of Indian bureaucrats. My brother-in-law, who was travelling first class with our mother and his family, (we two brothers were in the third class), was dilly-dallying in getting down from the train and check-counting the pieces of luggage. Meanwhile, on the other side of the platform, the mountain train was waiting to depart. The guard was waiting to flag off the train, which was already delayed. He became impatient and came up to my brother-in-law and shouted at him: "Do you want to take this train, or should we leave without you?" Then only we all hurried, and the porters too, and we boarded the mountain train. What a contrast to our experience while travelling to Grafing!

In Grafing

Grafing was a beautiful small village with the obligatory church and a market place, about three quarters of an hour train journey away from Munich. It is of course still a village, only it must be much more developed than 60 years ago. I got a room in a small private house of a widow, who was living in the ground floor with her son and his family. The first floor was rented out to the Goethe Institute, for two foreign students. I got one room and the other one was occupied by a Syrian, who was also going to attend the same course as I at the Goethe Institute. I saw the old lady at the beginning and then rarely. I also hardly saw the son and his family. I realized soon that they didn't want to be disturbed unnecessarily.

It was autumn and quite cold for an Indian. The old lady came next morning to show me how to heat my room. The heating system with briquettes would surely appear very primitive to modern-day Germans. I do not know, whether modern middle-class Indians living in, say, New Delhi, heat their rooms in the winter. But in those days, we in Calcutta, also situated in northern India, did not have any heating at all, not even in a very cold winter evening. We then used to wear two sweaters and otherwise tolerated the cold. But the Bavarian autumn cold was much colder.

With this system of heating, I could withstand the Bavarian autumn cold pretty well. But a problem arose six days later. It was Sunday. I could not go out because it was foggy and cold. Moreover, I wanted to stay in my room and read. But by the late afternoon, all the six briquettes the old lady had given me, were burnt out. When it again became cold in my room, I went to the old lady (sorry, I have forgotten her name) and told her I needed more briquettes. She was very displeased. She told me: "It is now only autumn and you are burning so many briquettes! What would you then do in the winter?" The disgruntled old lady gave me two more briquettes and said: you must live with this much. I really did not know then what I would do in winter. I remembered Shelley's poem as my only consolation: "If winter comes, can spring be far behind?"

A fellow-student of mine in the same course, Van from Vietnam, told us his story of suffering due to the heating system in his accommodation in Grafing. He and a US-American, who had come to Grafing just to learn German, were housed in an originally big longish room divided into two rooms and separated by a door. It might have worked OK in summer. But in autumn and winter there was a problem, for there was for the two rooms only one source of heat, and that was located in the room of the American. The houseowner himself managed the heating. When it gradually became cold, he put more wood in the hearth for the originally one big room. The result was bad for both tenants. The American sweated due to too much heat and for Van, it was still too cold. Van, let me add, came from South Vietnam, where there is never any winter.

There were many other foreigners who were learning German in Grafing. When I told them about my problem with briquettes on Sundays, they told me about their solution. They simply came to the institute, where one big class room was heated also on Sundays. There they did their homework and also enjoyed the company of other foreigners and classmates. From next Sunday onwards, I emulated them.

In Grafing, I got used to eating German-European food. There was no alternative unless one was prepared to take a lot of trouble. The Goethe Institute reserved a hall in a big restaurant for its scholarship-holding students. But also paying students came to that hall. There was no supermarket in Grafing, only one or two small grocery shops. It did not take me a lot of effort to start eating beef, although I was born a Hindu and brought up without beef. I do not know what the Muslim students did. But Ahmed, the Syrian classmate was a leftist like me. He probably ate also pork. Anyway, I soon liked many German dishes: *Bratwurst, Bratkartoffel, Schweinegulasch, Schnitzel* etc. etc.

With fellow students from the Goethe Institute in Germany (Lüneburg, 1964)
Photo credit: Saral Sarkar

But once I was really put off by a German dish: That evening, the cook offered oversalted soup to start with. Although the first ones who ate their first spoonful of that soup amply showed their distaste and sent the dish back, the cook continued to send his dish of oversalted soup to the late comers like me. I found it astonishing. I asked our teacher who also came to eat there whether the GI must pay for that soup. He only laughed with the others, who had tasted the soup, and said with humor: Yes, today's menu contains oversalted soup.

The GI with its many foreign students gave Grafing an international flair. The "elite" citizens of Grafing seemed to value that. In any case, they organized a get-together in cooperation with the director of the GI. The mayor welcomed us foreigners to his village and expressed the hope that we were feeling well there. I was selected by the Director of the GI to reciprocate on behalf of the foreign students with an oration. There was, as expected, a lot of talk about solidarity, peace and cooperation. I of course did not mention our problem with the number of briquettes. At the end, there was free beer for all.

A similar get-together between us, the future foreign teachers of German, and the German teachers of the nearest gymnasium (high school) was also organized by the latter. I do not remember any more whether it was in Grafing or in the nearby small town. We had to go there by a hired bus. At the end, there were conversations of a little higher quality between the two groups of teachers. They asked me about the use of learning German in India. I told them, at least I did not learn German in India for its usefulness in India, that I learnt it because I wanted to read German literature, apart from English literature. But, I said, it must be of use to Indian scientists. I do not remember anything more.

One Sunday, I went with Cruzito, a Nicaraguan fellow student, to the Church, just out of interest and inquisitiveness. It was my first visit ever to a church. I understood everything said there, and I went along with all the bodily gestures of the faithful. When it was all over, Cruzito told me he would introduce me to an old gentleman, who admired Indians very much. The reason for his admiration for Indians was that sometime in the past, another Indian student had saved a child from drowning and had declined to accept a monetary reward for his act.

Cruzito did introduce me to the old gentleman and his wife. He was glad to meet me and said that I should visit him soon. I readily agreed, because I wanted to have as many conversations with the natives of Germany as possible. But when I asked him when I should come, he hesitated. He said, he would let me know later. But then I did not hear anything from the old man.

Snowfall in Lüneburg

After finishing our two months' sojourn in Grafing, during which I had my first impressions of the German countryside, we were sent to a middle-size town in North Germany, Lüneburg. It was beginning of December, winter had begun. After my experience in Grafing in the autumn months, I was a bit worried. Because I had caught a little cold there. But I actually enjoyed the winter in Lüneburg. Firstly, because it was not so cold, secondly, because the heating system there was modern, namely central heating, and thirdly, because it snowed. I had seen snow lying on the meadows in Grafing. I was overjoyed to see that. But until then, I had seen snow falling only in American films. It was only seeing pictures of the thing. But in Lüneburg, I also experienced real snow falling, big snowflakes.

I could not go out on the very first day of snowfall, because it was already dark when we had finished the day in the institute, and it had stopped snowing. But I could see snow falling through the big glass window of our classroom. I saw how gradually three-four centimeters of snow accumulated on the branches of the trees in the garden of our insti-tute, how the green ground of the garden turned into a white carpet. On the way back to my accommodation, I intentionally took the path that had not been cleared of snow and walked gladly on the still fresh snow that made a crunching sound under my boots.

On the tobbogan in Lüneburg (1964). Photo credit: Saral Sarkar

Next Sunday afternoon, I went to the nearby park to enjoy a stroll on the snow that was still lying there. There were some more people doing the same, Germans all. But a noisy bunch of children around a hollow in the park attracted my attention the most. They were tobogganing down a slope of the hollow. They were having great fun. My childhood love for various kinds of sports was reawakened. I went to some of the kids and asked them whether I too could try it a little. They were friendly, and interested to hear that this dark-skinned grown-up foreigner wanted to play with them. They gladly gave me a chance. It was wonderful. Then they asked me to do it again. They insisted that I do it lying prone on the toboggan. When I was about to slide down, two kids just jumped on my back and we slid at great speed uncontrolled. Arrived at the deepest point, we were lying on the snow. It was great fun. I saw a man with a camera observing us. I spontaneously requested him to take a photo of mine lying on the toboggan. He obliged me, and a few days later I got my photo.

For the small town Lüneburg, it must have been something special that so many foreigners, would-be teachers of German in other countries of the world, were in town. The local newspaper even wanted to publish an interview with one of us. They selected my compatriot, Ms. Mani, a beautiful young woman from India. The interview appeared next day with her photo.

The director of the institute was also interested in holding an international cultural event with the foreign students as performing artists – not only with us, would-be teachers of German, but also with the ordinary German-learners. I had nothing to contribute to this event. I don't remember any Indian contributing anything. One Indian man, also from Calcutta, offered to sing two songs of Rabindranath (Rabindrasangeet). But he was not a good singer. His offer was rejected after the trials. But Indian culture was still represented – by an Indonesian female student who performed a beautiful classical Indian style temple dance with an earthen oil-lamp. Another beautiful dance I saw on that occasion was a Persian folk dance, in which a Persian male student, about 40 years old, played the role of a peasant, and a Persian female student played the role of the peasant's wife. They together performed a cheerful harvest dance. Remember, in their homeland, in 1964, it was the Shah of Persia who was reigning. The Mulla rule was still very far away.

From these two months in Lüneburg, I also have a bad remembrance, that of an accident. Lucia, a fellow student from Brazil, told me that there was an opportunity to travel to Lübeck by car and see there the house of the great German novelist Thomas Mann, which was serving as a literary museum and a memorial to the great author. I gladly accepted it, the date of travel being a Sunday. It was a Brazilian male student, Lucia's friend, who was driving a small VW-Käfer. It was a sunny winter day. Some gradually melting snow was lying on the asphalted road to Lübeck. Clearly, the Brazilian driver had no experience with snow-covered roads. He was driving too fast for such a road. At a curvy point on the road, it happened. We landed in a ditch on the roadside. It was fortunately a soft landing on softened earth. Nobody was badly hurt. With some effort, we all, newly arrived foreigners, could come out of the car.

We could not do much. In those days there was no mobile phone, nor telephone facilities at short distances. But car-drivers passing by stopped, enquired about our wellbeing, promised to inform the authorities and drove on. We had to wait on the roadside in mild cold until help came, police too.

The owner of the nearest car-repair shop had come with his machinery and instruments. He lifted the car out of the ditch and offered to make it again roadworthy. We had to accept the price he demanded. I do not know any more how much. I remember only that the failed travel to Lübeck cost me 60 Mark.

At the end of the two months' stay in Lüneburg, we, would-be teachers of German, were scheduled to finally go to Munich for carrying on with our higher studies. My feelings were already different from what they were when I arrived in Germany. The four months of living and learning in Germany and the international community in the midst of which I lived, had the effect that I already felt to be a world citizen and not an Indian in a foreign country. I now had more foreign friends than the total number of Indian friends I had in India. My friends now came from Korea in the Far East to California in the Far West, from Sweden in the Far North to South Africa in the Far South. I had a wonderful happy feeling. I felt at home in Germany, although I knew all the time that my homeland was India.

Chapter 7:
As Student in Munich

My feeling of living in a world community continued in Munich. The Goethe Institute (GI) had rented there a big house with many single rooms in the upper two floors, where we, the would-be teachers of German from foreign countries were accommodated. Our hostel was situated in the northern border district of Munich. I have forgotten its name. From there, we every day went by tram to Kaulbachstraße, in Schwabing (roughly in the centre of the city), where the teaching unit of the GI was situated. It was a beautiful old-style building at the edge of the famous „Englischer Garten", actually a huge park.

The students of our program were divided up into two groups, but we all had close contact with each other. We had all become friends. In Munich, I also came to know those who were not with us in Grafing and Lüneburg. So the internationality of the group became stronger. We all spoke German, but we came from different countries. Germany was also represented in the residential group by a sickly person who was not a student of the GI, but worked as an employee of the Max Hueber Verlag, publisher of the books that were used in the GI for teaching German to foreigners.

Excursus on Homesickness

I must here tell the story of one young man from Iran, who was also expected to become our friend, but could not. He and I shared a big double room, much bigger than the single rooms that my fellow students got. He came a few days after us. When he was showed into the room and introduced to me, I welcomed him heartily. But the young man did not reciprocate. I tried English, but that also did not help. He came with a violin. So I guessed, he would go to the music college after learning some basic German. I saw the young man rarely and only for a few days. I wondered, why the young man was so reticent. Maybe he came without any language competence other than in his mother tongue Persian.

When the young man had completely vanished, I asked a secretary of the GI what had happened to him. She told me, the young man was just 18 years old, and he was terribly homesick. He was sent to Germany because he was musically talented. But the young man could not bear life away from home. He simply went back.

Strangely, I never felt an iota of homesickness. On the contrary. I felt happy that I could come to Germany and study here, that all my fellow students were so friendly. Indeed, I felt a little sad when my student life in Germany was over and I had to go back home and start working in order to earn money. I asked my fellow students whether they felt homesick. They did, they said, but they never for a moment thought of giving up the study and going back home. All that they did in order to overcome that feeling was to cook native dishes and speak the mother tongue with their compatriots. I even liked German food and speaking German.

Let me come back to my main story. Also our lecturers, who lived in their own home but met us every day, became, so to speak, members of this friends' group, because they not only taught us literature etc. but also accompanied us in all our cultural study tours. When we, e.g., visited a museum or an art collection or looked around the famous churches and cathedrals of the German speaking world (which included Austria) they gave lectures on art and religious history of the region, and, inter alia, explained the difference between impressionism and expressionism in art, or Gothic and Baroque in architecture. We would also joke with them. For instance, Al Quader, a fellow student from Morocco, who was perhaps fed up with too many churches and too much church history, once called out to Frau Dr. Herbert: Frau Dr., there is another church there. It was a small unspectacular church. We all laughed loudly. Frau Dr. too.

Particularly Frau Dr. Herbert was a very cheerful person. She took care of our writing and speaking abilities. Of course, by the time we came to Munich to continue our studies at the Seminar for foreign teachers of German, all of us could speak German fluently. But we generally spoke simple German – fluent and with mistakes – in the context of everyday-life, and that did not need much effort, not any more. However, writing an essay in good German or taking part in a discussion on a serious topic – also an exercise for would-be teachers of the language – was not that easy, German being a very difficult language. Thereby we still made grammatical errors or chose wrong words and phrases, some more some less. It was Frau Dr. Herbert's duty to point out our errors and deficiencies, not a pleasant job. Yet she always did it with humor.

Later on in life, I found out, when I started writing essays and articles for Indian journals, how difficult it was writing one even in English and Bangla, the two languages that I had a good command of, and even when I was not pressed for time. It is not only a question of having enough time and having enough command of the language, it is also a question of whether the author has something to say, and whether he/she has enough knowledge of the subject matter. Think of it, there was no internet and no Wikipedia in those days. Of course, *Encyclopedia Britannica* and *Encyclopedia Americana* were there. But they were in the big libraries. And although newspapers and magazines were available to us, not many read one to keep abreast of what was happening in the world. In Munich, not all of us could write a good essay, some had difficulty in filling four pages with some thoughts based on knowledge of facts and figures. Some tried to fill the pages by writing in big letters, some had finished before the allotted time (one and a half hours).

Unfortunately, one of us also failed in the final exam. He was a good friend of all. He once told me: Saral, you know, when I go out with my German friends for a glass of Bier, they all say I speak very good German. But our teachers always give me bad grades. Another one of us, also a scholarship holder, failed. After a week or so of hospitalization due to some illness, he gave up and returned home. He was a professor of German in his homeland, had even written two books on German grammar, probably for his students. But in Munich, he was not good enough. Sad story. How would they show their face at home, I thought!

Another lecturer, whom I respected, was Dr. Rohner. He too was very friendly, but in a different way. He was our lecturer for German literature. His lectures were very philosophical, or, to say it in different words, deep going. He was a Kafka specialist, had written a biography of Kafka. His way of treating (and teaching) literature, leaving the superficial level of the story and seeking instead the subsurface statement on the human condition that the author was trying to convey, appealed to me very much. But exactly this way, I know from a conversation with an Indian student who went to Munich a few years later to do the same course, was regarded as bad. This Indian student thought Dr. Rohner was just a bagful of air.

With Dr. Rohner, we were reading, not Kafka, but Herman Hesses's *Steppenwolf* (Eng. Steppe Wolf). I read the novel with great interest and admiration for the author. Anybody who has read this novel of Hesse should recommend it to other friends of literature. But we also read with him Franz Kafka. I do not exactly remember what. I think it was the long story *Die Verwandlung* (Eng. Metamorphosis) around the absurd metamorphosis of a man into a beetle. This absurd story and its unfathomable insinuations and allusions on the human condition fascinated me so much that I decided to write my *Diplomarbeit* (Eng. Something like an M.A. dissertation) on Kafka. With this purpose, I also read his three novels and some more stories privately.

Dr. Rohner was an anthroposophist[*]. I am not going to explain or describe it here, because in 1965 I did not know what it exactly was. I/we only knew that it was a serious philosophy. Even so, his classes were not devoid of all humor. Once, he could even generate a loud laughter in the class. Choi, our classmate from South Korea, was one day sitting in the front row with a glum face. We knew from before that he was so. When, on that particular day, Dr. Rohner entered the classroom, he saw Choi's glum face and spoke to him: "Herr Choi, wie geht es? (Eng. Mr. Choi, how are you?"). In reply, Choi heaved a sigh of anguish and said "Ach Dr. Rohner, I am tired of life!" We others burst out in a loud laughter. But Choi was very serious that day. He asked in an angry grave tone: "Why are you all laughing? We immediately fell silent.

---

[*] Anthroposophy: A formal educational, therapeutic, and creative system established by Rudolf Steiner, seeking to use mainly natural means to optimize physical and mental health and well-being.

Meeting German Students in the Mensa. Eating Beef

In our world community of students of the GI, there was no German student. But I thought, having come to Germany as a student, I should also meet German students, at least some. This opportunity existed. One only had to go to the Mensa, the huge eating hall of the university, where students usually took their lunch in the afternoon recess and dinner at the end of the working day. It was of course meant for the university students, but it was accessible to all who wanted to have a cheap simple meal. That was of course my main purpose for going there regularly.

Many of my fellow GI-students, of course, preferred to eat their home-type food and cook it themselves, for which there was a kitchen in each of the two floors of our hostel. These kitchens of ours were also wonderful meeting and gossiping places. But the atmosphere in the Mensa, the opportunity one got there to meet many kinds of new people – students from many foreign nationalities as well as German students – was for me another attraction.

Of course, Indians, i.e., Hindus – had a problem with beef. And Muslims, generally, had a problem with pork. But I always saw some Muslim students eating in the Mensa. And a few Indian Hindu researchers too. I, born and brought up as a Hindu, ate beef from my very first day in Germany.

Once, Dr. Mukherjee, who was a teacher of German at the GI of Calcutta – apart from being a medical doctor, Yoga practitioner, and priest in charge of a temple – came to Germany for something and also visited the GI teaching center. I met him and out of deference to a senior colleague accompanied him to the railway station. Doctor Mukherjee, a Brahmin, asked me during the conversation in the waiting room, whether I have eaten beef in Germany. When I replied in the affirmative, he was very displeased. He asked me whether I was a Hindu. I could not reply to him immediately. In my embarrassment, I asked him instead: what was the difference between beef and the meat of a ram-goat, that all Bengali Hindus ate, including Bengali Brahmins. This time it was Dr. Mukherjee who was embarrassed. Or, so I thought. I remember his reply only roughly. In the general sense, he said: scientifically speaking, there was no difference. But religion was an altogether different thing. And there was also our cultural tradition. Both were important for him.

After seeing Dr. Mukherjee off, on my way back home, I thought about his question. I myself wondered: "Am I a Hindu?" Religiously speaking, No. In my childhood, I sometimes went into a temple as a sort of escort of my mother. Thereafter, never. In my youth, when I sometimes travelled in India, I went to a temple as a tourist, to see it as a piece of architecture, or out of pure curiosity. Moreover, I was an agnostic, an atheist, purely on logical grounds.

But my cultural tradition had not become unimportant for me. More-over, in the Hindu cultural tradition, there was also an agnostic or atheis-tic stream of philosophy. Debiprasad Chattopaddhyay has elaborated on it in his magnum opus *Lokayata*. Adherence to this non-faith has never prevented me from being a Hindu. I think, I can say, culturally, I have always been a Hindu. I have been brought up in the midst of this culture. After all, I have always loved to hear *Bhajans* of Meera, *Kirtans*, and especially *Rabindra-Sangeet* songs created by Rabindranath Thakur, who belonged to a stream of Hindu religiosity called *Brahma Samaj*. I could even sing Rabindra-Sangeet, many pieces of which belonged to the group "worship". And many of them were so touching that even atheists like me could not but shed tears.

One thing that surprised me on my very first day in the Mensa was that most German students, or let us say the average student there appeared to be older than his Indian opposite number. At first, I thought it was because of their well-built physique coming from their protein-rich meat diet. And I was perhaps seeing them in comparison to the shorter and weaker physique of rice-and-fish-eating Bengali students of Calcutta. Of course, the diet makes a difference. But later I came to know that German students studied longer than the average Bengali student of Calcutta. Un-like us in India, they were in no hurry to finish their studies as soon as possible and go seeking a job. They took their own time. Some of them were even married and had a child. Either their parents were well-off, or the state was paying their living and educational expenses. Of course, simply said, that was one of the manifestations of the basic difference between the rich, industrially highly developed and continually developing Western Germany and the still bitterly poor underdeveloped India.

But why were they so apolitical? I wondered. In 1965, I had the impression that they were all too content, too smug with their own life as well as with the state of their fatherland West Germany. The post-war prosperity the country enjoyed, also its youth enjoyed, seemed to have made them conservative, pro-American, in fact anti-communist. No experiments, they seemed to be saying. Whereas in the colleges of Calcutta, the students' unions were mostly in the hands of communists, most radical German students, so I heard, became only members of the Social Democratic Party (SPD), of the JuSos (the youth wing of the SPD). Whereas in India, advanced communist students were discussing/debating whether it had been good to call off the armed/radical struggles in the 1950s and take the parliamentary path, in West Germany they were discussing the merit of calling off the Cold War and initiating a policy of détente. Anybody who expressed radical leftist or capitalism-critical opinions, was cut off by being advised to go to East Germany (GDR).

Of course, these were only impressions I had from my random conversations with German students (and also with German elders). I had not come to Germany to do any research on my questions. Moreover, this changed in three to four years.

I read later, when I had already returned to India, that German students had in the meantime become more radical. One spoke of the new student generation of 1968. But it must be added here that for Rudi Dutschke and his comrades, the impulse came from outside, from the Vietnam War and the resistance of the heroic Vietnamese people against US-American imperialism.

Travels

Childhood experiences

In German, one should differentiate between *Urlaub machen* and *reisen*. The former mostly means to spend one's annual holidays in a resort: in summer, e.g., enjoy the sunshine and bathe in the sea at a coastal resort, or enjoy the fresh air and do amateur mountain climbing in a hill resort.

In winter, e.g., to enjoy the fresh air and do amateur skiing on snow in a mountain resort. But reisen means, to see interesting landscapes, visit places of interest such as historical monuments, museums to see famous art collections etc.

I myself had little interest in *Urlaub machen*. It was only in my childhood, on the initiative of my parents, that I, with the whole family, went to a sea resort on the Bay of Bengal, and two years later again to a hill resort in the Himalayas.

It was 1946. I heard that we shall go to Puri. I knew that Puri was a town with important temples. But I heard that we shall there also see the sea. I had already read a short version of our epic *Ramayana*, specially written for children. In this epic, there is a story of *Hanuman*, the great hero of the monkey-army of *Rama*, who was making a military campaign in *Lanka* (nowadays called *Sri Lanka*) to rescue Sita. When one day, during the battle, Rama's brother Lakshmana was severely injured, the Kaviraj (the doctor) said the latter's life could only be saved if extracts of *Sanjivvini Buti*, a particular medicinal plant, could be applied to the wound very soon. But that particular plant grew only on a particular mountain, called *Gandhamadan*, of the Himalayan range. Then Rama ordered Hanuman to try to get that plant as soon as possible. Hanuman started the journey immediately. He made great strides, actually huge jumps, to reach the Himalayan range. There he also located Mount Gandhamadan. But then he was at a loss. He did not know which one among the hundreds of plants there was Sanjivvini Buti. So he uprooted the whole mountain and rushed back to the seashore. He had very little time left. So, instead of using the bridge that the monkey-army had built earlier to reach Lanka, Hanuman took a mighty leap to cross the sea between India and Lanka. This great feat of Hanuman saved Lakshmana's life.

The child that I was then, I had thought that if Hanuman could leap over it with a mountain in hand, then a sea would be somewhat like a huge pond. With this image of a sea in head, I travelled with our family to Puri and reached the town next morning. Fortunately, we got a room in a house very close to the sea. As soon as we had entered the room and put down our luggage, Dilip and I rushed out and asked somebody: "Where is the sea?" The man just casually showed us the direction. We ran and after a minute, we stood stunned in front of the sea, the huge endless sheet of wavy blue water, five to six feet high waves breaking one after the other on the sandy beach.

The waves, I was told later, were in reality not that high, they only appeared so to a child of 10, who was, moreover, a little short in stature. The huge sea and its high waves breaking on the endless sandy beach: It was a whole-day-long huge happening.

I know, our parents also went to the temples and made their oblations. But we children, all six of us, spent almost the whole day on the beach, bathed in the sea holding tightly at the hands by the "Nunias" (fishermen-helpers), and collected mussel-shells.

Another similar childhood travel-experience, equally stunning, was our journey to the Himalayas. Father was sent to Darjeeling, 2185 meters above sea level. It was 1948. We travelled during our summer vacation, April - May. But Darjeeling was only the central town of the whole hills-region. Father was quartered in a "suburb" of the town, called Jalapahar, lying another few hundred meters above Darjeeling, and his office, of the military accounts department, lay another few hundred meters higher.

During our journey to the north, in the night, we crossed East Pakistan (now called Bangladesh), through the region where father's homeland was situated. I could not see it, the flat country with rice fields. I also could not see the famous old very long Sarah bridge over the river Padma. Next morning, we arrived in Siliguri, end-station of the broad-gauge Rly. line at the foothills of the Himalayas. There, the next lap of the journey on narrow-gauge line began. The small train crawled upward along the mountains. We could enjoy the full beauty of the mountains as well as of the receding plains.

But our most spectacular experience were the clouds. Because it was summer, we used to keep the windows open during daytime. And because it was just one month before the beginning of the monsoon rains, the clouds that were being formed by the summer heat were crawling upward along the mountain slopes. The clouds just passed through our rented house, since it was located on such a mountain slope. We could really feel them caressing our cheeks.

In 1965, during short holidays like Easter and Christmas, I made, with groups of German students, short bus trips for a few days to Rom, Venice and Paris. These cities, I thought, one must have seen in one's life. I could not go back home to India and not be able to say that I have seen the Vatican and the Eifel Tower and the Mona Lisa in the Louvre.

In Communist Lands

In the early summer of 1966, when my higher German studies had come to an end, I decided to make a few *Reisen*, travels, in Europe. Germans would use for them the composite word *Bildungsreise* (educational travels). For this time, I decided to see a little of communism in practice in the country of its origin, the Soviet Union, the Fatherland of Moscow-loyal communists. Of course, seeing the sea and seeing a part of the Himalayas for the first time, without having seen even a photo of the same before, could also be called an educational travel.

In Munich, there was a travel agency called *Studiosus*, which organized travels especially for students. I joined a mainly students' travel group that was planned to travel from Munich to the Soviet Union via Berlin and Warsaw.

The journey from Munich to West Berlin was uneventful, although it passed through GDR territory. Studiosus had apparently organized everything to the satisfaction of the communist authorities. There were three non-Germans in the group: a South African white young man (it was still Apartheid time), a Mexican young woman, and I.

We probably had to spend a whole day in West Berlin before we boarded the train to Warsaw. And I took the opportunity to make a sortie into East Berlin for a few hours[*]. That was possible even after the Berlin Wall had been built (1961). A foreigner (also a West German was a foreigner for them) could enter East Berlin from West Berlin for a few hours. He only had to pay a fee of 5,00 DM. And he could spend there as much hard currency as he wanted to. That was so, because the GDR suffered in those days from chronic foreign exchange shortage, so that they could

---

[*] Perhaps I saw East Berlin for the first time in 1965, during an educational journey to West Berlin organized by the GI for its students like me. But I do not remember it exactly.

not import many kinds of foreign consumer goods, which were coveted by its citizens, e.g., banana, oranges, etc. (*Südfrüchte*).

Big and splendid buildings and the usual landscape of a big city did not interest me. Also not famous museums. I had already seen enough of them in West Germany. I wanted to see rather unimportant residential localities. So I left the boulevards and walked through narrower streets and lanes. There I could see a grocery shop and a meat shop with the notorious empty shelves. So, I thought, it was not just western anti-communist propaganda. There indeed was shortage of consumer goods in the GDR. Many years later, when I narrated this to a GDR-sympathizer, he said: Who knows, if the prices had been very fair and very low, then everything could have been sold out when you saw the shops.

There must also have been a shortage of dark-skinned people in East Germany of those days. For I, a dark-skinned Indian, had a funny experience there: In a near-empty lane, I suddenly encountered a mother and a boy, roughly 5 years old. The boy gaped at me and sought shelter in the arms of the mother. Then he said: "Mum, look, a robber." The mum felt ashamed for her son, rebuked the boy and begged my pardon. The boy must have read children's story books, in which South Sea robbers were usually depicted as dark-skinned people.

I spent another two or three hours there, mostly in the big zoo of East Berlin. A GDR young man tagged himself on to me. All that I still remember from his talk with me is that he wanted me to write to him. Maybe he wanted to have a kind of pen-friendship with a foreigner from a very distant country.

There is nothing special to narrate about our short two days' stay in Warsaw. It was just sight-seeing, e.g., the Palace of Culture and Science, the huge and tall building – a monument to the victory of communism, or a gift of the Soviet people to the people of Poland, a sort of reward for accepting communism. At the end of the visit to Warsaw, when we boarded the train for our journey to the Soviet Union, something unpleasant attracted my attention: Our German tourist guide, who accompanied us, gave some money to the Polish local guide while shaking his hand – not so well hidden from us. I had not expected that in a communist country:

an employee of the state tourism organization accepting a *Bakshis*, or perhaps even a bribe from a citizen of a capitalist country.

For me at least, the journey to the Soviet Union (SU) got off to a bad start. We all had to get down from the train at the last Polish station bordering the SU. While the train was being prepared to be transferred to the broader railway track used in the SU, we had to pass through passport control etc. There, not only were our passports carefully examined, we also had to open our suitcases. Strangely, while all the others were allowed to pass through after only a cursory look at the contents of the suitcases, I was held up. The Soviet border inspectors turned every piece of my clothing and opened every piece of folded paper.

Now I became a little nervous. At the end of our studies, I had given up my room in Munich. I had planned to fly back to India immediately after the end of my last European tour. So, I had packed up everything in my suitcase that was valuable to me, among which were many letters of my parents and many photos that I had made in Germany. The Soviet inspectors saw/examined every photo. But they stood puzzled there, maybe they were also suspicious, when they opened the letters of my parents. They were not only written in Bangla, but also in Bangla script. They whispered among themselves. I wanted to help them in their work, in my own interest. I told them in English and also in German that they were letters of my parents and the script was Bangla, and that I have wound up my residence in Munich etc. etc. I could not make out whether they understood me. Then they called the Russian interpreter and guide, who would accompany us in the SU, and asked him something. I, of course, did not understand their conversation. But they finally let me get into the SU. My fellow travelers in the group were astonished that I had attracted so much attention of the border inspectors.

The journey from the Polish border station to Moscow started in the night. So, at first, I could not see anything. In the morning, when I got up and looked out, then also I did not see anything but empty land. From my readings on the Soviet Union, I had learnt much about Soviet agriculture. I had learnt that it was fully mechanized and organized in collective farms. I had also seen Soviet films in India. I asked the German speaking Russian guide why so much land was empty, where were the collective farms and tractors? The man smiled a little and replied, in the general sense, they were there where it was best to have them. Later I realized, with the huge land area that was in principle cultivable and the relatively small population (compared to India) that had to be fed, there was in the SU, unlike in India, no need to cultivate every acre of arable land.

In the SU, our tour program comprised visiting Moscow, Leningrad (nowadays called St. Petersburg) and Sagorsk (nowadays called Sergiew Possad). In Moscow, we did the usual sight-seeing: visited the Red Square, the Kremlin Wall, the Lenin Mausoleum. I remember we also went into the Kremlin area, where we saw the huge Bell of Moscow, and the huge canon. The bell, which was damaged, allegedly never rang; and the canon never fired a shot in any war. They stood there as monuments to useless megalomania. And, last but not least, we also saw the Bolshoi Ballet performing *Swan Lake* of Tchaikovsky – not in the also famous old Bolshoi Theatre, which was being repaired at the time, but in a modern very large theatre in the Kremlin. All these things I had read about in the Soviet-friendly magazines, of which there were quite a few in India.

We had one day in Moscow, on which we were not shown anything, but were free to do things we wanted. I decided to go to the Red Square again and see the embalmed corpse of Lenin lying in state in the Mausoleum. It was a long queue at the end of which I had to stand. There were many Russians in the queue (so it seemed to me), but also quite a few foreigners. I wanted to "see Lenin" not just out of touristic curiosity, but to pay my respect. After all, he led a successful revolution against an oppressive and exploitative system. What came out of it after his death, was not his fault.

For three years, also Stalin's embalmed corpse lay there in state at the side of Lenin. But in 1956, in the wake of destalinization, it was removed from the mausoleum and buried in a normal grave at the Kremlin wall, which too was a honorable place. While seeking Stalin's grave in the whole row of graves at the Kremlin wall, I saw many well-known names[*], which I had come across while reading the history of the Russian revolution.

---

[*] I had learnt the Cyrillic script as part of my preparations for this journey.

After destalinization, under Khrushchev's leadership, the SU sought de-escalation of tensions between the two superpowers, there was a lot of talking about peaceful co-existence, peaceful competition of the two systems etc. Although at the same time, in 1956, the nationalist revolt in Hungary was suppressed, it was believed in the outside world that in the SU a new liberal-socialist era had set in. It was this belief that motivated groups of inquisitive Westerners to visit the SU and see things for themselves. Ours was one such group.

Yet, somehow, they had become suspicious of me. That free day, I was simply going around on the Red Square and making photos. I saw an old man selling lottery tickets. I was surprised that even in the socialist SU people thought of becoming rich through good luck in a lottery-draw. I took a photo of the old man without him noticing it. Then in one corner of the Red Square, I saw a two-story log-house, probably uninhabited, from some previous century. I found it interesting, thought it was good that they left it standing intact. But after a while, I suddenly saw our German speaking Russian guide in front of me. I greeted him. But he straight-away criticized me, without mincing his words. He said that I was all the time seeking negative things for subjects of my photos. What was wrong, he asked me, if an old man tried to improve his pension by selling lottery tickets, what was wrong if the authorities left a log-house standing? There were so many great things and monuments in Moscow, why didn't I take photos of such things etc. etc. He then went away without giving me a chance to say something.

I was not afraid. I was somehow sure that they had not found my name in any of their lists of Western spies. They must have thought that I was a bad, unfriendly tourist. But that was a petty matter for them.

During our stay in Moscow, we were invited by the students' association of the famous Lomonosov University to meet them and have an exchange of thoughts, or a simple conversation or whatever (I did not hear exactly what). We had to ride in a lift many stories up in a high-rise building until we arrived at the right place. The students' association president of the Lomonosov University, accompanied by some other students, welcomed us. He introduced himself as a student of psychology. I do not remember any more what conversations took place. It must have been boring, otherwise I would have remembered something.

But one thing I still remember: Already as a student in Calcutta, I had read a little popular literature on psychology: Pavlov's experiments with dogs, his behaviorism theory, and then Freud's theories and the Marxist rejection/critique thereof. These books had been written by the famous Indian philosophy-scholar Debiprasad Chattopaddhyay*, a communist, for the benefit of young students. I asked the psychology student, the President of the Students' Association, whether then, in 1966, especially after destalinization, psychology professors had a better opinion of Freud's theory, whether they teach also psychoanalysis of Freud. The young man was visibly very displeased. He gave a curt, unfriendly reply: "Yes, yes, we know about Freud." That was all. I had the impression that the meeting was just an unpleasant duty for the Russian students.

The visit to Sagorsk was more interesting. The town, just two-three hours bus ride away from Moscow, was/is a famous pilgrimage site, site of a famous Cloister of The Holy Trinity. We came (were rather brought) there just as tourists, but also many Russians were there that day. Of course, elderly Russian Orthodox Christians, but they were genuine people, genuinely faith-inspired pilgrims. I could see that on their face. In contrast, I could not see similar expressions of genuine faith on the face of Soviet communists of the Brezhnev era.

Let me quote here a joke on Brezhnev that I read somewhere, of course in the Western media. When he had reached the zenith of power in his country, Brezhnev once invited his old mother to visit him in Moscow. The mother came, or was rather brought to his son's dacha in Moscow. Brezhnev showed his mother everything around in the house: his high style-furniture, his big drawing room, the first-class carpets on the floors, his most comfortable large bed, his guns, the hunting trophies on the walls etc. All the while, the old mother remained silent. Brezhnev became impatient. He asked: "Mother why don't you say something? Don't you like all this?" The mother broke her silence after a while. She said: "Son, I like all these things. But what will you do if the Reds come again?"

---

* I have written about him in chapter 3.

The Russians had planned our visit to this unknown town for us. They wanted to show us, that there was freedom of religion in the Soviet Union. We saw that. There was nothing else to see in Sagorsk. We were then carted back to Moscow.

The last leg of our journey to the SU was that to Leningrad. It was almost like a pilgrimage for me. In 1966, I had not yet apostatized, not yet fully renounced my faith in socialism. A little hope still lingered. Moreover, Leningrad, the city, had not yet changed so much. It was for me still the city of the Revolution of 1917, still the city of Lenin. So, dutifully and half-faithfully, I visited all the places and site-seeing objects that were associated with the Russian Revolution: the Winter Palace, the then residence of the Czar and seat of his government, which had to be stormed by the armed revolutionary workers and soldiers to overthrow the system; later it became a part of the Hermitage Art Museum; the cruiser Aurora, from which the first shot of the revolution was fired; the Peter and Paul Fortress, the Smolny Institute, etc. In 1966, I still knew these names and the associated stories, which I had read in John Reed's book *Ten Days that Shook the World*. I also saw a film on the storming of the Winter Palace, but I cannot say any more whether it was before or after my journey to the SU.

My travel-companions were probably not so interested in these nondescript sites. They probably were more impressed by the Hermitage and the great Art Museum, the Summer Palace etc., which all I too saw as a routine matter.

What impressed me more were the very long summer evenings – result of the very northerly location of the city and the many canals and small bridges. I took long walks in the streets in such evenings before returning to the hotel.

To England

After returning from the SU to Munich, I had to wait two days, before embarking on my next journey. I had good luck in Munich. An Egyptian student of Germanistik – his name was Radwan – with whom I had become friends, had taken a big, costlier room with two beds in the same hostel as ours. I had given up my smaller room in the hostel and, with

Radwan's permission, kept my second suitcase packed with German books in one corner of his room. When I returned and told him that I must wait two days before departing for London, he spontaneously offered me the second bed of his room, which I gladly accepted. After all, I had to count every D-Mark that I could save for my journeys.

The relationship between India and Great Britain (GB) had been, I may perhaps say, dialectical – on the one hand antagonistic, because the British waged many wars and committed many breaches of promises to conquer India, and on the other hand, it was GB that had brought the industrial civilization, the sciences and modern humanistic thoughts to India. There were many Indians who were grateful to the British for the latter. But there were also, particularly after the beginning of the independence movement, many who hated the British and wanted to throw them out by using bombs and an independence army. That was at least one reason, why I (perhaps all Indians) by all means wanted to visit GB, particularly London.

A cousin of mine lived in those days in London. I had written to him to find a cheap hotel room for me. But he invited me to stay in his simple apartment. It was a two-room apartment, in which one was the bedroom of my cousin, and the other was his drawing room and kitchen. I got a portable bed put up in the drawing room. I accepted it gladly, because it was free, and my cousin and his Irish wife received me with a hearty welcome. I did not need more, because I was going to spend the whole day seeing London.

I need not here describe what all I visited and saw there, because London's touristic attractions are perhaps known to all who would read my autobiography. But let me mention the three things that fascinated me most. One was the Rosetta Stone in the British Museum that enabled linguists to decipher the Hieroglyphic script of the ancient Egyptians. It fascinated me, because I too "deciphered" for myself a new language, namely German. Another was the *Speakers' Corner* in the Hyde Park. Mostly, missionaries of small Christian sects spoke there to small audiences, who were just tourists like me. There were also political activists of lost causes, who criticized the imperialists and capitalists, who did not take their cause seriously. I sympathized with them, because I too was one like them.

One or two such speakers had also brought their table, on which they stood while speaking. Their comrades held up placards. One Christian missionary had even made a special invention. He, incidentally, an Indian, had fitted a tall ladder with wheels, so that he could easily drag it while coming to Hyde Park.

The third thing was the most fascinating of all, the visit to the British Library, which was, in 1966, still an integral part of the British Museum. While seeing the exhibits in the Museum, I remembered that after getting my Bachelor's degree, I was taking a course in librarianship. But then I got the job in the Bank and thought a bird in the hand was worth two in the bush. But the curiosity about how such a huge library and documentation center worked had remained and was reawakened at the sight of the portals of the British library.

I had registered myself for a short, guided tour of the working rooms of the library, which was offered free to librarians and would-be librarians. But I came just one minute too late, and the tour-group was already somewhere inside the premises. I thought I should not give up and appealed to the personnel at the entrance to make an exception for me, because I had come to London only for a few days. An employee of the library, who apparently had no particular work to do at the moment, was forbearing with me. He told me to come with him. He made a guided tour extra for me, showed me many things that I had not expected to see. When we were on the second floor of the high dome, he called me to come to the railings and pointed his index finger down at the reading room on the ground floor and said: You see that chair, third from the right (or somewhere else), that was where Marx sat every day and wrote his *Das Kapital*. I was overwhelmed.

I also visited Cambridge, the famous University town. Frau Dr. Herbert, who was one of our lecturers in GI, Munich, was living there with her Welsh husband, who was teaching something at one of the famous colleges. She had invited me to visit her and be her guest in her cottage home. She showed me around in the town, its famous colleges and the river. I remembered that when I and my brother Dilip were about 9- and

11-years old children, my father once told us that if we were good in learning, he would send one of us to Oxford and the other to Cambridge. Now I was in Cambridge, but only as a one-day tourist.

Chapter 8:
Back To India – Via Egypt

After concluding my tour of England, I returned to Munich, visited Radwan, the generous Egyptian friend, in whose large hostel-room I could again sleep two or three nights. I had earlier told our secretary in the GI office, Frau Steiff, that on my flight back to India, I wanted to make a one-week stopover in Cairo, and so I had requested her to book for me a flight that would make that possible. She had done that. It was not per Lufthansa, the German airlines, but per Japan Airlines (JAL).

I do not remember exactly when – whether it was after returning from my Russian tour or after returning from London – I went to the central office of the Goethe Institute (GI) to collect my papers. I already had an appointment as lecturer at the Goethe Institute, Hyderabad (India). It was scheduled to be formally opened when I and the simultaneously appointed would-be director of the institute, Dr. Ohlau, would arrive in Hyderabad.

Fortunately, I met Dr. Ohlau in the central office of the GI. When we met, he had already heard about me and that I would be his colleague. He spontaneously invited me to an evening party of all the Germans who were being sent or soon to be sent to foreign centers of the GI. It was a mere drinking and chatting party. The German GI personnel to be sent abroad to different GIs wanted to get to know each other. I was there the only non-German. I chatted with them. Those who heard me were totally surprised that I spoke German fluently.

In Egypt

I broke the journey in Cairo for a week. In Munich, I had requested Radwan to help me prepare my stopover there, which he did. He did more. He wrote to a relative of his, a cousin brother, to find a cheap hotel for me in Cairo, and gave me the details of how to reach the address, where his relatives lived.

The first thing I experienced after landing in Cairo reminded me that I had come back to the Third World. The man, who was the officially appointed currency exchanger, tried to cheat me. He gave me a few Egyptian Pounds less than what I should have gotten. When I protested, he gave me without further ado two more Egyptian currency notes.

I had to be tightfisted with the money I had for the one week stay in Cairo. So Radwan had advised me to always travel by bus rather than by taxi and gave me the route-number etc. of the particular bus journey to the house of his relatives.

It was like in Calcutta. The bus from the city center to the suburb where Radwan's relatives lived was jam-packed. It was however no problem for me. I was young and full of energy, and the friendly people helped me to accommodate my suitcase in the bus.

I got a friendly reception in the house of Radwan's relatives, a middle-class family. Radwan's cousin brother then accompanied me to my hotel in the city's central area. Again, by bus. The hotel was a relatively old building. Remember, it was 1966. I got a longish big room. The hotel boy, actually an elderly man in a long robe (usual in those days in Egypt), served me dinner and, next day morning, the breakfast in the room.

After taking breakfast, I immediately set off on a bus journey to the pyramids. I do not have to describe the Pyramids and the Sphinx; they and their photos are so well known. But I also spent several hours there observing the scenes at the edge of these landmarks of ancient history. I left the desert zone around them and went toward a canal, at the edge of which stood a village. There were trees and other greenery there. I shot some photos of the village on the canal-side and the villagers who lived there. But at one point somebody protested. I did not understand the words, but understood the sign-language. What he meant was that I must not take photos of the people. But another man, whose photo I wanted to take, had no problem with that. They started a small quarrel. But I dropped the idea, particularly because there were also some women there, which made it a sensitive issue. I walked away, but saw more of the canal zone where there were a few more farmers' houses. That was an interesting sight; water and a greenery in the middle of the desert. I do not remember much more. After all, it was almost 60 years ago.

I went back to the pyramids area, saw everything in more details, climbed a few steps up the Pyramids. The steps were actually awe-inspiring huge blocks of Stone. That was enough for me. I returned to my hotel in Cairo. Next day, I went to the famous museum, another routine tourist activity.

The day after, I went exploring the city of Cairo, the old city. Since I have had and would have so much to do with the Goethe Institute, I was also interested to visit the GI in Cairo. Sometime in the late afternoon I found it and went in. And most unexpectedly, I again saw Dr. Ohlau there. He too had wanted to do some tourism in Cairo and made a stop-over there. He had of course made much better preparations for that. But he unexpectedly got an invitation from a German colleague to be his guest. When I met Dr. Ohlau, this colleague, a deputy director or so of the GI Cairo, was with him. Dr. Ohlau asked me where I was lodging. I told them the name of my hotel. But, naturally, they had never heard of it. I told them, it was a simple and cheap hotel, something I could afford. The German Cairo-colleague immediately invited me too to stay with him, as Ohlau was doing. His family, he said, was holidaying in Germany, so he had enough room there for two guests. I accepted the invitation gladly. It was, of course, more comfortable, I had good company, and the host had a car, which he used also for us. He apparently took leave to care for his two guests.

I do not remember well what else I/we saw in the rest of my time in Cairo. Only one thing I remember well: an excursion deep in the desert. I always had that desire. There is a desert region in India too, in the province of Rajasthan. But I never had an opportunity to travel to that region. I had made a sea voyage when I was still younger, from Calcutta to the Andamans across the Bay of Bengal, but never a trip to the desert. I found the desert trip in Egypt great. I missed, however, the sand dunes, that I had expected to see. It was all along a gravel-and-sand desert, so no dunes. Our host, however, showed us a different landmark, a waterhole in the desert. It was a large hole that the traders who crossed the desert in earlier centuries, had to dig in order to find water in a depth of some 10 meters. When we saw it, the sand at the deepest point was just wet. That was all.

On our way back, the host asked me whether I could drive a car. I could, I said, but my Indian driver's license was not there with me. Apparently, he was not feeling well. Maybe he had headache. Why he did not ask Dr. Ohlau, I could not understand. Anyway, the host continued to drive until we came back to Cairo. I do not remember what else I/we saw or did in Cairo. The river Nile of course, but it was nothing special for me like the desert. After all, I came from Bengal, the land of many rivers, and Calcutta lies on the Ganges.

In Calcutta, for a Few Days

On the seventh day of my stay in Egypt, I flew back home. But not straight to Hyderabad. I first wanted to spend a few days in Calcutta with my family.

My father and my brother Dilip had come to the airport to receive me. I was so glad to be on home soil again. But, on the other hand, I was also sad that the best time of my life was now over. I already knew that in India, I would not ever have such a good time as I had as a student in Germany. When I came out of the gate at the Calcutta airport, I first went straight to my father and dutifully did my *"Pranam"*, i.e., touched his feet and symbolically put the dust of his feet on my head. Father, again following the ritual, put his hands on my head and then caressed me a little on the cheeks. That was (still is, I suppose) the usual ritual for such occasions. But I must admit that at that particular moment, for a few seconds, I did become emotional, although the reality in our childhood had been very harsh. Dilip and I embraced each other. I think I had long ceased to do the ritual Pranam for showing respect to Dilip. We simply had a loving relationship. At the time of writing this, now, I have tears in my eyes. For they are all gone, my parents and the siblings.

At home, in Ballygunge, all those who could come, had been waiting. Also the nephews and nieces. The others came in the evening, after their working hours were over. The rituals described above were repeated. Mother was visibly very emotional. I think, among my siblings, only my eldest brother could not come. He was living in a village in faraway Maddhya Pradesh, with his family. It was simply too difficult for him.

Meeting Former Bank-Colleagues

Two days later, I went to Liluah to meet my former bank-colleagues in the Punjab National Bank (PNB). I have written in an earlier chapter that many of them had come to the Calcutta airport to see me off when I flew to Germany. I had not written to them from Germany. Nor did I inform them that I had come back and would meet them in PNB, Liluah. When I reached my former workplace, at around 11 o'clock, the first one who saw me, said aloud, "Oh, see who has come! Herr has come." When I had been working with them as a colleague and they knew that I had been learning German, some of them had given me the nickname "Herr", the only German word they knew. The former colleagues were all totally surprised, but also overjoyed to see me again. They all put off their work for a few minutes, surrounded me, and shook my hands one after the other. One of them immediately sent an assistant out to buy some sweets for me, the usual way in India to greet a person respectfully at home. Those who could postpone their work for some time, did it and chatted with me. The others used the recess hour, called "tiffin time", to chat with me. That was one of the smaller branches of the PNB. So I did not have too many ex-colleagues to meet. At the end of the tiffin-hour, I brought the meeting to an end and went back home. Before going, I and they reciprocally wished each other all the best. They told me to come again, when I would have come to Calcutta.

I did not have much time left in Calcutta. The next two to three days I had to spend visiting relatives and receiving visits. Then it was again time to pack the suitcase and to board the train for Hyderabad, where I had to do a lot of things in the beginning. But the Hyderabad story I will narrate in the next chapter. Let me first finish, here and now, the story with the PNB and my job there, although it dragged on for another six months.

Not knowing how the job in the GI, Hyderabad, would be, I had not yet formally resigned from my job in the PNB, where I had been granted unpaid leave for two years. This leave was not yet over, when I started working in the GI, Hyderabad. Then, a month later, having found the new job satisfactory, I sent my letter of resignation from the job in the PNB. But, in India, it was not that easy to resign from a job either. Some junior officer of the PNB wrote back that I have to first rejoin the service there and then apply for resignation. I do not here want to tell that nonsensical story in detail. In short, when I got some vacation in the Christmas time of 1966, I went to Calcutta to settle the matter, but also to spend some good time there with my family and friends.

In Calcutta, one day I went to the regional office of the PNB, where the matter of my resignation was lying undecided. Following the aphorism *Kleider machen Leute* (Clothes make the man), I put on my best clothes, even wore a tie. When I entered the regional office premises, the very first man I saw there was an ex-colleague of mine in PNB-Liluah. He knew my story of going to Germany, but did not know that I had come back. He was surprised to see me. After a few minutes of usual small talk, he commented: "Why did you come back at all?" In reply, I could only smile a little.

Then I met the Regional Manager of the bank. As good luck would have it, it was the same Mr. Ghosh, who was our branch manager in Liluah, now promoted to this higher post. As I narrated earlier, when I was a clerk under him, he valued my ability to write good English, but thought I was somewhat arrogant. Anyway, this time, he was not meeting me as his subordinate clerk. He heartily welcomed me and had a little conversation with me about my stay in Germany and my higher studies there. He told me that he had read my correspondence with the head office in Delhi and had found it good that I got the study leave. He called the junior officer in his room and asked him what the problem was. The man said something that I don't want to repeat. In any case, Mr. Ghosh ordered the junior officer to accept my resignation. The official matter was over. And he asked me some more things about my future etc. Finally, he put the most important question: How much was the salary at the GI? When I told him it was Rs. 750 in the beginning, he was very impressed.

That was the end of another chapter of my life.

Chapter 9:
Fifteen Years in Hyderabad
Part 1

The Bicycle City

I had agreed to report for duty in Hyderabad on the 1st of July 1966. I think I arrived there one or two days earlier. I got down from the train at Nampally station and went out to the courtyard. I was immediately surrounded bicycle-rikshaw drivers, who all wanted to take me to my destination at a price that I would consider to be fair. From where I stood, I did not see any motor taxi. So, I took a cycle-rikshaw and mentioned a price that I was prepared to pay – without even knowing how far from there my destination, the Goethe Institute, was. The particular driver immediately agreed. He almost snatched my suitcase from my hand and told me to follow him to where his cycle-rikshaw was parked.

I want to remind my readers, it was 1966, about 60 years ago from now. India was still very underdeveloped, and the people, even middle-class people, were very poor. Hyderabad has always been a capital city – when I came there, capital of Andhra Pradesh (now of Telengana). But the streets were not dominated by motorized vehicles. Taxis were rare. There were of course buses, but there was hardly any time table for them. Nobody knew exactly when they would come. So about 90 percent of those who needed some transportation help, depended on the ubiquitous hirable cycle-rikshaws. Most young and able-bodied people used their own bicycle.

When I say cycle-rikshaw, it was actually a tricycle, driven by pedal-power, i.e., manually. In Calcutta, even in the mid-1950s, the street scene was dominated by motorized vehicles and electric trams. There were taxis for hire at almost every important traffic center and street junctions. Rikshaws were there too, not cycle-rikshaws, but old Japanese-style, two-wheeled and hand-pulled ones. They were generally used for transportation help within the small radius of a particular locality – mostly by old ladies, mothers with children, and also by men when they had to transport some luggage.

We must remember, Hyderabad had been for a very long time the capital of a feudal state in south-central India, ruled over by a Muslim dynasty stemming from the olden days of the Mughal Empire in India, whereas Calcutta was, until 1912, the capital of British India and the second largest city of the British Empire. Many Hyderabadis thought that those who came from Calcutta exuded a kind of not so well-hidden arrogance and superiority feeling.

I had been to this city earlier, in 1956, when my father was working in the South-Indian center of the Military Accounts Service. His office was located in Secunderabad, the part of the city, which was more modern-looking because it was built much later by India's British rulers as a cantonment town. We – mother, Dilip, I, and Khuku, our youngest sister – went there to visit father during our summer vacation. One day, Dilip and I decided to take a trip with hired bicycles from our accommodation in Secunderabad to the old city of Hyderabad. After some riding, we found ourselves approaching a large street-crossing somewhere in Hyderabad. It must have been the largest street-crossing in the city-center. We had no particular plan, we did not know where we wanted to ride to. We just wanted to see the old city of Hyderabad. At the crossing, in the melee of some one thousand bicycles, we got confused and also a little scared. To avoid that melee, we simply turned left. And immediately we heard the whistle of a policeman. What we had done was perhaps against the traffic rules, which also existed, though only on paper. But we paddled away fast. And nobody chased us. Bicycles also had no number.

From where we were accommodated in Secunderabad – third floor of a new building – we could look down on the main thoroughfare of the twin city. Every morning around 9 o'clock, it was rush hour of office goers. Several hundred bicycle riders toiled their way up to office along a slightly upward slope of the street. Among them were also a few young women. All in all, I think the twin cities of Hyderabad and Secunderabad deserved the title "Bicycle city per excellence", at least, seen from to-day's viewpoint, particularly from the viewpoint of environmentalists.

But, in 1956, the twin cities also had a few more attractions for us. In front of our first accommodation in Secunderabad, at the edge of the city in a beautiful tree-covered area, across a road, was a large open space. On holidays, people played there cricket, which was a great attraction for Dilip and myself. And, apart from that, we once saw a display of cavalry soldiers of the Indian army, real horse-riding soldiers, who had put on beautiful turbans for the occasion. They showed several horse-riding skills.

Goethe Institute alias Max Mueller Bhavan

From Nampally station, I went straight to the Goethe Institute in Ramkote, and reported myself there. Mrs. Siddiqui, a European woman, secretary of the institute, was there. She was expecting me. She said, Dr. Ohlau had also arrived, but was at the moment not there. Mrs. Siddiqui recommended a hotel room for the time being and promised to help me get an apartment for rent. She also booked a room for me in the hotel. Seeing that she was very busy working, I got up and headed for the hotel, again by cycle-rikshaw. I wanted to have a little sleep in the afternoon.

Just a note on the name of the Institute. Of course, it was the Hyderabad branch of the Goethe Institute. But some years ago, some Germans had thought that since Max Mueller was more famous in India than Goethe, it should be appropriate to call the GIs in India *Max Mueller Bhavan* (Bhavan = house). It could be understood as the house in which the Goethe Institute was located.

Mrs. Siddiqui had already advertised for the new courses. Many young and old people had registered as desirous of learning German. When the classes started, I came to know them personally. Unlike many in Calcutta in 1961, when I joined my first course, the Hyderabad students were not people seeking a job opportunity in Germany. I think that wave of actively seeking a low-level technical job in Germany was over, or it had not reached Hyderabad at all. My students in Hyderabad were mostly university students, also a few university and college lecturers. Some were medical doctors. But there were also ordinary educated people among them. They all thought that it was somehow good to improve their educational qualification, that knowledge of German – rather a certificate from the Max Mueller Bhavan (MMB) – would stand them in good stead in their profession or even otherwise.

With the help of Mrs. Siddiqui, after one or two weeks, I got a two-room apartment for rent. It is perhaps informative to write here about the hotel in which I lodged till then. When I went to the counter to pay my bill, the counter-man charged me more than what I had agreed to pay. I protested against the extra charge. The counter-man said in reply: "But you have had guests in the night! The extra charge is for them!" That was either a plain lie or a case of mistaken identity. In the end, I just paid the correct amount and went. Many weeks later, when I had found some friends in the city, I told some of them this funny story. They asked me for the name of the hotel. When I told them the name, they laughed out loudly and meaningfully. I wondered what they actually wanted to say. Finally, one told me what it meant. That hotel was notorious or renowned for entertaining guests who wanted to spend the night with prostitutes. I was astonished that Ms. Siddiqui did not know that. But how should she have known? She had little knowledge of and contact with the local population. She socialized only in the small European community of Hyderabad. Maybe her four children, born in her marriage with the Indian Muslim gentleman Siddiqui, knew better.

Loneliness, and Friends in Hyderabad

At first, in the first few months after coming to Hyderabad, I felt very lonely. In Calcutta, I all along lived with my family, even as a grown-up young man. Good or bad, it was my family. I was never alone. That was important. In Germany too, I almost always had friends around me and they were of various types and from various countries. It was an enormous enrichment of my horizon that I heard about their life in Brazil, Chile, Argentina, Bolivia, Sudan, Ethiopia, South Korea, Vietnam, Indonesia, Afghanistan, etc. etc. And the Germans were, of course, everywhere.

There were only two exceptions: The GI never invited any Russian or anyone from a communist country. And I avoided meeting a student from Pakistan. He was, of course, not in our teachers' training course. But he went to the same institute – for what, I could not find out – and he lived in a room in the same hostel building. I met him once by chance at our tram-stop. We greeted each other dutifully, two brown people from neighboring countries. But just a few days ago, it was in 1965, war had broken out between India and Pakistan. What an embarrassing situation! The first sentence was said by the Pakistani: "You know, I hate this war." I said just two words: "I too." And then we went our way in different directions.

In Hyderabad, in the institute, there was no time to chat with the two colleagues. I went to the institute after lunch, in order not to fall asleep in the afternoon, which was difficult due to the warm and humid weather. But both Mrs. Siddiqui and Dr. Ohlau were busy doing their duties, and in the evenings, I had my classes.

Yet, some of my students of the first class of the evening used to come early. I could chat with them and enquire about their backgrounds, their views etc. I could also chat with the students for some time in the small pause between the two evening classes. I gradually came to know more about them. Most of them came from science and engineering milieu. Many were engineering students; many were students of some branch of science. Particularly women students were versed in Biology (Botany or Zoology), one was a Master of Chemistry. Three were doing some research, one already had a scholarship for higher studies in Mathematics in Oxford. A few were students of medicine. One was already a medical doctor. Once, having heard that I was not feeling well, she brought her stethoscope next day and spontaneously examined my health.

Among my students were also four lecturers in physics at the University Science College. Because they were approximately my age or a little older, we could become friends, particularly because I, coming from the arts and humanities stream, showed interest in questions of physics. I once asked them: How do you know that there are electrons; After all, you cannot see them! Or can you? Mr. D. replied that I should come to their University Physics lab, he would then show me how they see electrons. I did go to their lab. But all that I remember from that visit is that he showed me an instrument, switched it on, and a small bright green point of light became visible on its screen similar to a TV-screen. Mr. D. said then: here you see the electrons. I did not understand how this small bright point of light proved the existence of electrons orbiting the nucleus of an atom. But Mr. D. was a man of few words. I simply thanked him and went back home.

One day I met a Bengali man at the market. I heard him speak with his son in Bangla. I introduced myself to him, also in Bangla, as a newcomer to Hyderabad and asked him whether there was in the city a Bengali cultural association. He said there was one and gave me the address and the timings of opening of its office, actually a chat room and a small collection of Bangla books.

At the next opportunity, on a holiday, I went to that office in the evening, and indeed I met there some members of the association. Thereafter, I regularly went there, but only on holiday evenings, and chatted with the Bengalis who had come – just to overcome my feeling of loneliness. Most of the members of the Bengali society whom I met there were not the political type of people who could like me, nor whom I could like. Yet, some of them invited me to come for tea etc. With some of them I also became sort of chatting friends. Almost all were middle class people, family fathers with children.

I also took part in the religious festivals and cultural events of the Bengali community, sometimes even volunteered with manual work to organize them. To perform a play on an improvised stage during a religious festival like, e.g., Durga Puja (worship of Goddess Durga), was the most important and popular cultural activity of the community. For such a show needed many actors, and, after all, saying some sentences as one usually does in everyday life has never been so difficult. But singing and dancing events were rare, for such things needed training and regular practicing. Sometimes, such artistes and theatre groups were invited from Calcutta. Going to such events was my only cultural entertainment.

One of my Bengali friends was a young man, B., who was working in a private compo any. Just then, he was looking for a cheap room for rent.

Since I, a bachelor, was living a simple life in a two-room apartment and could spare one of them, I spontaneously offered him one. I offered him the room at the rent of one-third of the total rent and agreed to bear the rest two-thirds myself. It was good for both. He had his cheap room, and I had company of a young man, who respected me and, in course of time, became a sort of a friend.

B. left me after two to three years and rented his own apartment. He also revealed the reason: he was going to marry soon.

With two friends from Germany in Hyderabad (1973). Photo credit: Saral Sarkar

Later, I came to know from my student-friends that many of them, even engineers working in renowned state-owned companies, lived with two or three other friends or colleagues under this kind of arrangement as long as they were bachelors. I once visited such a friend and found that four of them were sharing a room. Their beds were rolled-up and put in a corner to make room for two or three plastic chairs. The bed-rolls would again be rolled out on the floor in the late evening when they would go to bed. I could not see, where their suitcases and other things were and where their clothes were hanging. I remember, in our childhood, in our then four-room house, we three brothers shared a room. The eldest brother had a single bed. Dilip and I shared a double-bed. These were not bed rolls, but proper cots. But that was in our childhood, we were not earning anything yet. The three sisters shared another room.

Such a system was common in India. We were simply poor, poorer than the average young people in, say, Germany. But we also had a culture, in which asceticism was generally regarded as a virtue. Spendthrift lifestyle used to be frowned upon.

One such engineer-student, S. from Bangalore (Karnataka), became one of my best friends. He visited me often on Sundays and other holidays. I also visited him once in his family home in Bangalore. He had invited me. (I got there a proper bed on a cot). I liked him very much. I could discuss many things with him, get some technical and scientific questions answered. Sometimes I could draw his attention to deeper scientific issues like, e.g., the Entropy Law.

S. was a great traveler. When I proposed that we travel to the Himalayas, which was my heart's desire for a long time, he immediately agreed. Together with some other pilgrims, we travelled to *Kedarnath* and *Badrinath*, the two famous and important temples of the Hindus deep in the Himalayas. Kedarnath is situated at a height of 3584 meters, Badrinath at a height of 3133 meters. The last leg of the journey involved marching uphill, from early in the morning to just before the onset of darkness, along the roaring Alakananda, a tributary of the Ganges, which however could not be seen because it was flowing downhill in a deep gorge.

S. was a devout Hindu. He, naturally, offered his "Puja" (oblation) in the temple. I, of course, went into the temple, but only paid my homage to the Himalayas, to *Giriraja* (the king of the mountains). Some years later, S. told me (or perhaps he wrote to me) about his journey also to *Gangotri* and *Jamunotri*, the points of origin of the glacier-fed rivers Ganga and Yamuna. I envied him for that. I had seen the Western part of the mangrove-forested delta region of all these rivers of North India situated in the South of Bengal (the jungles of the Sundarbans), where they flow into the sea. I would also have very much liked to see the glaciers where they originate. But, as if to make amends for that omission, I took some extra trouble to see the Mount Everest. I do not know any more in which year it was, nor what the occasion was: I was in Kathmandu (Nepal) for something. There I availed myself of the opportunity to fly with a tourist group in a small plane high enough, from where we could see the Mount Everest.

Another student who became a good friend was V., a geologist, who was working at the University Science College as a lecturer. I learnt from him a lot about the geology of the Earth. He was a close neighbor and visited me often. He too, as long as he was a bachelor, lived with his sister and her husband. So, I could not visit him.

I used to walk back home every evening after end of the teaching day. Many students of the last class formed a group because they went in the same direction. In effect, they accompanied me – down the street from the institute to the main road. During this walk we enjoyed jokes and somebody or the other told a funny story. I too had a funny story to tell, which later became one of my standard jokes on Hyderabad:

P. was a good student of mine, an intelligent young man. He, incidentally was a son of an editor of the city's daily newspaper called *The Deccan Chronicles*. One summer afternoon, I was standing on the balcony of my apartment in Himayatnagar. I suddenly saw P. on the street. He was looking for something. I called out for him and asked what he was looking for. He greeted me and said, he was looking for an address, but could not find it. He asked me whether I knew where it was. I could not help him. After about one hour, I again saw P. in front of my house. He again said he could not find the address, although he went all around in the locality. Nobody could help him. It did not surprise me at all.

I knew many people who had suffered like this. In Hyderabad, the houses had funny addresses. E.g., the address of my house was 3-6-378, Himayatnagar. Now Himayatnagar was the name of a locality, not of a street. In that locality, there were perhaps 500 houses. In effect, it was no address at all. How could one then know where the house was?

The second part of the joke was: when I had first suffered like this, I wrote a letter to the editor of *The Deccan Chronicles*, which was not published. I had also offered to help overcome these difficulties, free of cost. But nobody replied.

Among such students, some became good friends, particularly those who lived in the same locality, namely Himayatnagar.

I could not enjoy the local culture, the culture of my Andhra friends, because I did not understand Telugu, their language. I was often criticized by them for not trying to learn Telegu. But I had a good and truthful excuse, namely that learning a new language needed sincere effort and much time. I knew that from my experience of learning German. But I did not know how long I would live in Hyderabad. English and a smattering of Hindi and Urdu was all I needed for my daily needs.

In the course of a few years, I also came to be acquainted with some members of the academic and social elite of Hyderabad. I do not remember exactly how, but some of them became my friends. They were highly educated, well-stablished, and prominent citizens of Hyderabad: a lawyer practicing at the High Court and his wife, who was a lecturer in English, a medical doctor, a lecturer in physics, a professor of political science with a Ph.D. from Paris, a professor of economics with a Ph.D. from Germany, a high-level government scientist etc. etc. Some of them would later play a role in my life. I shall write about that at the right places.

My Political Friends

As described above, in the beginning, I had two different friends' circles. Later, gradually, I acquired a third one, a political one. While conversing with my students outside class hours, I had spoken about my native province West Bengal, about Kamrabad and Calcutta. I must have somehow let them understand that I had leftist sympathies. And one of the students must have been a busybody, who must have told the students of Osmania University that Mr. Sarkar of the MMB was a leftist or a communist or socialist or something like that.

I do not remember any more the exact details of how I came to know the students, who were members and activists of one of the radical left groups. Somehow, one of them (let us call him R.) met me somewhere, maybe in the University Arts College. I asked him about their activities and their thoughts and positions. It was I who asked and R. replied. He said they supported the communists[*], and they spread the message of the revolution among students. He also said that they were interested to learn the theory of Marxism-Leninism. But in the Osmania university, among the teaching staff, they could not find anybody, who had the knowledge required or was prepared to help them.

He then suddenly asked me whether I could teach them the theory. I was taken aback. I could not reply immediately. I, of course, knew a lot about all kinds of communist movements in India and the world, but teaching the theory of Marxism-Leninism was another thing. I told him, I had of course read something on the subject, had also read the first volume of Marx's *Capital,* but … R. roughly said that would be more than enough, that they, the students, did not know anything. I asked him, why their party leaders didn't teach them the theory. R. replied, the leaders were all underground, they hardly came to the city. And if they came at all, they came under camouflage. I ended the meeting for that day. I needed time to think about the matter, and about myself and my life.

1966 was a crucial year for all communists of the world who looked to China for inspiration – i.e., for the members and leaders of the parties that called themselves Communist Party of India (Marxists-Leninists) [CPI (M-L)]. The group of R. was associated with one of the factions of CPI (M-L). That was the year when Mao-Tso-Tung initiated the *Cultural Revolution* in China. And within two years, his admirers in India started an armed revolt in some rural areas, which they, however, boastfully called the beginning of a revolution. They repeated the Chinese communist slogan: "A single spark can start a whole prairie fire." I found this slogan, applied to India, too verbose. It was based on a complete misreading of the situation in India.

I have now shared with my readers the salient points of my life and thoughts till 1966. I cannot say exactly when I met R., in which year. But

---

[*] All such radical communists were popularly known as *Naxalites.* But there were also divisions among them. Another such students' group was called *Revolutionary Students' Union (RSU).*

it was surely sometime in the second half of the 1960s or a year or two later. That was when I had to take another important decision of my life. I was of marriageable age, well placed in life according to Indian middle-class standards. Father had written to me, asking whether he should now look for a good bride for me. To reply to father's question was not difficult. I had replied No, that was not his business. Dilip told me later that father was deeply offended by my reply.

I remembered a Bangla drama performance, that I had seen in Calcutta: *Ebong Indrajit*. It was the story of four young men, friends, who were very close to each other. Three of them – Amal, Bimal and Kamal – grew up in the normal course of life, founded a family each, begot children and got entangled in the twirls of life: Any time of the year, this or the other child was sick, this or the other child failed in the yearly school exam. Some one of the three friends got heavily indebted and wanted to be helped by the other friends, some one of them got reprimanded by his boss for frequently falling ill etc. etc. Indrajit, however, developed differently. He did not found a family, had fancy ideas and ideals in head, but was free from the entanglements of life that the other three experienced. The drama consisted of several funny scenes of occasional meetings of the four. I detested the average life of middle-class Indians – as depicted in the life of Amal, Bimal, and Kamal in the drama – although I belonged to this class.

After R.'s visit, some more left-radical student-activists – both young men and women – visited me. In the course of the following two to three years, they found me sympathetic to them, and they became my young friends, close friends. I started going to their public meetings. I actually went, whenever possible, to all public meetings, discussions, conferences and cultural events of all kinds of leftist groups and parties, also of those who were opponents of R.'s group. I especially went to the events of the Moscow-oriented CPI, whenever their chief political intellectual, Mr. Mohit Sen, spoke. Sen, incidentally, lived in Hyderabad. I became somewhat generally known in the city as a sympathizer of the cause of socialism.

The rooms of my small three-room apartment in Himayatnagar were too small for any large gathering. But groups of up to five people could find place, and they came often, also individually. I also knew people from the moderate communist parties, and young student activists of radical parties opposed to R.'s. But they were not close friends of mine. I also had friends who kept company with all left parties and groups.

That was also right. After my deep disappointment in 1956 with the Stalinist version of cruel communism, I had distanced myself from all communist parties and groups in India. I had then busied myself with getting my Bachelor's degree and getting a job to earn my livelihood. I have already narrated in the previous chapters the story of these and subsequent years of my life. But I could not also betray the cause. I remained a socialist in the *general sense*, and I postponed the question whether, realistically, there was any chance that humankind would ever achieve the ideal stage of communism[*].

I had always been a thinking and reading type of man. But in real life, one does come in contact with many people who put questions, and one cannot postpone an answer, one does often have to say immediately, or at least soon, Yes or No. So, when I was asked to give a talk or take part in a discussion, I could not say No. It was of great advantage to me that my German teaching classes were all held in the evening, and I was generally free in the daytime, and the university classes were all held in the daytime.

But the young friends and their party leaders in the underground had obviously overestimated my capacities and underestimated the difficulty of learning Marxist theory. One day, I got the request, passed through R., to teach, in seven days, four young girls, members and activists of the radical students' group, the essentials of Marxist economic theory. What nonsense, I thought. But I could not say No and thus dampen their enthusiasm.

These young girls – between 20 and 25 – were undergraduate students or had only finished their B.A. They came soon, in the afternoon. I knew them all, and they also felt at home. So much so, that one soon fell asleep and the others showed other signs of tiredness. I adjusted my first class

---

[*] Marx/Engels quote about this ideal stage of communism: "From each according to his ability, to each according to his need."

to their level of existing knowledge (almost nil) and their level of tiredness. But it was all useless. I later talked with their student leader – a very bright young girl of the same age-group – about the utter futility of the effort. Maybe she and the participants in the class realized it too. Anyway, they never turned up again for learning Marxist economic theory.

But they and other members of the group often turned up in my apartment, for Himayatnagar was somewhat centrally situated and easily accessible. They could simply take rest there, and also make tea for themselves and me. And in addition, they had a good chatting partner in me. They of course thought that these mere chats were discussions.

Among my friends in Hyderabad, there was a group of seniors, all from my age-group, all from the academic and social elite of the city. I have mentioned them above. I used to meet them often. The occasions were many – social as well as political. Sometimes it was just an invitation for dinner (with or without some reason), sometimes, one of them needed some help. Or some prominent person from some other city came to visit our prominent lawyer friend, K. G. Kannabiran, who was also a prominent civil liberties activist. I remember, once Mr. Namboodripad, the then general Secretary of the CPI (M), came to visit him. We, the senior group of friends, were invited to meet him. Sometimes a friend from abroad came to visit one of us and she/he wanted to meet the friends' circle of her/his Indian friend.

Let me finish this section with a funny story. Once, I was invited to take part in a socio-political discussion, which was to take place in M.'s large drawing room. The beginning was agreed to be at 4.00 PM. It was a hot summer afternoon. I came at 4.00 PM and rang the doorbell. I had to wait a little before M. opened the door. She was still wiping the sleep from her eyes. She greeted me with the words: "I knew, it was Sarkar. Who else would come exactly at 4.00, if I say 4.00! "This was typical India and typical Hyderabad.

Meeting Maria again in Poona

I came back to India in 1966. Then, in 1967, I was again invited or rather asked to go to the Goethe Institute in Poona. This time to take part in a summer-seminar for the Indian lecturers of German. I do not remember any more what all we did or heard or learnt in that seminar. But I can safely say, that for all those Indian lecturers of German who had earlier spent four or even just two months in Poona in the hostels of the MMB with their gardens and free green space, it was a great joy to be there again, a great joy to go to the cafeteria (Bund Café) at the Boat-Club Road and chat with colleagues for long hours over a cup of coffee, or to take a walk along the Mula-Mutha river.

But for me, also this visit to the GI-Poona was of great significance, for a different reason: Here I met Maria again, this time as a colleague. It was Maria, who had made the program and it was she who was the leader in realizing it through her contributions.

Occasionally, after the lecture-and-discussion events of the seminar, in the early evening, some of us – both Indians and Germans – went to a Chinese restaurant in the cantonment part of the city. Apart from taking dinner there, we also continued to discuss the things touched upon during the seminar events. One evening, we were discussing, in the superficial style usual in a restaurant, about, of all things, religion. I had already made known that I was a socialist and not religious. I did not know till then that Maria was a serious and pious Catholic. She suddenly asked me, in the general sense: if you are a socialist, then you must be having ideals. Where do you get your inspiration from, if you have no faith in something higher? I do not remember exactly anything more than this much of that discussion. Why I am narrating this here is that it triggered off an exchange of a few letters between us.

If my memory serves me right, this kind of a summer-seminar was repeated in 1968, and I took part in it gladly. Most probably, our serious private discussion on God, religion, socialist ideals, etc. was repeated/continued whenever the context and the opportunity arose. But then, in 1968, Maria's five-year contract with the GI ended, and she did not renew it. As she told me later, not that she was fed up with India or the GI. But her old mother, whom she loved very much, was frequently falling ill. She wanted to be near her mother. She went back to Germany. Our discussions and correspondence gradually developed into a friendship.

Chapter 10:
Fifteen Years in Hyderabad
Part 2

Maria

In those days, without a computer and e-mail, it was very difficult to keep up communication. Every personal letter had to be hand-written. Typewriters were there only in offices. In 1966, when I returned from Germany to India, I brought along my small portable typewriter that I had to buy for writing my diploma thesis. But I did not get used to typing personal letters. Maria too wrote all her personal letters per hand. We both liked it that way.

The contents of our letters were no longer only our analysis of or opinions on theoretical, religious, political or philosophical issues. They became also and increasingly personal – what happened in personal life, what I felt etc. Maria wrote that she had quit her school job. After having seen India and experiencing life beyond Germany, she could not imagine going back to the small world of middle-school service in small towns of Rhineland-Pfalz. She started studying at the university. She wrote that her future was uncertain, that she planned to live the next few years off her savings, that she had been able to make enough savings from her well-paid job at the GI. I believed she could. I had seen in Poona how simply she lived in her two-rooms, which were actually two garages converted into an apartment.

I started feeling love for her. I still did not think of marrying, let alone marrying Maria, who lived in Germany, while I lived in India. But one day, in a very personal letter, I did write truthfully that I loved her, without telling her that I wished to marry her. I must have expressed it awkwardly. I know today, how young people do that in Germany, i.e., express their love. I roughly also know how modern young people do that in India, if they at all choose their life-partner themselves. But in those days, in India, it was absolutely rare, particularly at such a great physical distance. I had in mind only a sort of felt love relationship, nothing more. I cannot really recall how it went on after that. I only remember I had a positive feeling that she reciprocated.

It was 1972. Maria wrote that she was coming to India in the summer and that she would visit me. I was very glad and invited her to stay with me. But at the same time, I was also nervous. I introduced her to some of my Hyderabad friends as my friend and former colleague. I also showed her the city of Hyderabad and its interesting tourist spots. We also had many discussions. She spent five days with me. But we did not sleep together. I gave her my bed to sleep in and I myself slept on the floor of the drawing room in a rollable bed. Then Maria continued her journey to her other friends – to Bangladesh and to Poona.

I must have made a positive impression on Maria during that visit of hers. She visited me again next year, i.e.,1973. This time she stayed longer, maybe four weeks. This time we became serious, we slept together like a couple. But my bed and bedroom were both too narrow for two people to sleep in. So, I designed a flexible bed to be made of plain wood. The two parts of it could serve in daytime as couches for the drawing room. In the night, placed side by side, they could make a bed for a couple. I also got quilts made for the couches.

I again invited my Hyderabad friends and told them that Maria was my partner (maybe I used the term girl-friend), that we were a couple, though not married. That was no problem for my highly educated and modern friends. They immediately liked Maria. Particularly my female friends, who had already become feminists, became close friends with her. But also their husbands, who were also my friends.

Political Friendships and Their Unforeseen Effects

As I wrote above, most of my young political friends were members or activists or at least sympathizers of one or the other radical left students' groups, if not also members, of the Maoist left parties. Also some of my senior group of friends were sympathizers of the left parties, but not members.

Now, in the late 1960s and early 1970s, and also several years after that, a Maoist insurgency against landlords in particular and the ruling classes in general was going on in some rural parts of India. The umbrella term used for the insurgents and their fellow-travelers was "the Naxalites", stemming from "Naxalbari", the name of the village in North Bengal, where the insurgency had first erupted. They had many urban sympathizers and supporters, particularly among students and other middle-class young people. Also the group of seniors among my political friends, including myself, were generally assumed to be sympathizers of the Naxalites. We were at least regarded by the then ruling parties and their police as such. To what extent this assumption was based on facts, I cannot say even today. And in those days, nobody put questions about the depth of anybody's sympathies for radical leftist parties, or about the kind and extent of help they gave to such parties. If anybody was a member of such a party, it was not clear.

In the case of Kannabiran, our renowned lawyer friend, his sympathies were public knowledge, because he, after all, was defending in the courts many of the accused from this radical leftist spectrum. Moreover, he was known all over India as a leading activist in the sphere of defending human rights and civil liberties (sometime later, he was unanimously elected as the president of *People's Union for Civil Liberties*). But what could be said about the others? Not much, apart from the fact that we were all friends of the radical youngsters and other radical leftists, and that we read their journals and other publications.

About myself, I can say today that already in those days, I was not convinced of the correctness of their analysis of the situation in India. They used to say/write (quoting Mao) that "a single spark could start a prairie fire". That was nonsense, wishful thinking. India was not a large dry prairie. Of course, there were many "sparks", i.e., fiery speeches and writings by middle-class communist revolutionaries. But the amount of "dry grass" that existed – even in the hotspots of the insurgency such as Naxalbari and Srikakulam – was too little.

I knew somewhat the history of both the Russian Revolution (1917) and the Chinese Revolution (that achieved success in 1949). Both took place in the context of wars: the Russian Revolution in the context of the

First World War and the Chinese Revolution in the context of the Japanese imperialist wars of aggression (1930s to 1940s). In the case of the Russian Revolution, large sections of the demoralized Russian soldiers and navy sailors changed side, joined the communists and overthrew the bourgeois government in one night. In the case of the Chinese Revolution, the communists had built up a whole army, the 8th Army, that did the Long March from the South to the North in order to fight against the Japanese invasion army. In India, in Naxalbari, the few communist revolutionary peasants were in the beginning armed with just bows and arrows.

It was in the wake of this insurgency, in the summer of 1975 (exactly speaking, on 25th June 1975), that the central government declared a state of national emergency in the whole country. Whatever the government might have stated as reason – I do not remember any more all the details –, the immediate real cause of it was of course just power struggle within the political class and within the ruling Congress Party. But ultimately, the government also utilized the declaration of emergency, with its suspension of several fundamental freedoms, for suppressing the Maoist insurgency. All over the country, many "Naxalites" were arrested. Arrested were also many of their academic and intellectual friends. At least in Hyderabad, it was so.

This is not the place to write the history of India of that epoch. Other authors have done that already. In the context of these autobiographical memoirs, I only want to narrate what happened to me and my close friends. Many of my young friends went underground. Some could carry on their revolutionary activities from there; others lost contact with their leaders and bided their time somehow, somewhere. Four of us seniors were also arrested. The police came at midnight.

One of us, Shatrughna, suffered much. He was arrested and also detained in jail for months. He was especially targeted, because he was the publisher and chief editor of a periodical that he had himself started and named *News and Views On China*. For whatever reason, he had thought that it would be good to let it appear as the product of a collective. So he chose three other "editors", whose names also appeared as co-editors. I was one of them. Not that I was a wholly sleeping partner. I once also contributed an essay under a fake name.

I and another "editor" of the periodical were interrogated in the night and let go home in the morning. We were told not to leave Hyderabad, and that we would be arraigned. On what charge, they did not tell us then. In any case, the title of the periodical was for the police a sure indication that the editors were Naxalites. That was enough guilt in the emergency days.

While we, the other three, were waiting at home to be arraigned, the chief editor Shatrughna was lingering in jail. Not only he, but a few months later also his wife was arrested and detained in the women's jail. I did not know the finer points of law that allowed this different treatment of the four editors.

I continued to go to work as usual and did not tell anybody at the GI about my arrest and subsequent arraignment on charge of sedition. Fortunately, my teaching duties were only in the evening. So I was free in the daytime to go to the court hearings without having to apply for a holiday. I wonder what my co-accused did with their employers. They were all college teachers. So they, I suppose, were protected by some job-security law.

Now, toward the end of my life, I can write about these things calmly. But, as far as I can remember, also in 1975, when I was arrested and subsequently arraigned, I was not really agitated nor nervous. But I was definitely worried. I had thought I could lose my job at the GI. But, since I was working in a private institution, I had already been living with this possibility, from the very beginning. That was the reason, why in the first four years of the 1970s, I had learnt French through intensive private study. I had thought, if I lost my job at the GI, I would offer to teach both French and German as a private teacher, in my own institute.

We, naturally, handed over the case to our renowned lawyer-friend Kannabiran. It was his special domain: cases involving defense of human rights and civil liberties. He knew what to do and what to say in the court. I do not want to narrate here the arguments and the counterarguments that the public prosecutor and the counsel for the defense proffered in the court. I also do not remember them anymore. I thought our case was simple: the right to express opinions in journals had not been abolished through the declaration of emergency. In any case, Kannabiran could convince the judge that we were not seditionists, as charged. We were all acquitted. But Shatrughna could not enjoy his freedom for long. He was again arrested and detained in jail under the Preventive Detention Act. From time to time, he was of course granted parole for a few days or weeks, but after the few days, during which he could breathe freely and meet us, he was again put in jail. His days of suffering could finally end only after the emergency was lifted in March 1977.

Maria – a Visiting Relationship

After eight years of teaching German in India, in 1974, I thought I had earned the right to get a scholarship for a short study trip to Germany. It was granted. So I flew to Germany in the summer, which is in India in April and May. I planned it so that I could first live with Maria a few days in Cologne and then go to my first station Iserlohn. The latter town is situated close to Cologne, so I could spend the weekends with Maria. She was of course very happy with this arrangement.

Every Monday morning, I was in bad mood because I had to leave Cologne and take a short train trip to Iserlohn, where I got a guest-room with a family. And every Friday afternoon I was in good mood, looking forward to spending the weekend with Maria.

The working hours of the weekdays I had to spend at the GI doing hospitation, sitting in on classes and observing the teachers teach German. That was a very boring thing, but was one of the intended purposes and conditions of the short scholarship. I was supposed to learn the latest methods of teaching German from my German colleagues in the GI there. In fact, however, they had nothing to teach me. Their method, in general, was a bad one, and few of them were really good teachers. I was happy, when the period at this station was over.

The second station was in Munich, my old love, where I felt at home, where I had my first success in life. There, the participants, who were all teachers of German from various countries, heard lectures on various subjects: German literature and arts, German politics and economic problems (as results of the oil crisis), all at a very high level. The lecturers expected a discussion after every lecture. But they were mostly disappointed. Sometimes I raised a point or made a comment. And they were almost grateful to me for making the semblance of a discussion possible. At the end of this station, I could spend a few more days with Maria. But then I had to fly back to Hyderabad, where my students were waiting for me. It was end of May.

Around a month or so after my return to Hyderabad, I received a letter from Maria informing me that she needed an operation, that she had something in her belly, and was going to the hospital next day. Naturally, I was worried. I wrote back wishing her quick recovery. She, of course, recovered, but not quickly. When she visited me next time – that was in November or December 1974 – she told me that it was not a quick recovery. It was a myoma (a uterine tumor) the surgeons had to operate away, but they also had to operate her uterus away. She said she had wept bitterly, that she had expected a consoling telegram from me. I felt guilty, but I had no knowledge of the name and address of the hospital where she was being operated. Her friends who got access to her apartment got my letter and brought it to her in the hospital, days later.

In Hyderabad, it has always been pleasant weather in November–December, rain-free and not hot as in summer. Maria proposed that from now onwards, she would visit me in this season and I must visit her every summer, when it is too hot in India, but most pleasant in Germany. It was a very attractive idea, but I could not afford it. I told Maria, my salary was good for Indian standards, but flying every year to Germany was too much for me. She said, she was now earning a much better salary as a college professor and so she could pay for my flights to Germany. I could not say No. After all, already in 1973, we had become a couple without a marriage certificate.

Let me look back a little and complete Maria's side of the story. Returning to Germany in 1968, she went to the nearest large city from her village, namely Cologne, and rented a room, not an apartment, in the attic of a house in the inner city. Her immediate neighbor was also a female university student. She met the professor and head of the department of sociology, Prof. René König. Her training diploma of a middle school teacher was regarded as enough for going to the university. Moreover, her feminist inclinations had already led her in Poona to make a sociological study of the reasons why her grown-up female students at the GI, Poona, were learning German. This paper, which had been published, impressed the old generous professor. Maria completed her sociology studies unusually fast, and that too with a Ph.D. In 1973, when she visited me, she was already a college lecturer.

I do not remember any more, whether I visited Maria in April–May of 1975. Maybe, maybe not. But Maria came, as agreed earlier, in November–December, despite the bad political situation in India during the emergency. It was then that we started worrying about our visiting relationship. From a friend who kept company with all kinds of political people and groups, I heard that police agents were asking him about the white foreign woman whom they could often see with Sarkar. Obviously, they were watching me. And I also did not care, particularly after the acquittal, to avoid political meetings etc.

Marrying Maria

Sometime after returning to Germany, Maria wrote to me that she wanted to marry me, that she could not live on like this, with this uncertain relationship etc. etc. It was end of 1975 or early 1976, when Maria wrote this. The autocratic emergency rule in India was going on with full force. People were being persecuted. In this situation, I thought it would be good if I could say in reply to any query of police agents that Maria was my wife. It would not force us in any way to give up our respective jobs and independence. It would not force us to choose to live together either in India or in Germany. So I replied that I agreed, that it would be the best in the given situation. Maria had about six months' time to think and rethink about the matter, because I took time to report our desire to marry to the local marriage registrar.

Maria came to Hyderabad in the summer of 1976, in the German summer vacation time. With the agreement of the marriage registrar, I had set a date for the event, it was to be on 17th September, 1976. I had requested two good friends to be witnesses – one was Mr. Burman, a high-level scientific officer of the government of India, the other a university professor of economics, Prof. Shantilal Sarupriya. I was in good spirits. But then suddenly Maria had doubts about her decision. In the morning of the date set for the event, she said she wanted to postpone the date. She would not like to marry, not that day, etc. I was astounded and at the same time angry. I did not ask her why she suddenly changed her mind? I told her she was making herself a laughing stock, and also making me a laughing stock of my friends and acquaintances. I told her, she could also later break off the marriage, get herself divorced in Germany. But today (that day) she must go through with the ceremony.

Marrying Maria (1976). Photo credit: Saral Sarkar

Then, again suddenly, as suddenly as ten minutes ago, she changed her mind. She agreed to marry. Thank God, she did not change her mind a third time. In the afternoon, about a quarter of an hour before the appointed time, we arrived in the house of Shantilal, the appointed place of the official ceremony. The registrar of marriage came on time with his assistant. The papers had already been prepared. The word of consent was uttered, the signatures were put on the papers. The marriage was done. I heaved a sigh of relief that nobody present could hear. After the officials were gone, a little of the traditional Indian part of the ceremony was gone through. The garlands that my friend Shantilal had bought were exchanged between Maria and me. My Bengali scientist friend Burman, following the special Bengali tradition, had bought for Maria two bangles cut out of conch shell. He personally put them around Maria's forearms. He added the comment (only in the general sense): "You are now a Bengali *Bodhu* (bride). After all, you have just married a Bengali man. Like it or not, you must wear them all your life, unless your husband dies first." That must have sounded funny to Maria. Also to me. For, the same morning, just a few hours ago, I had told Maria that she could later get herself divorced if she thought that it had been a bad decision.

Shantilal, the host of the ceremony, had bought a lot of Indian sweetmeats for the occasion. His wife distributed them among the five grown-ups and two children.

Chapter 11:
The Last Five Years in Hyderabad –
Prelude to Living in Germany

After living a few more days with me in Hyderabad, Maria had to go back to Cologne to her work. It seemed to me that she was now reconciled to her new status as a married woman, married to an Indian. She even appeared to have been happy that I had prevented a scandalous blowing off of the official marriage ceremony. Due to the emergency rule that was still in place, I desisted from inviting my political friends to a private social party. However, they all were well informed. Only, I did not tell anybody about Maria's last-minute dithers. A few common female friends came and congratulated us.

I had not taken a day off from my job at the GI. And I had not told anybody there about my marriage. I quietly continued with my work. But it was increasingly becoming difficult for me to work there. While the first director of the GI-Hyderabad was almost a friend of mine (we two had started the work there), the second director was an unfriendly man. The latter tried to behave as a boss, also toward me. And that was impossible for me to swallow. There were frequent low-level verbal skirmishes between us, particularly as I was the trade-unionist in that small institute.

All told, I was unhappy with my job at the GI. Not only the then director was a bad guy, but also the two German ladies, who were working there, were not particularly my friends. Also, the work I was doing there, teaching basic German year after year, could not give me any job satisfaction. In all the years I have been teaching German, not a single student of mine showed any interest in speaking German with me, or reading a German story. The certificate was all that they wanted. It was also understandable. In India, there was nothing that could not be read or studied in English, nothing important for which one needed German. Yet teaching German was my bread and butter. That was what I was officially qualified for. And I had to earn my livelihood.

As a solution to part of these problems, as described in the previous chapter, I had already thought of starting a private language institute of my own. As a more concrete step toward that, I grasped an opportunity to own a bigger three-room apartment, where I could live as well as teach three languages plus spoken English. A state-owned company produced a plan for a housing colony in a good location of the city. I thought of booking an apartment there. Maria would also like living in a larger apartment, I thought, when she would come to Hyderabad.

In the meantime, my political friends, who had been kept imprisoned during the emergency rule under the Preventive Detention Act, were released in 1977, when the emergency rule was declared over. Those who had been employed, had not lost their jobs. They went back to their respective jobs, as if nothing had happened. Of course, we all welcomed them back to freedom and to our group of friends. Moreover, in the next general election, the autocratic Congress Party of Indira Gandhi was defeated. Whole India was happy, it seemed.

I had a special reason to be happy. The housing colony plan had in the meantime taken concrete shape. And also my friend Shatrughna thought of buying an apartment there.

Maria and I continued with our visiting relationship – since 1976 registered as a marriage, which however did not make any substantial difference in the relationship. Only, the atmosphere of freedom and return to democratic rule in India did our heart good. We could again invite friends free from worries, and the friends also invited us. Particularly Maria was very popular and much loved among women, my friends or not.

I do not think, I went to Germany in the summer of 1977. The emergency was revoked in late March of that year (21.03.1977), too late for preparing the journey in April–May. But in 1978, I did. From that visit, I still remember a story very much. It involved Maria's then very old mother:

The old lady lived in her own house with the family of one of her daughters – Trudel, Maria's youngest sister. Maria had a very intimate relationship with this sister and her family, not the least because she loved her mother very much. One day, after my arrival, Maria and I travelled to Auel, her ancestral village, to visit her mother. The family knew me from my earlier visits. But the old lady, my mother-in-law, was a little demented. This time, Maria introduced me to her mother, who was sitting in the rather dark kitchen, in a special way and as a very special person. She said: "Mum, look, this is my husband". Her mum replied in a jocular style: "What! You too have finally got someone!" This was an allusion to Maria's long spinsterhood. Maria then asked her mum, also in a jocular style: "Isn't he a beautiful man?" The old lady replied humorously: "Oh, I do not know what I can say. After all, I do not see anything other than his white teeth!" She was also right. She saw a dark-complexioned man in a relatively dark kitchen. This was how I too became a member of the extended Mies-family.

In that year, 1978, Maria and I went to Geneva. Maria to attend a conference of the ILO on women's labor, I just accompanied her. At the end of the conference, I heard from Maria that the ILO was requesting her to do a study of the labor of housewives in India. I told her to immediately say yes to it. She could use my Hyderabad apartment as her research base, and I assured her that we could easily find there some women as her assistants.

It worked out well. Maria got the assignment from the ILO, and also the required study-leave from her *Fachhochschule* (College of Social Work and Social Pedagogic). It was also good for our relationship. Two years after marrying, we got a chance to live together for about a year rather than a few weeks. We found two young Hyderabadi women, both from my circle of friends, to work as her assistants and interpreters. We also found a woman to work as her office assistant. The Administrative Staff College, located in Hyderabad, provided her an office in their big premises. It was from this research project that her famous study *Lace Makers of Narsapur* resulted. Maria has written about all these things in her autobiography[*]. So there is no need for me to write more.

---

[*] Mies, Maria (2009): Das Dorf und die Welt, PapyRossa Verlag

New Politics in Germany

In the previous chapter I have written about my two-months visit to Germany in 1974 and on my memories from those two months. What I did not write about in that chapter was that in 1974, a new wind was blowing in German politics. I had only heard a little about that when I was there. But in 1978, I got more time to enquire about it. And I also got very interested, so much so, that I collected some written materials and saw some TV documentary films on it. It was the anti-nuclear-energy movement, which was being organized and sustained by ordinary citizens, not opposition parties. Associated with this particular movement were also agitations on several other questions, which later came to be known as the ecology movement. This umbrella term actually covered several particular protest movements that thematized particular negative environmental effects of particular projects, but also the general negative effects of the industrial way of living and producing goods and services. These particular movements were also organized and sustained by the affected ordinary citizens of the region. Actually, most often, the opposition parties of the day agreed with and supported the projects.

I had read the book *The Limits to Growth* by Meadows et al. already in 1972 or 1973. So I could see these movements as more or less inspired by the contents of that and similar other books, e.g., Herbert Gruhl's *Ein Planet wird geplündert*, (Eng. A planet is being plundered), 1975. Actually, I was convinced of the correctness of the conclusions of these books. Yet, it struck me as surprising that it was ordinary affected citizens who were protesting and demonstrating – knowingly or unknowingly, in the spirit of the contents of these books.

I asked Maria, who had by then advanced to the status of a leading feminist theoretician of Germany, what she and the feminist women's movement thought about these movements. Her reply sounded like a general support. It sounded like they supported these movements because the latter were protesting against some dominant views in government and society, which the women's movement was also doing, namely against the patriarchal society. But I shall come back to this topic in a later chapter.

Going back to Hyderabad, I collected some more materials on the subject from the German newspapers and journals available in our GI, and wrote an article on the *Citizens' Initiative Movement in Germany*. The longish German version of the same was published in a journal of the Indian teachers of German with a limited circulation. But the shorter English version was published as a report in a famous Indian journal called *Economic and Political Weekly* (EPW)

The shorter English article immediately attracted the attention of some prominent Indians – academics, as well as political activists – who had been shaken by the emergency regime of Indira Gandhi. These people were thinking of a kind of people's movement without affiliation to any political party, that would rise up against the regime, whenever the latter would try to impose on the country something unjust and atrocious as exemplified by the emergency regime.

The academics and intellectuals among them were mostly also working in or associated with a research organization called *Center for the Study of Developing Societies* (CSDS), the director of which was Prof. Rajni Kothari of the University of Delhi, a famous political scientist of those days. They founded an organization called *Lokayan*; which also had a monthly magazine called *Lokayan Bulletin.*

An associate of this group, actually a high-ranking administrative officer, came down to Hyderabad to meet me. During our talk, I narrated more about the CI movement in Germany, things that could not all be packed in a short article. When the visitor told me about their thoughts on building up such a movement in India, I really did not know what to say. On the one hand, I did not want to discourage them; on the other hand, I knew about the great difference between the situation obtaining in the highly developed, rich industrial country West Germany with its well-educated citizenry, and the situation in India with our masses of bitterly poor, illiterate or lowly educated people, who constituted the citizenry here. I remember I just hinted at this great difference, but I also offered to cooperate with them if they tried to build up such a movement.

I do not remember exactly in which year, but I was still living in Hyderabad, when Maria brought me the sensational book *Die Alternative* (1977) of Rudolf Bahro. After reading it, I thought leftist Indian readers should also get acquainted with the contents of this challenging book. I proposed to Krishna Raj, the then chief editor of *Economic and Political Weekly*, that the EPW should publish not just a review of, but a longish review article on the same. He readily agreed and proposed that I write it. It took me more than the usual effort to write this review article. But it was worth it. It was also my introduction, so to speak, to critical theories of socialism.

Maria brought me another such book, this time a thin volume: *Weltniveau: In der Sackgasse des Industriesystems* (1979) [Eng. World Standard: In the blind alley of the industrial system] by Otto Ullrich. But I will write about these things in the next chapter.

The Students Movement

Another series of things that were happening in West Germany in the late 1960s and 1970s and belonged to the category *New Politics* was the *Students Movement*. I had of course been a student in Germany from 1964 to 1966, and went regularly to the Uni-Mensa in Munich, but I did not see any such thing happening or even brewing up. That was because it started in right earnest only in 1968.

That was the year in which Maria went back to Germany and started studying sociology. She wrote in her letters to me positively about this students movement, in which she also was participating. I too found it wonderful that students of West Germany, a part of the Western imperialist alliance, were protesting and demonstrating against the aggressive war campaign of the Americans in Vietnam, that they were actually supporting the cause of the liberation struggle led by the North Vietnamese. They were in fact lionizing Ho Chi Minh, the leader of communist North Vietnam. I remembered that, while studying in Germany, I had three South-Vietnamese fellow students, who, after completion of their studies, were supposed to go back and teach German in their schools. They never said anything about the war that was going on there. Of course, that was understandable. They were after all civil servants.

The students were also demanding a truthful and deep discussion on and analysis of the Nazi past of their people. They were demanding of their parents' generation that they reveal their personal roles in that horrible era. They were not prepared to hear: let bygones be bygones.

They also demonstrated against the old traditional university system. I heard a slogan of theirs in German that reads, "Unter den Talaren: Muff von tausend Jahren" (Under the academic gowns: thousand years old stifling air). I did not understand it at first. I wondered, what could these leftist students have against the academic gowns of the professors of the past? Or against academic tradition? Wasn't Kant a philosopher of Enlightenment? And didn't Marx learn dialectics from Hegel? But later I learnt that their criticism was directed against the authoritarian manners of the professors.

Maria's Distress Call and My Dilemma

Maria's *Lace Makers of Narsapur* had made her very famous. And it was then that the Institute of Social Studies (ISS) in The Hague was looking for a suitable scholar to found a department of women's studies. It was Maria, who got the job – that of a senior professor. So, my next trips to Europe, to visit Maria, were to The Hague. But we, particularly Maria, utilized every opportunity to go to Germany – on weekends and other holidays. The Hague is a beautiful city, particularly its seashore. But, especially Maria felt homesick and wanted to visit her family in Auel and friends in Cologne. I played along. After all, I knew more people in Germany than in Holland.

Sometime in 1979 or 1980 – I do not remember exactly – Maria wrote that she often felt very lonely, although she was surrounded by so many fans and female students. She missed me very much. She wrote that it did not make sense that we lived separately, though we were married, that she could not continue with this visiting marriage etc. In short, she wanted me to come to live with her, permanently live with her.

It was a problem for me to reply to Maria's appeal, which sounded like a distress call. It was, on the one hand, good to hear that she needed me. And I would also love to live with her. But, on the other hand, if I went to live in Germany or Holland, I would become, to start with at least, an unemployed middle-aged man. And I would become dependent on Maria, my wife, for my livelihood – the worst imaginable status for an immigrant in Europe. So far as my qualification was concerned, it was respected and valued in India. But, I knew, nobody in Germany really needed a middle-aged foreigner with good proficiency in German. And in Holland, I would need to learn a new language.

I knew about Maria's fickle-mindedness, which she had once demonstrated on our very marriage day. Moreover, divorce had been a common occurrence in modern Europe. If that occurred to us, I thought, after I had given up my job and gone to Germany, then I would have to return to India as a jobless and incomeless man.

With Maria in India. Photo credit: Saral Sarkar

I thought through every possibility, for several days. I could not any longer keep her waiting for a reply. Then I wrote back. I wrote that she must return to her old job in Germany, for I was not prepared to live in Holland. Maria immediately agreed. She was after all homesick. She was prepared to quit her job in The Hague, that had brought her international reputation. I also asked her whether she could use her influence in her friends' circle to get me a job in Germany. I, however, knew that she was no good in practical matters. I did not really hope to receive a positive reply to this question. And in fact, I didn't receive any. Maria replied that I ought to come and search for a job myself. I decided to take the risk and try my luck. I suddenly became fatalistic.

Rajni Kothari's Offer

I have described above how I became known to the circle around Prof. Rajni Kothari, the director of *Center for the Study of Developing Societies* (CSDS). He was at that time the director of an international research program of the United Nation's University (UNU). His task was to organize studies on peoples' movements in several countries. It was surely his own idea.

I do not know any more what brought me to Delhi just at that time. Maybe it was my summer holidays. Or maybe Maria had come to India during her Christmas holidays, when I too had some free days. Maybe Maria and I had gone to Delhi in search of a publisher for her Dissertation on Indian women, which I had in the meantime translated into English. I had first written a review of the dissertation which had already appeared as a German book, and it was published in the *Economic and Political Weekly* (EPW). In any case, I went to the CSDS and met my new-found friends. Prof. Kothari asked me in a very general way what I was doing at the time. I told him I was going to give up my job and would henceforth be living with Maria in Germany. Then he made the offer: Since I was in any case going to Germany, I could as well do a study of the peoples' movements there. After all, I already knew a lot about the subject etc. etc. He was obviously referring to my article in the EPW on the citizens' Initiative Movement. I agreed to do the study, but I said I required a formal letter or a contract or some such thing. He promised to send me one.

Chapter 12:
Living in Germany – Part 1

I arrived in Germany in early January 1982. Maria came to the Frankfurt airport to receive me, with a flower. She was obviously very happy; the long tension was over. We both hoped that it would go well with us here-after.

I had left many things behind: my well esteemed profession, my job in the Goethe Institute with its better than usual salary, my close friends, my circle of political friends, and many social contacts. In Cologne, I needed to build up everything from scratch. I of course knew some friends and relatives of Maria, but only superficially.

I had been to Calcutta to visit my siblings and close relatives who lived nearby and bid farewell to them. They were both sad and happy. Sad, because they knew I would no longer be able to come to Calcutta so frequently as till then. Happy for me, because from now on, I would be living together with Maria as a proper family. But now I had a new duty: to regularly write longer letters to them.

New Political Activities: The Peace Movement

I have always been somewhat of a homo politicus. So I soon started going to meetings and demonstrations. West Germany was in those days very agitated over the so-called "Doppelbeschluss" (double resolution) of the NATO, of which the country was a member: In December 1979, the NATO had resolved to deploy in West Germany US-American interme-diate range ballistic missiles (called Pershing II) as well as cruise missi-les, both capable of carrying nuclear bombs. The idea was to restore the balance of nuclear threat, which, according to the NATO, had been dis-turbed by the deployment of Soviet SS-20 nuclear missiles in Eastern Europe. The second part of the resolution proposed also negotiations for nuclear disarmament.

Peace activists had argued that such deployments in Western Europe would provoke the Soviet Union to strike first without warning, in order to destroy such missiles. But the West German government and the federal parliament accepted the deployment resolution of NATO. Peace activists then started organizing a series of small and big rallies and demonstrations against the deployment. In spite of its now being a decision of the state, they hoped to prevent the deployment proper, as the peace activists of some other Western European countries had succeeded in doing.

I came to Germany when this movement was in full swing. I heard a lot about it from Maria and her friends, who too were regularly taking part in it. I heard about the first huge rally on the lawns of the Bonn university. It was soon no longer only the issue of deployment of the nuclear missiles that was being discussed and debated, but increasingly also the basic question of how to bring peace in human society at all. There were people who were protagonists of principled non-violence, protagonists of not using violence in any case. Their slogan was "Frieden schaffen, ohne Waffen!" (Let us bring peace without weapons!).

To such a peace activist I once put the hypothetical question, what they would do, if the Soviet Red Army attacked West Germany and tried to occupy the country. He replied, they would put their hands in the pant pockets and watch the Red Army coming. Thereafter, they would react with non-cooperation and nonviolent resistance as Gandhi did in India. I wondered that the activist knew so little about India, so little about the failure of Gandhi's ideal of non-violence. Yet, I felt nothing but admiration for him and the peace movement. After all, it was great to have at least some ideal.

In the summer, or perhaps late spring of 1982, the West German Peace movement organized another huge rally against the deployment of nuclear missiles in West Germany, again in Bonn, but on the other side, the eastern bank, of the Rhine. Maria and I participated together with two or three other friends.

I do not remember the words said by the prominent invited speakers. But I remember a funny thing that I observed in close proximity of where I sat on the lawn. A technical glitch in the large loudspeaker system was delaying the beginning of the speeches. The technicians – all men – were trying to mend the glitch, but it was taking time. It was this delay that some female participants in the rally (probably feminists) utilized to taunt the male technicians. They started singing a slogan in an intentionally distorted tone and pronunciation: "Männer und Tächnik", "Männer und Tächnik." The lack of peace between men and women of the same people had already begun to manifest itself[*].

But all these rallies and demonstrations were in vain. The nuclear missiles were deployed in West Germany.

The Ecology Movement and the Green Party

Already as a child, I was aware of an aspect of the ecology problématique. Only I did not know that it was called so. One day, in Kamrabad, Dilip and I, then 11 and 9 years old respectively, were standing on the bank of the *Jhil*. I presented my little problem to him. Look, brother, in the beginning, mother and father were two people. Then we six were born. Now we are eight people. But father's income has not grown fourfold. How can it work? Dilip was smarter. He replied: "You are stupid. Look at the Jhil. When it is hot season, the water level is here (he showed with his hand the water level). But then in the rainy season, millions of drops of water fall in the Jhil and the water level rises (he showed the level with his hand). Then in the following months, water level falls again. What happens? Nothing." I was not really satisfied with Dilip's reply. But I could not say anything against his argument. Little did I know then that we were talking about two different things. Dilip was talking about the steady state of the Jhil. And I was worried about the limits to growth of world population.

The Green Party of Germany (*Die Grünen*) had already been founded (1980) when I came to Germany. I had already read about it in India – in the German newspapers and magazines available in our institute. I had already been attracted by its program, because I was convinced of the

---

[*] I have dealt with the causes of such conflicts in my book *Factors of Conflict and Conditions of Peace.*

correctness of the assertion made by Meadows et al. that there were limits to growth.

I asked Maria about their whereabouts, for I wanted to meet them. But Maria could not help me. She knew less about them than I. In the years when there were neither computers, nor internet, nor Wikipedia, and the Greens were still in their infancy, it was not so easy for a newly arrived foreigner to find them in a large city like Cologne.

After arriving in Cologne, my first part-time job was in an organic food shop (Bioladen), where I had to mix muesli and pack the product in paper bags. I had hoped that I would get information from the customers about the Green Party's office and activities. But such muesli eaters were not interested in party politics. And they knew less about green politics than I. Moreover, the owner of the shop told me that my job was to mix muesli and not discuss green politics. So I left the job soon after.

One afternoon, Maria and I had just left our home in Blumenstrasse and were on our way to the little park nearby, when I spotted a young man in Probsteigasse (Blumenstrasse was a side street of this side street) cycling in the wrong direction of that one-way street. I told Maria to stop, and I followed the cyclist with my eyes. Strangely, I had a hunch: a young man on a bicycle riding illegally in the wrong direction of a one-way street could be a Green. And if he got down in that street, then it could be that he was going to a meeting place of the Greens. And indeed, a little further away in the Probsteigasse, the young cyclist got down and entered a house. I made a mental note of the spot, and then we went our way in the opposite direction.

In one of the next afternoons, I went to the spot in Probsteigasse. I looked at the houses there. A rather dilapidated house seemed to be the one the cyclist had entered. And I was right. At the glass window of a room facing the street on the ground floor, I saw a large poster of the Green Party.

I went in and greeted the man at the table. I told him, that I already knew something about the Greens from the media, and that I now wanted to know more and meet them personally. The man sold the party program to me. He said I spoke so good German, and asked where I came from. That is how our personal-political conversation began. I told him how I found this office of the Greens. He laughed loudly and said he was the cyclist I was talking about. It was Albrecht Kieser, who, in course of time, became a good friend of mine.

Another two or three days later, I went again to the Green Party office. This time I found a different young man there. I asked him what had happened to Albrecht. The young man replied: "Nothing!" It was simply his turn today to run the office. I was surprised. The young man, a Belgian student at the Cologne University, explained that the Greens could not yet pay for a secretary. That is why unemployed and student members were rotating voluntarily for the office work free of cost, that is why the office could not open every day, and not for more than two to three hours.

As a Party Member

Their "poverty" made me feel pity for the Greens. I also wanted to become a member of the party. I had an assignment from the United Nations University (UNU) to do a study of the peoples' movements of West Germany (see chapter 11). I thought, through my membership of the Green Party I could have easier and better access to information on the peoples' movements and their activists. Actually, I was not so keen to become involved in usual party politics of the Greens. My personal political focus was particularly on the ecology movement and fundamental questions of ecology.

So, I became a member of the Green Party, and I offered my voluntary labor for running the office in Cologne. I offered to work four hours in the afternoon and all six days of the working week. It was easy for me. The office was barely two minutes' walk away from our home in the Blumenstrasse, I was unemployed, and in the afternoons, Maria was mostly in her college.

The Greens were overjoyed. I too was happy, for this way, within a few months, I learnt a lot about political life in West Germany, especially about politics in the Green Party and the ecology movement. Of course, I also had to read a lot in order to know the antecedents of both, but that was no problem. I had time and books and brochures were relatively cheap, partly even distributed cost-free.

My office work was also interesting. Not only did I have to do all the usual office work: reading letters, and replying to them, answering phone calls, filing papers and documents etc. etc. But I also had to meet people who just came to talk with a real live Green. Many were first surprised to face a dark-complexioned person in the Green Party's office. (Remember, it was early 1982, just two years after the Green Party was founded). When they expressed their wish, and I replied in high German that they were at the right place and asked what I could do for them, they perhaps did not know at first what to say. They usually put some standard questions and wanted to immediately fill out the membership application form. But I also put my standard question to such people: whether they had any idea of the program of the Green Party. Most people had only a vague idea of it, gathered mainly from newspaper headlines and TV news. I usually sold them first the party program and then gave them a membership application form. I requested them to first read the program and then decide.

My approach was not really to the liking of the local party leaders in Cologne. They wanted the Greens to rapidly become a big party, but they could not say anything against my argument. I told them that it was not good if anybody and everybody who could sign on a piece of paper could become a member, that a member should at least agree with the basics of the party's program.

I worked in the party office first as a volunteer. But in March 1983, in the federal elections, the Greens got more than 5% of the votes and so won several seats in the Bundestag. That also brought them some state funding, which enabled them to pay me a salary of 400 DM. And I could moreover share the job with a colleague, each doing half the job. In those days, I also worked as an irregular part-timer at the *Deutsche Welle*, where my job was to do translations from English and German into Bangla. I also wrote some texts that were broadcast for the listeners in Bangladesh and West Bengal. But I gave it up after about half a year, because it was such a stale and senseless job. I then had enough free time to take part in ecological political activities and collect materials for my research project.

I worked in the party job for five years. I could observe in this period the progressive electoral successes of the Greens and simultaneously their continuous political regression from the "bearer of hope" to a "boringly normal party" (*stinknormale Partei*).

Theory Deficit in the Green Party

A popular slogan among the Green Party people as well as among activists of the ecology movement was "Think globaly, act locally" (*Global denken, lokal handeln*). I found it, these words, very good. "Act locally" was clear. When some issues or disputes came up, and it was necessary to protest, then one had to protest and demonstrate at the location of the dispute. For example, when the authorities decided to build a nuclear power plant at Wyhl, it was necessary to demonstrate in Wyhl and the neighborhood, Kaiserstuhl, where vine growers thought they would be badly affected. But when one says *global denken*, it is not always clear, what is meant. Is it spatially meant? Or is it thematically meant? When, e.g., one protested and demonstrated against the proposed nuclear power plant (NPP) in Wyhl, did one protest because of the danger of a blow-out and subsequent widespread radioactive fallout (proliferation), as it later happened in Tschernobyl in 1986, or did one protest against continuous growth of energy generation and consumption?

To take another example, when in the 1980s, a general discussion and debate on the desirability versus opting out of nuclear energy was in full swing in Germany, one solution popularly envisaged was to replace all the NPPs by building gas power plants. The solution envisaged huge quantities of natural gas imports from the Soviet Union. It appeared to me as very odd. In a letter to the editor of a monthly journal, which was popular among Greens, leftists and anti-nuclear-power activists, I pointed out that the solution so proposed was no example of thinking globally. The proponents were actually thinking only locally, proposing a solution for Germany only. If they were thinking globally, they should be calling upon the leaders and citizens of the Soviet Union to replace all their NPPs by gas power plants. After all, natural gas was abundantly available in their country. Moreover, at least in this case, nobody among the discussants was thinking of reduction in power production.

Soon after joining the party as a member, I observed this deficit in their theoretical thinking, which existed also in the thinking of eco-activists outside the party. I thought, this point should be discussed thoroughly. So, although I was a new member and a foreigner too, I proposed, for Cologne, a *study group* on the topic "ecology and economy". As far as my knowledge went, in the German party system, such a tradition already existed. But such groups dealt with particular concrete problemareas of practical politics – of the city, of the province, or of the whole state. And they were probably also called working groups. My purpose was to help create theoretical clarity. Hence, it was called a study group.

I was very glad that some 15 – 20 people reported for the study group. About their background I had only a vague idea. There were among them working people, often with a family, students, and there were also two young academics, who had studied political economy and were still associated with the university as something – as assistants or as researchers working for their Ph.D. They were all against deployment of nuclear missiles in Germany, generally speaking, peace activists, against nuclear power plants (NPPs), and generally for environmental protection.

As the initiator, I had to take up the organizational task of proposing the date, time and place of the first meeting and proposing the first text to be read by all. At the first meeting I also gave the introductory talk, explaining why it was necessary to go deep into the question.

I remember I proposed as the first reading material the introductory chapter of the book *Wachstum oder Askese: Über die Industrialisierung der Bedürfnisse*, by Klaus Traube (Eng. Growth or Asceticism: On the industrialization of needs). Already the title "Growth or Asceticism" summarized what I wanted to be the basic question for the study group.

I do not remember any more what the participants said after my introductory talk, nor what their contributions in the next two meetings were. I only remember how the study group ended soon. At the third meeting, somewhere in the middle, a participant said, in the general sense: Saral, you think you are a theoretician and you must teach us theory. But in three months from today, the next federal election would take place (in March 1983). We have to campaign for the election, for that we need to form a working group, and not a theory study group. Those who want to do election campaign work may come with me. He stood up and went. About half of the participants went with him.

Parliamentary Arm of the Movements

The politics of the Green Party was supposed to be guided by the motto, as they formulated it themselves, "We are the parliamentary arm of the movements". That sounded so good. They meant to say: you ecology activists, you anti-NPP activists, you peace activists, you women's rights activists, you Third-World solidarity groups, you anti-imperialists, you all need a voice in the federal parliament, yes, indeed, in all parliaments of the country, in the provincial parliaments, and even in the city, town and village parliaments. Without a voice in the parliaments, where everything is decided, you and your positions can be easily neglected and your demands easily ignored. So, make use of your votes; vote for us, and our deputies would transport your opinions and demands into the centers of power.

This sounded convincing. And many movement activists and their supporters not only voted for the Greens and their candidates, but also became members of the party. In fact, when the Green Party was formed in 1980, the initiative came from several leading people of the peace movement and initiatives mentioned above. Many of them, not only of those who took the initiative, but also of the ordinary supporters of such movements had previously been members of the established parties. The radical leftists, those who were at the forefront of the anti-NPP movement and often staged violent demonstrations, were members of small communist parties. They were not just anti-imperialists, but also radical anti-capitalists. This constellation – to be truthful, an opportunistic alliance – would later lead to hard inner-party disputes and controversies, and often to resignation of the outvoted minority of radical sections of the membership.

Not only were the radical leftist sections of the party outvoted, but also the radical ecological ones. Although originally, the Green Electoral Lists and also the Green Party were inspired by the growth-critical writings of the early 1970s – *The Limits to Growth* by Meadows et al., *Ein Planet wird geplündert* (A Planet is Being Plundered) by Herbert Gruhl etc. – the majority of the ordinary people who became members of the party were hardly radical-ecologically motivated. The most important thing that such people cherished in life was peace, social peace, law and order, and *economic prosperity*. They had been shocked by the violent confrontations between the police and militant anti-NPP activists. They were in favor of reforms for more environmental protection and safeguards against pollution, but they could not think of a complete aboutturn from the long-standing growth-capitalist system, not even a gradual one.

And they took no stock in ideas like an anti-party party. They wanted the Green Party to be a party like the other ones, a boringly normal (stinknormale) party. This generated a temptation for opportunists, for people who sought a usual political career and a chance to rise quickly in the hierarchy. The party was taken over by the "Realos" (realpoliticians, pragmatists). This transformation of the party was summed up in a sentence spoken out by a "Realo" leader in a speech he gave at a party conference. He said defining the role of the Green Party: "The party is party and the movement is movement. They are two different pairs of shoes." Since I was on the side of the radical-ecologists, I first gave up my job in the party office, then I also quit the party. That was in 1987. There is no need here to go into more details of that story. I have written a whole book on the subject[*].

Several years later, in 1998–99, the Green Party also lost its virginity in respect of war and peace. When it was founded, in 1980, it was the peace party. Under the leadership of the Realos, in 1998–99, when it had become – as a coalition partner – a ruling party at the center, it decided in favor of Germany taking part in the NATO's war against Serbia.

A Note on Rudi Bahro

I have written in the previous chapter that I had published a review article on Rudolf Bahro's book *Die Alternative* (1977) (eng. title: The Alternative in Eastern Europe). Upon publication of the book in West Germany, he was exiled from the GDR and was allowed to go to West Germany.

---

[*] Sarkar, Saral (1994): Green-Alternative Politics in West Germany. Vol. 2: The Greens

Almost immediately thereafter, Rudi (his pet name among friends) aligned himself with the ecologists, who were in those days still rather radical. Originally, in the GDR, he had been a dissident socialist, and also in West Germany, he remained an anti-capitalist. He also joined the Green party, when it was founded. This combination – anti-capitalist and radical ecologist – earned my respect. Because of his fame, he almost automatically became the leader of the radical ecologists. I came to know him personally, and he knew me personally as one of his close supporters in the party.

But he was a very exuberant type of man. And that was reflected in his political speeches at Green Party congresses, many of which I heard, in his writings and also in his personal conduct of life. His fame and many successes as author and speaker may have turned his head. Finally, he became esoteric. He even started quoting Acharya Rajnish ("Bhagwan") after visiting the latter's Ashram in Oregon (USA). His closest friends started getting disappointed. One of them even thought that Rudi wanted to become a Guru.

I regretted this development of Rudi. It also harmed the cause of the radical ecology movement, which lost a leader. I parted company with him. But the question remains: Is radical ecology such a wayward ideal that it is bound to isolate its protagonists from the realities of life, from average human beings? Is it bound to fail, has it no chance, because it is an impossible cause?

I shall try to go into this question in the next chapter.

Chapter 13:
Living in Germany – Part 2

After Leaving Party Politics

After leaving the Green Party and quitting my job there I felt free to collect my thoughts, which were sprouting from time to time, and think them through. I had no obligation to defend the politics of the party, which I had as long as I worked for them in the office.

I had been a friend of the radical ecologists and radical peace activists, both within and outside the party. But I was not satisfied with them in one respect: They were always planning this or that action and were also happy after carrying them out. But they were hardly thinking, as far as I could know, why they were not gaining ground in the society as a whole. Why they even lost ground that they had occupied at the beginning, first to the moderate environmentalists, and later completely to the Realos. They were hardly thinking of developing a vision of a radical ecological and radical pacifist society.

Of course, Rudi Bahro was a big thinker. He was all the time thinking in terms of the society at large. But, as I have written in the previous chapter, he later, in my opinion, went astray and developed into spirituality. Toward the end, he was advocating the creation of ecological-spiritual communes as a solution to social and ecological problems. He appeared to have become a sort of Guru for some Germans who were searching for spiritual something. I was once invited by him to take part in a gathering of his admirers, where the assembly was supposed to discuss about ways and means to attain, at least to approach, the goal of an ecological and peaceful society. It was in Worms, where he had bought a house. He was of course the main speaker, but another person, who did not fully agree with him was also invited to speak. The assembly was, in my opinion, a total failure. Most attendees had nothing to say on the announced subject of the gathering. They were more interested in meditating together. What they were meditating on, that however nobody else could come to know.

My Writings

Already after joining the Green Party and starting to run their office in Cologne, I had begun collecting data and reading for my study of the people's movements in West Germany. I did not have to try hard. Most of the data, so to speak, flew into my lap. The only problem I had was to find enough time for reading the plethora of papers and books. Soon I learnt a lot about the basic positions represented in the Green Party and its programs, about German politics and official policies, about the views of the Greens on them, and about their alternative proposals. I thought that was enough and felt prompted to express my own thoughts in debates and discussions – both in the party and on other fora. But I eschewed any political office at the party level. I only often let myself be elected as a delegate to party congresses and conferences, so that I could get to know what discussions and debates were taking place at the provincial and federal levels. There I also got opportunity to express my radical-ecological positions.

Simultaneously with such political activities, I started writing. I began with the book on the origin and development of The Greens[*], because I was, immediately after my arrival in Germany, in direct contact with them, could observe/experience all the major happenings in the party. I also started writing essays and articles on matters mentioned above, even interventions in the form of letters to editors, and published them in Green Party magazines, in political journals standing close to The Greens, and newspapers. I cannot today name their titles, nor the journals in which they appeared. They were published in printed ones in the pre-computer era. I of course collected copies of them, or most of them, in a carton box, but I never had time to make a list.

---

[*] Sarkar, Saral (1994): Green-Alternative Politics in West Germany. Vol. 2: The Greens

Travels

When I came to live in Germany, Maria was already famous as a feminist author and speaker. Since then, she was getting many invitations to speak at conferences, also from abroad. Moreover, she had relatives in Chile, Brazil and the USA, whom she visited. She often asked me to come along with her, so that I would not live alone in Cologne while she was travelling. I did that gladly. This gave me opportunity to see some parts of the world, to give her company, and also to help her while on travel. Of course, these travels with Maria interrupted my work on my books. But I also wanted to see the world. Years later, when Maria had become known as an eco-feminist and I as an eco-socialist, we often both got invitations from the same place and same people to speak at the same conference. I remember such invitations from Barcelona and Andora.

My family menbers in India (my siblings and me). Photo credit: Saral Sarkar

And all the while, my love for my family of origin and Maria's special interest in India, her Indian female and feminist friends, and relatives through marriage with me stimulated us to visit India every two/three years.

Memorable among such travels were, just to name a few, crossing the Atacama Desert in Chile with Maria's brother Hermann, who lived there and owned a middle-size business, seeing one of the deepest and largest mines of the world, the Chuquicamata copper mine; and a salt lake – both in Chile. In the USA, where we visited Maria's sister Katrin and her husband, the most memorable were the visits to the Grand Canyon, Petrified Forest, Meteor Crater, etc.

Work on my UNU-assignment had been going on all these years. The volume II, that on The Greens, had been temporarily completed first (in 1984 or 1985, I think) – completed but not concluded, because The Greens in those early years were not only fresh and alive, but also kicking. I submitted this draft version to my UNU friends in Delhi during one of our India visits. They were quite happy about it, simply because the gentleman who had been assigned the task of doing a parallel study on the people's movements in India, had not yet submitted anything.

Two to three years after that, I also submitted the volume I, that on the new social movements[*]. I was in a very happy mood, also told people around me about the two volumes. I expected them to be published soon under the title *Green Alternative Politics in West Germany– Vol. I and Vol. II*. But then began a long period of agony. The Indian gentleman, whose newly-founded publishing company got the contract from the UNU to publish the two books, was a political man, who stood close to the UNU group in Delhi, but was very incompetent as a businessman. He dilly-dallied for several years, and never managed to publish even the first volume. He later even stopped replying to my letters. The UNU people in Tokyo finally cancelled the contract with him and gave it to a new company, also an Indian one. The main point in getting the book published in India was to keep the cost of production as low as possible. The new company published the two volumes in 1993 and 1994 respectively.

---

[*] Sarkar, Saral (1993): Green-Alternative Politics in West Germany. Vol. 1: The New Social Movements

The two volumes were not a big success on the market. Particularly because they were academic books. And also because of lack of publicity. The UNU did little in that regard. Information on them appeared only in an obscure bulletin on UNU publications. Later however I came to know that they were being regularly recommended as useful reading whenever the political science department of a university offered a course on social movements.

My Analysis and Conclusions

During the 1980s and 1990s, while writing my essays and articles and the two volumes on green-alternative politics, thoughts were continuously shooting through my head. They did not always, not all of them, find expression in my essays and articles – partly because they had not ripened, not yet been thought through, and partly because the right occasion was not there yet.

After my two volumes on green-alternative politics had been published, I had more time to collect my other thoughts, bring them to an order, present my analysis of the general world situation, and sketch the vision of a future peaceful human society that would be based on our recently gained knowledge on limits to growth. My two volumes on green-alternative politics were mainly descriptions, perhaps also a little analysis, of struggles for or against something as they were being waged in those days. Most people who were taking part in those struggles, were still stuck, I thought, in the traditional ideas of progress, peace, equality, socialism, liberation, democracy etc. But an absolutely new situation had arisen *after the discovery of limits to growth*. Not only those traditional ideas, but actually the very basis of those traditional ideas had become obsolete. Those traditional ideas were all based on the unquestioned, tacit assumption that the world economy and the economies of individual countries would continue to grow, i.e., material production and consumption of goods and services would continue to grow. That has been the *growth paradigm*, as I call it.

At the latest since 1972, however, i.e., after the publication of the book *The Limits to Growth*, a new paradigm, which I call *Limits-to-growth paradigm*, should have formed the new basis of all socio-economic, socio-political and socio-psychological thinking – be it thinking on a future good society, be it on the future dangers to any human society, be it on environmental protection, be it on balance and peace between living beings in nature, in fact thinking on any serious subject related to humans and their societies. But the *imperative* need of this radical change, called *paradigm shift* in scientific language, had not been clear to the majority of environmental and peace activists.

Their demands, slogans, opinions, proposals of solutions etc. were, as before, based on assumptions of the growth paradigm. They were related to *policy decisions* at the central, provincial, and local governance level, which too were based on assumptions of the growth paradigm. The imperative of this paradigm shift had not been clear also at the international level, in the UN for example, not even at the level of highly placed social scientists.

As speaker on a conference in Italy. Photo credit: Saral Sarkar

I have already given above an example from the anti-nuclear-power movement. Another example, actually a basic conclusion, from the socio-political sphere would be the *imperative of revival of socialism* as an ideal and *necessary* form of human society. Since the demise of "official socialism" (AKA "actually existing socialism") in 1989–1991, it had become quasi-impossible for a leftist to stand for socialism, particularly in Germany. But in a capitalist society, nothing can function unless the freedom of capital owners to legally get rich (often at the expense of others), and the possibility of blamelessly becoming poor – e.g., through redundancy – are guaranteed. Such a social system absolutely needs continuous economic growth to ensure at least some *social peace.* Under the paradigm of Limits to Growth, however, an economic policy of *purposely reducing production and consumption* (nowadays popularly called *"degrowth"*), and *reducing population* – worldwide and, especially in overpopulated countries – is imperative. When production contracts, distribution must become egalitarian in order to ensure *social peace.* This will inevitably necessitate also rethinking and massive changes in secondary economic policies, such as price policy, employment policy, social welfare policy, actually in every area of policy. In order to ensure international peace, a lot of transformation in international relations would also become imperative.

Today, it is almost impossible to know how all this could become realizable soon. But is it not the duty of thinkers to think what appears today to be unthinkable?

Three more points became clear to me since the 1970s:
(1) Economic prosperity in the usual sense and good health of the environment are inversely proportional to each other. We humans as a whole must become "poorer" in the usual sense so that health of the climate, of the oceans and the rest of nature can be restored.
(2) In other words, green growth, sustainable growth, is a nonsensical idea. And
(3) there is no reversing the flow of non-renewable resources toward exhaustion, because the Entropy law (called the Second law of Thermodynamics in the area of energy) is an inexorable law of nature.

My Theory-Book: Eco-Socialism or Eco-Capitalism?

I cannot say any more when exactly I came to these definite conclusions. Surely, they did not occur to me like a flash in the sky. That took time.

176

Particularly the idea of sustainable development (or green growth) within the framework of capitalism, that Green Party politicians dangled like a carrot in front of the voters, was a big obstacle. But not only shrewd Realo Green politicians, but also many a scientist, otherwise honest thinkers all, dangled this carrot. They just obstinately refused to accept the truth that there was no other way to save the environment but to pursue a policy of a contracting (de-growing) economy. I remember a sentence from a book by a famous German scientist, which I often quoted in my speeches and writings[*]: "To tell Europeans, Americans and Japanese that they should wear sackcloth and ashes and forgo prosperity, is a strategy condemned to failure."

It was obvious to me from all that was known about the hitherto prevailing socialism that also this conception of an ideal society was not compatible with the requirements of an ecological economy. But I thought, socialism being essentially an egalitarian conception of society, it should be possible to conceive a *different kind of socialist society* that can be harmonized with an ecological economy. I thought, if I succeed in conceiving one such thing, then it should be called ecological socialism, in short "eco-socialism".

A particular German author, Otto Ullrich, and the thoughts presented in his thin 160-page book *Weltniveau – In der Sackgasse des Industriesystems* (1979) helped me a lot in coming to my analysis and my conclusions. Particularly the following quote from his book influenced me very much:

"There is no *lower* limit of the 'development of productive forces' below which socialism is impossible, but there is an *upper* limit. The level of industrialization that has been reached today by the FRG and the GDR is creating, via technology, a social structure that by itself makes a socialist relationship between humans impossible." (p. 102, emphasis in original.)

---

[*] v. Weizsäcker, Ernst Ulrich (1989), Erdpolitik, p. 14

It was again Maria who brought me this fresh publication from Germany when she visited me in 1979. I read it immediately and was highly enthused by its contents. Again, I offered to write a review article on it and an Indian theoretical journal called *Alternatives* published it.

On the basis of further reading and further thought, I soon became convinced that, actually, a socialist order of society was an *essential primary condition* for citizens to accept a contracting economy for the sake of protecting the environment from the onslaught of our own species.

I had already been expressing such thoughts in short lectures, essays and articles. Now I decided, it was 1994, to write a whole book that would expressly be called *Eco-Socialism*, in which I would elaborately present my argumentation for my conception.

But I thought, in order to make my argumentation for eco-socialism comprehensive, it was also necessary to add my answer to the question, why the traditional model of socialism, as had been applied in the Soviet Union, failed at all. For this part of the book, which I put at the beginning, I had to do some more research-like reading, much more than what I had already done. In short, I found two factors that had been responsible for the failure:

(1) limits to growth, that necessarily existed in all industrial economies, and ecological degradation that also necessarily happened in the Soviet Union, because no industrial economy can function without degrading the environment. And

(2) moral degeneration that had gradually set in in the Soviet society leading to its transformation into a class society.

For making the book comprehensive, I also added a chapter on the question why eco-capitalism cannot work – whatever one may call it: green capitalism, sustainable capitalism or ecological market economy. And I also examined in short two other alternatives: market socialism and Gandhism.

I also wrote in the book why I did not have faith in the hype about so-called renewable energies, solar and wind energies. They were (still are) not, in my opinion, renewable at all, of which I was convinced after reading the works of Nicholas Georgescu Roegen.

After concluding the book, while I was corresponding with Robert Molteno, the publisher and chief editor of Zed Books, London, he informed me that in France too there was somebody who was talking of *decroissance* (which is nowadays being translated into English with de-growth). I was very glad that the idea of a contracting economy was so spontaneously occurring also to other thinkers.

Eco-Socialism or Eco-Capitalism? was published in 1999. It has been (and still is) my most important theoretical work. By writing it, I tried to lay the first and ultimate theoretical foundation of the idea and vision of eco-socialism. Although even in the 1980s, some leftist Social-Democrats and small leftist students groups had tried to do that, their work had remained just attempts. Nothing final had come out of that work. Mainly, I suppose, because they could not stomach the need for the economy to contract. But I admit, I do not remember the discussions of those days any more.

My book was also accepted in the world of books as the theoretical foundation of eco-socialism. It has been translated into four other languages: German, French (in internet), Chinese and Japanese. Unfortunately, in French, the book did not appear as a book, because the two professors of the University of Liege, who took the initiative to get the book translated by their students of German, did not take the responsibility to find a publisher, and I had no contact in the publishing business of France or Belgium.

In this connection, it is worth mentioning that on the occasion of publication of the Chinese translation by the Shandong University Press in 2008, the political science department of the University organized an international conference in Jinan on the subject of the book. I was invited there as the chief guest and the main speaker. There, a number of students of the higher levels and professors and lecturers sought to have private discussions with me on the subject. I had a feeling, just a feeling, that my conversation partners felt embarrassed that although China was being ruled by a communist party, the country was known in the world to be a highly successful capitalist country.

I was also invited to Beijing, but this time by the Beijing Agricultural University. There too I gave a lecture on my subject. But I avoided to mention the point that China pursued a capitalist economic system. After all, all Chinese people knew that truth. Anyway, in both Jinan and Beijing, the hosts tried to show utmost respect to me, and fulfilled all my sightseeing interests by ordering a few students to help me whenever I asked for some help. In Beijing, standing on the Tien-an-Main Square, I experienced the notorious smog of Chinese cities. It was actually a sunny day; I could see the sun's round disc on the firmament, look straight at it. Yet, down on the square, there was no bright sunshine.

Origin of My Other Theory-Book: The Crises of Capitalism

I had studied some economics in college as a part of my studies for the Bachelor's degree. That was in India in the second half of the1950s. After graduation, I had no further reason to have interest in standard economics. Only Marxist economic theory interested me. But that was because in India of those days, up to the end of the 1970s, all one could think of as an alternative to capitalism-related bourgeois economic theory was "Marxism-Leninism-Mao-Tse-Tung-Thought". So an intelligent, educated, middle-class Indian searching for an alternative economic theory had to read Marxist economic theory.

But after immigrating to Germany, due to my association with The Greens and the ecology movement, I again got interested in economics, but more in ecological economics. That was the time when I read, e.g., Herman Daly's *Steady State Economics*, about John Stuart Mill's stationary state etc. These were compulsory readings for one like me, who was writing and planned to write a book on eco-socialism and eco-capitalism.

But there were also eco-Keynesians, Gesellians etc. etc. I remember, I wrote a critical article each on Keynesian and Gesellian economics. The latter thinker (Silvio Gesell) was relatively popular or rather well known among the Green-Alternatives.

The 1990s were also the time when globalization of the world economy was making rapid strides – not to the liking of the ecos and the Greens. Around that time, the OECD took the initiative to draft an international agreement on globalization. It was called *Multilateral Agreement on Investment* (MAI). When the clauses of the draft became known, one could see that it proposed to deprive the signatory states of the right to intervene in investment-decisions and -agreements of large corporations in foreign countries. When we in Cologne read about it, we immediately started a campaign against the MAI (1997). Maria assembled her friends in our drawing room (I too took part in it). We understood our campaign as a general movement against globalization, not just against the MAI or particular clauses thereof. The movement became global and gained in strength. In 1998, the initiators, OECD and some governments, dropped the idea. It was a great triumph of a global people's movement. When ATTAC was founded in Germany (2000)[*], we joined the organization and became the ATTAC's local group.

Maria as speaker, at a "polit-action". Photo credit: Saral Sarkar

---

[*] ATTAC is the acronym of the French *Association pour une taxation des transactions financière pour l'aide aux citoyens* (Association for taxation of financial transactions in the interest of citizens).

It was then that I started intensively reading on economic theories. I also had time to do so, because I had finished the manuscript of *Eco-Socialism or Eco-Capitalism?* I got the manuscript typed by our next-door neighbor Hermine Karas and sent it to Zed Books (London) in mid-1997.

The next 10 years I spent reading and writing occasional articles on issues in my areas of political activities. Writing had become easier. First, Maria was goaded by her female friends into buying a computer. Then I too bought one.

A Short Digression on Maria's PC

Maria actually never wanted to buy a PC. As for letters, she was satisfied with her electric typewriter. Her longer texts she wrote by hand, and then gave them to Hermine for typing, who already had a PC which she used for typing Maria's texts. We both were in principle against using more and more high-tech apparatuses. But once, one of Maria's women friends told her: "How can I communicate with you unless you have a PC?" Maria, of course, hated the idea, but she also hated the idea of losing contact with her friends. So she agreed. The said friend of Maria sent her young son, who had started a small computer business, to sell a PC to Maria and install it. He did it. Maria had her laptop on her table, but she had absolutely no idea how it functioned. She tried to use it just as a better and smaller electric typewriter, and so muddled up everything. The young son of her female friend did not show up at all any more. Later we heard that he went to Berlin to study something there. So it became my work to learn rudiments of the new technology from friends, who happened to visit us and teach Maria how to use her PC.

Let me come back to the theme of my second theory-book:
In 2007, the manuscript of the book was already written. But I had not started asking publishers yet. I was hesitating. Because, firstly, I was not at all known as an economist; and, secondly, economic theory was supposed to be uninteresting for political activists. I had, for that matter, written the book in German. I had thought, since I live in Germany, it might be easier for me to find a favorably disposed publisher here.

I probably would not have found a publisher for the book if a new and very serious global economic crisis had not broken out in 2008. I hope this crisis has not yet disappeared from the memory of my readers. So, in short, I did find a small publisher in Germany[*]. But I had to support it by purchasing 150 copies of my own book and try to sell it. I had, however, better luck in the USA. A political publisher located in Berkeley showed interest. It found financial support from a nature-loving and politicized ex-industrialist. It got the German book translated in Argentina by a young woman, who had studied in Austria. The English translation appeared in 2012[†]. I even got a royalty two times. 500 Dollars and 100 Dollars, So they must have sold it relatively well.

The philanthrope who supported the American publishers was Doug Tompkins. He was also quite well-known in Germany. Doug and I first met in San Francisco at an international conference on alternatives to globalized capitalism organized by *The International Forum on Globalization* (IFG). I have forgotten in which year exactly; maybe it was in 2008, the year in which the global financial crisis broke out. The conference was financially supported by Doug, who himself took part in it. The IFG has been an alliance of leading activists, scholars, economists, researchers, and writers. It analyses and critiques economic globalization's cultural, social, political, and environmental impacts. I was invited to the conference to give a talk on my theory and vision of eco-socialism. There I met several prominent US-Americans, who had, in my view, something important to say on the subject. I remember only two names among them all: one was Richard Heinberg, a high-level authority on energy questions, whom I respect very much, and another was Joel Kovel, author of the book *The Enemy of Nature* (2002). Joel Kovel has also been an adherent of eco-socialism. I had met him a few years earlier in New York (when exactly? I think soon after my book on eco-socialism had appeared in London). In New York, that time, our friend George Caffenzis (professor of political science) had organized a book presentation for me, and Kovel had presided over the meeting.

---

[*] Sarkar, Saral (2010): Die Krisen des Kapitalismus. Eine andere Studie der politischen Ökonomie

[†] Sarkar, Saral (2012): The Crises of Capitalism. A Different Study of Political Economy

Kovel did not become a friend of mine. But Doug and I later became good friends. Every time he came to Germany for something, mostly to Berlin, he requested me to meet him, which I gladly did. Doug had appreciated what I had said in San Francisco. And I was surprised that he, an ex-industrialist and multi-millionaire, could turn into a critique of capitalism. For quite a few years until his death, we had a sizeable volume of correspondence. His (second) wife, who too was an ex-industrialist, had put her money into their common philanthropic fund. That fund promoted nature conservation projects in the deep south of South America.

They both appreciated and agreed with my particular reasons to reject the possibility of a solution of the ecological problems within capitalism, but probably not with my vision of eco-socialism. Doug did not say anything about that, but his wife once said: "Saral, you are dragging a rock behind you". She meant the term "socialism".

Chapter 14:
The Plagues of Old Age

Maria Got Epilepsy

During the Anti-MAI Movement and during our participation in ATTAC and the Anti-Globalization Movement, Maria was still very active – both as a political writer and speaker and as a political organizer. But gradually we both noticed – I cannot say exactly when it began – that Maria was occasionally getting fits of epileptic attacks.

Maybe I should have known much earlier. One night, around 2 o'clock in the morning, while she was sleeping and I was still awake, she started giving out strange sounds and wildly throwing her arms above and around. I had no idea what was happening. After a few moments she became quiet, but did not respond to my efforts to awaken her. Then I called the emergency medical relief-team and the friendly neighbor Hermine, who came soon. She too could not awaken Maria. When the emergency relief team came, she had woken up. I told her what I had observed and that she must now be taken to the hospital. She was totally surprised, but acquiesced.

Next day morning, in the hospital, I talked to the doctors. As far as I can remember, they said they could not find anything wrong, but they wanted her to stay another day for further examinations. Next day, again they could not say what was wrong with Maria.

We had forgotten the incident and Maria had long returned to her usual activities, when, one afternoon, in the presence of another person and myself, she suddenly fell silent, head hanging, and not responding to anything. She recovered from this state within minutes, and everything was as before. She could not say what had happened. But when such a thing happened again next week, I decided we must go to her family doctor. The latter must have surmised what it was and referred Maria to another doctor who was a psychologist or neurologist (I do not remember exactly). It was from him that we learnt that she had epilepsy, old-age epilepsy.

This doctor treated Maria for several months, but we could not see any improvement. On the contrary, she started occasionally collapsing to the ground – sometimes she fell with a thud. All the time, it was I who was worried, not Maria. I feared, she would one day be badly injured, but Maria laughed it away. I proposed that she wore a cyclist's helmet to protect at least her head. She found it ridiculous. I started escorting her to places as far as possible. If she went to a function, political or social, I had to stay there to the end. We were living then in an apartment on the second floor of an old building. I asked Maria to tell me every time she wanted to go down or up the stairs, so that I could hold her by the arm and prevent her from falling and rolling down the stairs. But she pooh-poohed the idea away.

Maria insisted on carrying on with all her usual activities, even without being accompanied by me. Two–three times it so happened that I was at home and I received a call from her from somewhere. She said, she was now coming back home. When I wondered why she was calling me at all for coming back home, she said she was calling from a hospital. She had had a fit of epilepsy while coming back home, had been lying on the pavement, until some passers-by noticed her and sent her to a hospital.

Two or three times it so happened that people who had invited her got panicky when Maria had a fit. They had no earlier knowledge of Maria having this illness. They thought Maria was dying and called me frantically, asked me to come immediately. I had to quieten them and tell them to tell the doctor that she had epilepsy. Once, in Trier, I suppose, she had been invited by a women's group to give a talk. She had gone alone. After the welcome address, she was called to give her talk. She sat at the table, took out her papers. Some two hundred people were waiting for her to start speaking. But nothing came out of her mouth. After a minute or so, she fell down from the chair. Again, panic in the audience. I got all this information through a frantic call from the hosts. They had sent her to the nearest hospital and been waiting for a word from the doctor. Again, I had to quieten them. Next morning, I got a call from the hospital that Maria was OK and had decided to travel back to Cologne alone.

I do not remember well the chronological order of these events. Sometime in-between, the specialist doctor, who had been treating Maria till then, gave up and referred her to Prof. Dr. Elger of the University-clinic Bonn, whom he respectfully called "the Pope of our discipline". Maria was examined there for ten days as in-patient. These ten days, I travelled everyday morning from Cologne to Bonn and returned only in the afternoon. Thereafter, the Professor referred her with his recommendations to a specialist doctor in Cologne, who had been one of his students.

This treatment went on. I do not know any more for how many years, until I could say, toward the end of 2012, that Maria's condition had stabilized, that she was not having epileptic fits any more. But she had to continue taking the medicines, two times every day, and without fail. I had to supervise that she did.

We Changed House

We had been living, since my arrival in Germany in 1982, in an apartment in an old house (Blumenstrasse 9) in the central city; Maria since longer. The house had been built in 1876. It needed a total renovation, which had already begun. In view of the risk that Maria could fall down the stairs, I had proposed to the owners to build a lift, at least to our second-story apartment. But they refused.

We had come to love this house and our apartment. Not only because of its old age, but also because of its central location, its closeness to everything important to life: main railway station, main post office, main department stores, the famous Cathedral, a market center for daily needs, two parks etc. etc. Moreover, Maria had spent a large and most important part of her life in this house. I too had in the meantime spent my thirty most important years in this house. All our books and the most important writings were written here, all our political activities were planned here and also executed from here. It was the central office of the Anti-MAI movement. Our next-door neighbors were our best friends.

But, firstly, because of the noise generated by the renovation work and, secondly, because of the lack of a lift, we decided to change house.

It was hard for us, but then our best friend and next-door neighbor, Hermine, left the house and found a good apartment at the southern edge of the city, in the area called *Klettenberg*. After 5 to 6 months, we followed suit in January 2013. Since then, we (now I alone) have been living in our present apartment in the same housing colony built by *Caritas*, a charitable organization of the Catholic Church of Germany. It is a beautiful colony in a quiet area surrounded by much greenery. The colony itself has a little park of its own. What is also of importance to old people, the *old people's care home* of Caritas is also located in this colony. The tenants here must all be at least 60 years old. They usually come here to live till the end.

Maria Suffered from Dementia

In 2013, Maria was 82 years old, and I 77. We were both happy. No longer politically active, Maria still remained in contact with her younger and active friends, who often visited her. And her epilepsy was under control. I was taking care of her, was also registered as her care person. So she did not have to bother about anything, because I was in any case the manager of the household.

Because I was at first doing all the household work – Maria, of course, helped me in cooking – and also going out for walks with her, I found little time for any intellectual work. I only found time for an occasional article on thoughts that occurred to me in connection with my political convictions. In addition, I started or continued with reading on the question of Conflict and Peace.

But soon we found a helping hand, Mrs. Schmidt, a married woman, who took over most household jobs except cooking. I still had to do all the care work for Maria, dispensing the medicines to her, to do all the cooking, and going out for walks. But I found some more time to write articles and comments. I opened (or had perhaps already opened) a blogsite of my writings and called it Saral Sarkar's Writings[*].

But, unfortunately, this satisfactory arrangement, which had made us both happy, did not last long. Soon after her 85th birthday, celebrated with

---

[*] https://eco-socialist.blogspot.com

many of her old and new friends in the community, she started often complaining about forgetfulness. She did not use the word "dementia", but I knew that many old people suffer from this problem. And, after all, Maria has had neurological problems originating in her head, that is, her epilepsy, which was not really cured, but only held under control by means of medicines.

With Maria on my 80th birthday (2016). Photo credit: Saral Sarkar

I found a specialist doctor in our locality, Dr. Ghaemi, a neurologist, who also treated dementia. When we first went to him, one of his assistants subjected Maria to a memory test. Maria told me later, she had become angry, because the assistant put "stupid" questions that she naturally could not answer. I understood the situation: The assistant had put standard questions prepared for average people leading a normal life. But Maria was not an average person, nor had she ever led a normal life. Many of the questions must have related to experiences that Maria had not made.

Anyway, Dr. Ghaemi prescribed a drug, but he also told us that it would actually only slow down the progress of her dementia, but the disease could not be fully cured. I felt so sad for Maria, for her tragic fate. After her years of suffering from epilepsy, she now suffered from dementia. I think I dispensed the medicine to her for about five years, along with all the other medicines against epilepsy and high blood pressure. For about five years, i.e., as long as she remained at home under my care.

I Had a Heart Operation

In the meantime, I also suffered from heart problems. I had to go regularly to my family doctor and occasionally also to a cardiologist. But one day evening, in December 2019 – I was 83 years old – I had to rush to the hospital. I called the emergency medical relief, called also Hermine, our old friend and also in the colony our neighbor, called the two nieces of Maria who had promised to take over charge for care for Maria, if and when I would no longer be able to do that duty. Then, when Hermine came, I climbed into the ambulance car and they brought me to the hospital Evangelisches Klinikum Köln Weyertal.

There they examined me thoroughly for several hours. I had thought, after the examination they would give me some new or additional medicine and send me back home. But they didn't. They said, I should sleep now in Weyertal and next morning I would be transferred to the University Clinic. Asked why to another hospital, the Doctor said: because they had better facilities. I understood, I had something serious.

In the University Clinic, they again examined my heart thoroughly, and then sent me to an intensive station. To make a long story short, a few days later, I had to undergo an emergency operation, an open-heart surgery through which three bypasses were constructed.

In the Uni-Clinic itself, nobody cared to tell me anything about the operation. I heard of it only incidentally from a charwoman of the clinic who was cleaning my room. My friends came to visit me, but they too did not tell me anything about the heart operation. And apparently, somehow, none of Maria's numerous relatives had thought it was his or her duty to visit me. Maria, however, my demented wife, who was temporarily housed in an old people's care home in Rodenkirchen (in Cologne), came to visit me twice. She was brought to my bedside by a niece of hers. Maria perhaps had not heard or had heard but not understood that I was seriously ill. She had thought that I was worried about her welfare, which I indeed was despite my own sufferings. Maria tried to allay my worries, she told me again and again that I should not worry, that she was being sufficiently taken care of. After each of these very short visits, she had to leave me alone. She was after all dependent on her niece who had brought her to the hospital by her car.

Since nobody was caring for me, I myself took the initiative and asked the doctor during one of her rare visits when she would discharge me, when I could go home. She answered, next week Friday. When the next Friday came, two nieces of Maria came, one a little later. Apparently, they, as next of kin, had been called. When they were asked, they said, there was nobody at my home to care for me; so I could not go home. But I insisted. I thought I had recovered enough, I could care for myself – with the help of my friends, if necessary. Actually, I was frustrated. The hospital personnel were very unfriendly, had, anyway, no special love for me, they did only the minimum that was necessary. The doctor finally said: "This hospital is not a prison, if you want to go, you can go. You only have to sign some papers." I went back home on that very Friday, early evening.

My home-coming was a total disaster. I had thought I was ready to go back home. But my home was not ready to receive me. It was some day in January. 2020. The apartment was bitter cold, the central heating system had been turned off, and the refrigerator was totally empty. I could not get out of my winter coat. But the telephone was working. I called my friends and told them about my situation. I requested them to bring me some food for the evening.

The friends came, they also brought some food for me. But they told me frankly that I had made a mistake, that nobody could give me the care that I still needed. Some of them had in the meantime called the emergency medical relief. The ambulance came soon after. Without saying a word, I allowed myself to be pushed on a wheelchair out of home and back to hospital, to hell, I thought at that moment, again to the University Clinic.

Fortunately, in the University Clinic, I landed in some other department or some other section. I did not naturally understand why. In the Uni-Clinic, the doctors never explain anything to the patients. In the previous department, before I was discharged, I had been asked whether I had a place in a convalescent home. That meant I was cured, but needed some rest and good food and exercises etc. But here I was again, on a normal sickbed in a normal three-bed hospital room.

Fortunately for me, this time, Biggi took pity on me. Biggi (Brigitta Perings) is the eldest daughter of Maria's late eldest sister Agnes. She visited me often. Then she somehow organized that I would be transferred to a better hospital, which was especially meant for old patients, to the St. Hildegardis Hospital. And she also organized that I would get the better treatment that I deserved as a privately insured patient: a bed in a two-bed room and treatment by the principal consultant (chief physician) of the department.

This time, fortunately, the chief physician told me, what I was suffering from, namely from an atypical pneumonia. Because it was atypical, it was difficult to treat. But after about four weeks, he had success, and I could now go home. The doctor, however, strongly recommended that I subsequently go to a convalescent home, which I agreed to. Biggi organized that too.

Between discharge from St. Hildegardis and going to the convalescent home, I had three days of waiting, which I did at home. In this treatment pause I visited Maria in her care home in Rodenkirchen. Maria was overjoyed to hear that I had finally left the hospital. She immediately laid claim to living with me together, when I finally come back home. It was important for her, for she had heard whisperings among her visitors and "well-wishers" that it would be better for her to live separately from me in a care home, that then her visitors could come freely anytime to visit her. I too, of course, wanted to live with her in our familiar home in Karl-Begas-Strasse 3. I promised to her, we will do that.

Our New-Found Happiness Ended Soon

After spending about four weeks in the convalescent home, I finally came back to normal life at the end of February 2020 – after about three months of absence. I had arranged that Maria would be brought back home on the same day as I, in the afternoon. So, we were reunited. We were both overjoyed and we lived totally happily thereafter, almost.

I took over complete charge of the household, and Maria was at first happy that she was not responsible for anything, not even for helping me in cooking. I also did not dare any more let her do risky things like cooking and vegetable peeling with a knife. For, even earlier, she often forgot that she had put something on the stove, and then the food started burning; often she cut her finger while peeling potato. I also took over the complete work of sorting her medicines, which, earlier, she was at least trying to do. She found it admirable that I could quickly sort her as well as my medicines without looking at the medication plan. In short, she became totally dependent on me. And when I went to do marketing, I had to prepare her for my short absence, just for some 45 minutes or so. When I came back with the purchases, I always found her waiting for me in front of the house looking intently at the entrance gate of our housing colony. She must have spent the 45 minutes anxiously, afraid that I may not return.

But soon she started getting bored. She lost interest in reading, because she forgot the content of the first sentence, when she came to reading the second. She lost interest in seeing TV, because she did not understand what the pictures were conveying. She wanted to do something, but I could not give her any work. Only when the grocery van came to the colony and parked just in front of our house, she wanted to go and buy something, anything, thus feeling herself useful for something, meeting other old women. I let her go and buy something, necessary or unnecessary, that didn't matter. Very often she wanted to go out for a walk when I was busy doing something. She simply could not accept any restrictions on her movements. She always said she would just take a short walk around the houses in our colony. I had to allow her to do that, but had to remind her that she should take the walker. Mostly, she came back home without any problem. But one afternoon, she went too far and could not come back home. After more than half an hour, she came back with a young woman. I asked the woman what she wanted. She smiled a little and said, she brought my wife back home.

Maria was also often falling, at home and outside, even when she used a walker, even when I was keeping watch and guiding her through the streets. I could myself treat the smaller injuries. Sometimes, however, the injuries were so severe that a trip to the hospital became necessary, sometimes in the middle of the night. At this stage, she had become so weak, that she could not get up by herself, once she had fallen, even if she was not injured. In such cases, she did not call out for me. She simply waited for me to discover her and bring her back on her feet again. Toward the end, I could not lift her alone any more. I too was becoming ever older and ever weaker. I had to seek help.

When I had an appointment with one of my doctors, I had to take her along, because I could not let her stay at home alone. She waited patiently in the waiting room, while I underwent the examinations. Once, about one year after the big heart operation, I had to go to the hospital again with some heart trouble. I had to take Maria along. I had to persuade the hospital people to allow her to stay in the hospital as long as I stayed there. They registered her as a patient of blood circulation trouble. I had to undergo a small operation with a catheter, through which they planted a stent in my heart. We came back after about ten days. Toward the end of our stay there, we could even have our two beds in the same room. These were a few happy and amusing days.

The decision, however, was gradually ripening in my mind that I must now prepare her for the fulltime care home. First, we brought her to the day-care facility of the care home for two days a week. I would thereafter accept my appointments with doctors only on these two days. But Maria resisted. I could not persuade her to go to the day-care center with me. Finally, I had to request Biggi and Mrs. Klimecki, the Caritas care person of the old residents, to help me. Somehow, Maria did not resist, when they asked her to go with them to the day-care facility. I went in the afternoon to bring her back home. She was always elated, when she saw me waiting for her. We also arranged for a young woman to come two times a week in the late afternoon to do some conversation with her. When the weather was good, they went to the little park for two hours.

In the last three years of our living together, February 2020 to December 2022, Maria's dementia worsened rapidly. She could not recognize any old friend. When they came to visit her, she would insist that I should also sit there, because she could not herself carry on any conversation with them. That was my task, I knew them all. Once a young female Professor of women's studies came from London (SOAS University) to personally present Maria her new book, which she said was inspired by one of Maria's earlier books. This honor too Maria could not really appreciate.

Sometimes, when her old friends were narrating something, she would suddenly start loudly singing an old hit-song: "Blow boys blow, from Californio". When Prof. Silvia Federici, our best American friend, came from New York to visit her, I invited her to stay with us. She gladly did it; but Maria could not exchange even one nice sentence with her. And then, in the middle of their get-together, Maria suddenly got up and dashed out of the room. I followed her into her room and asked her what had happened. Maria replied in a loud voice: Why should she be there. What did she have to do with that woman?

I realized then that the time for the physical separation had come.

Chapter 15:
The Last Days of Maria

Toward the end, somehow, Maria was frequently coming to think of death. She told me often: "Saral, du darfst nicht vor mir sterben. Denn dann wäre ich total verloren." ("Saral, you must not die before me. Otherwise, I would be totally lost.") That was also true. I thought I replied very well. Every time she said that, I gave her a kiss and told her: "Maria, sei versichert. Ich bleibe bei dir bis zum Ende. Nur, Frage ist: wessen Ende?" ("Maria, be assured, I will remain at your side till the end. Only, the question is: whose end?")

Fact was, I too was thinking of my end. I had already had two heart attacks. One generally believes, a third heart attack is mostly fatal. What would happen to Maria, if I would again have to be rushed to the hospital. The neighbors would surely inform Biggi. But she would also need time to arrange something.

So I started thinking, what I should do. In view of the progressive deterioration of my health, I started getting doubts that I would be able to remain at her side till the end, my end. Maria was of course totally demented and confused. With age, she was also becoming ever weaker. But otherwise, purely healthwise, she was OK.

I thought, if we could not live together in the same household, the next best thing would be to put Maria on the waiting list for a room in the old people's care home of Caritas, just one minute's walking distance from our apartment. I had to decide soon. For in 2022, Maria was 91, and I was 86, a very ripe age to die for averagely healthy men. I applied for a room for Maria.

Sending Maria into "Exile" in the Care Home

It was my duty to reveal it to Maria, whose else? It was my duty to prepare her for the transfer from home to "exile". I was sure, she would feel it like being exiled. In the story of our epic *Ramayana*, when Rama had to go into exile, it was a tragic event for the whole citizenry of the Kingdom of Ayoddhya. It was they who were weeping and crying. But Rama was not weeping. For him, it was a happy exile, because he was being accompanied by his wife and brother. Maria's "exile", I was sure, would make her totally unhappy. For she would be alone there. I could not imagine how lonely she would feel there. For I could not enter into her soul, nor could she express it through a conversation.

Whenever I got a chance, I told Maria that I was ill, that I had a heart condition, that any day I might have to go to hospital. I thought it would prepare her for the care home. But to no avail. She did not understand anything. And even if she did, she would forget everything within two minutes. Naturally, it was difficult for her to understand, for she did not see me lying in bed. She saw me going around and doing everything.

After about two to three months, I got a room for Maria in the care home. Now it became earnest. Biggi took charge of making the room ready for Maria. But I could not make Maria accept the idea, because I simply could not bring myself to tell her yet that she had now to leave this beloved home of hers.

Finally, the day came. It was 6th December 2022. When Biggi came, Maria and I were sitting in the drawing room. Biggi asked me, whether I had told Maria. I had not. Then Biggi applied her authoritative voice on Maria. She said as a matter of fact: "Maria, Saral is ill. He must now go to the hospital. And you must now go to the care home." Maria was not at all taken aback. It appeared to me that she had seen through our lies. She stood slowly up and said in a clear dry voice: "Ja, ja, ich weiß, ihr wollt nur mich los werden." ("Yes, yes, I know, you only want to get rid of me.").

I swear, it was wrong, a thousand times wrong. But this was what she felt, and this was what she also spoke out. It hit me like an arrow in the heart. My heart started bleeding. It is still bleeding, while I am writing these lines, my eyes full of tears.

Biggi held Maria by the arm, and the two left the house – Maria in the slow penguin-like steps as was her wont in those days. As for me, I was so overwhelmed with so many feelings and so confused that day that I would not have been able to say what I did thereafter, if anybody had asked me in the same evening. I guess I followed them into Maria's room in the care home. And then? I do not remember.

Maria in the Care Home

I must have visited Maria the next day, the 7th December. But I do not remember anything particular from that visit. On 8th, I had an appointment with my cardiologist, Prof. Dr. Franzen. It was meant to be a routine visit. But at the end of all examinations, after looking at the data, Dr. Franzen told me that I had to go immediately to the hospital. Unless I did that, I ran the risk of getting a stroke. He added, I was 86 years old, so I might die from the stroke. I made a gesture of resignation, that meant to say, if one died at 86, then what could one do? Dr. Franzen got a little angry. He said, if I did not die, but survived the stroke, I might live on with one side of my body paralyzed. I readily agreed to go to the hospital. Dr. Franzen did not give me any time to go home and pack up some necessities of daily life. He himself told her secretary to immediately order a taxi for me, and when it came, to help me get into it. Before I left, he gave me some tablet to swallow, for the way to the hospital, as he said.

This time I had to be treated in the hospital for about ten days – a short time compared to the previous occasions.

After returning home, the first thing I did next day was to visit Maria in the care home. And thereafter every day in the afternoon, around 15.15 hours, when I guessed she, with all the other residents of that floor, had had her tea. Every time, I surprised her very much, because I came from behind. But every time, she not only recognized me but was also overjoyed to see me.

I spent about two hours every day with her. Maria was of course very old and totally demented, but she was still very lively. She asked me a lot and herself talked a lot and loudly, unlike some other demented and less old women, whom I saw there. She was old, weak and demented, but not sick. She still walked up and down the long hallway without any help. We had brought her walker in her room, but she never used it. I guess she had forgotten what it was for at all. I was afraid that, without the walker, she might fall, and what then? If she fell in the hallway, she would be noticed by somebody. But if she fell in her room with the doors closed?

I was worried, particularly because in the past, in such cases, she never called out for help. I knew that from my experience with her at home. She waited patiently, as if she knew that help, i.e., Saral, I, would come soon. When I asked a care-sister, she replied that every now and then one of them looked into the rooms. Who knows whether it was true?

I noticed that she was very proud that she had a husband (perhaps because the other old ladies on the same floor, whom she saw everyday were widows.). Once, when I came just after their teatime, and she had stood up to go to her room with me, she pointed at me with her finger and told the old lady who was sitting at the same table opposite to her: "This is my husband." The other lady laughed mildly, and just said, "Yes, Yes, I know."

The others surely knew that Maria was totally demented. That meant that nobody could have an averagely reasonable conversation with her. I saw that some four or five old ladies had formed a kind of chatting club. But Maria could not be integrated into that club. She was very lonely in that story of the care home. The only other person, who was lonely there, was an old man, a rarity in the whole care home.

She also could not go out for a walk, because, even with a walker, she was in risk of falling. I too could not take her out, because I myself was too weak and had to use a walker. Moreover, I was afraid that if I did that, she would refuse to go back to the care home and want to go with me to her own home. Only a strong person could have taken her out, holding her by the arm. I could only once see her taken out in this way. The strong woman who had taken her out also rang the doorbell of my apartment. I came out and saw Maria with that woman. She asked Maria whether she would like to go in. But she refused.

I knew by then why she refused. Maria had thought – yes, strangely, even with her high level of dementia she was thinking – that the reason why I "wanted to get rid of her", and why she had to live in the care home, was that I wanted to divorce her and live with another woman. When other female neighbors and old friends visited her, she told them that Saral had separated himself (hat sich getrennt). When I visited her, we used to have a standard, often-repeated, conversation: Maria asked: "Saral, are you married?" I replied: "Yes." Maria asked: "Do you have children?" I replied: "No.". Then I said: "I am married with you." She was surprised as well as overjoyed to hear that. Then she said: "What? You are married to me?" I: "Yes." Maria: "I am your wife? You are my husband?" To both questions I had to reply "Yes."

But then my trouble began. Maria said: "But then we must live together!" I then had to repeat my lies, that I was sick, that I was living in a hospital, where there was no place for my wife, etc. But although highly demented, Maria could not be fobbed off so easily. She developed ideas for us living together. She said we could ask the hospital authorities to put just another bed in my room. She could sleep there. She could also nurse me. (Actually, we really did it once. Had that remained in her head?). When I replied that it won't work in a hospital, she said, then she would ask the Caritas people to put another bed in her room, and I could sleep there. This way we could again live together. I agreed, and asked her to demand that of the Caritas, and left her for that day.

Two or three times we had another conversation. Maria refused to accept my lies. She did not believe that my illness was the reason for our separation. She said she knew the reason: "Yes, I treated you badly. Yes. I was too often away from home. You had too often to live alone." That was true, but that was not the reason. Surprising, that she was thinking so much about the reason of our separation, but never thought that the reason could have been her dementia and old age.

We usually had a nice two hours' time during every visit. It began with tender embraces and kisses. Then nice but repetitive conversations. Often, suddenly Maria would start singing loudly her most favorite song "Blow boys blow from Californio." But there was always trouble, when it was time for me to go. She would not let me go. She held fast onto my arm and said: "I also come with you." Or she said "Take me along!" It did not help that I promised to come again. She always followed me. Sometimes she said she would come only up to the hallway door. When we were there, she wanted to come to the next door, then up to the lift. At the last door of the hallway, I had to become hard, had to tell her rudely: "No further". She of course stopped, and I could close the door behind me. But through the glass I could see tears in her eyes. Tears also poured out of my eyes.

Maria's Death Comes

So it went on till mid-May 2023. On 6th February, we "celebrated" her 92nd birthday a little. In the beginning of May she fell once, Biggi and I visited her in the hospital. She still had her strong will, was determined to get down from her bed. The medical personnel had to give her a sedative injection. She was sent back to the care home. Nothing more could be done in the hospital, they said. She fell a second time, was sent to the hospital, and again sent back to the care home. In the third fall (within one week), she broke a pelvic bone (Beckenbein). The hospital sent her back again. The fracture would/must heal by itself, they said.

But it did not heal. Maria breathed her last breath early in the morning (3.00 hours) of May 15.

Chapter 16:
My Life After Maria's Death

On her last day before death, I went to her bedside with Biggi. I knelt down and caressed her face with both my hands. She looked at me; it was a strange look with very widely opened eyes. I wished that she said something.

So I asked her: "Maria, do you recognize me? Who am I?" She understood my question, and replied slowly in a strangely broken deep voice: "Yes, you are my most beloved one." ("Ja, du bist der Allerliebste von mir."). She perhaps could not recall my name any more, but she knew who I was. These last words of hers said to me were the greatest prize that I have ever received. I will treasure them until my death.

Suddenly, it seems, I have become a little superstitious. Suddenly, it seems I believe a little in a life after death, in a "Hereafter" ("Jenseits"). In the beautiful info-card that we sent to Maria's close relatives and best friends, there is a quote from Kant:

> "Wer im Gedächtnis seiner Lieben lebt, der ist nicht tot, der ist nur fern. Tot ist nur, wer vergessen wird." ("One who lives in the memory of his loved ones, he is not dead, he is only faraway. Dead is only one who is forgotten.")

So, I often imagine, after my death, when I have landed in "Hereafter", I go straight to Maria, embrace and kiss her and tell her: "Maria, my most beloved one, from now on, we will live together under the same roof. I will ask our Governor to put another bed in your room. I will sleep there, and I will nurse you."

Yes, I imagine it.

The Rituals After Her Death: The Funeral

There were many things to be done immediately after her death. Biggi and Jakob were all the time at my side. We had already taken the major decisions, long before and during Maria's last days. Only the work remained to be carried out. We divided up the tasks. It was Maria's desire, expressed to me long before she became demented, that she should get a traditional burial. Biggi and Jakob took up the responsibility for organizing a good one.

It was my task to inform the family and friends and to stay at home to receive the possible condoling visitors. I formulated the info-letter and sent it by e-mail to all on my mailing list, to be followed by a beautiful card sent by post. It read:

> Dear friend(s), in deep sorrow and with tearful eyes I have to inform you that Maria, my wife has passed away. After about a week of light suffering due to injuries caused by falls from the bed, she died peacefully in sleep – in the night of 14th – 15th May, 2023, at around 3 o'clock.

On the funeral day, 25th May, we had got special permission to use the condolence hall of the South Cologne burial grounds for one full hour. So we could request two of Maria's best old friends to deliver a condolence speech each: Dr. Ute Projahn and Prof. Veronika Bennholdt-Thomsen. I contributed a recorded Bangla song of Rabindranath Thakur, which he had written and composed for exactly such occasions[*].

What I found best on the occasion was the song "We shall overcome" (most prominently interpreted by Joan Baez), that Josefine, a former student of Maria, also from the Eifel, Maria's beloved home district, had proposed to be sung by all on the coffin's way to the burial place. Josefine herself began the singing. The others, some 200 to 250 funeral guests, many of whom had come from many distant places outside Cologne, sang with her, all the way to the grave. The place before the funeral hall reverberated with their chorus. It was a fitting tribute to Maria's memory. She was after all, a fighter for every good cause – all her life. It was the great tragedy of her life that, due to her progressive dementia, she could not

---

[*] A translated version of this song is located at the end of this chapter.

but withdraw herself from her struggles in the last ten years before her death.

But, in spite of this tragedy, she had not been unhappy. She was not living alone (until I put her in the old people's care home, where she had to spend only the last five months of her life). I was there at home with her, her self-chosen husband from India. I tried to make her as happy as possible in the given circumstances. In the very advanced stage of her dementia and turbidity of mind, she often said: "Saral, *es ist mein großes Glück, dass ich dich habe.*" ("Saral, it is my great good luck, that I have you.")

But in December 2022, it was I who put an end to her sense of happiness, I had to. And that was, in turn, the cause of *my* great unhappiness (mein großes Unglück). That was my great misfortune.

My mourning

Now, Maria is beyond happiness and unhappiness. Who knows how she is feeling in the far-away country "Hereafter" (Jenseits). But I am living alone in this world, inconsolable in my grief. I cannot forget that Maria did not want to go to the care home. I cannot forget her entreaties that I take her back home, when I stood up for going at the end of every visit. I cannot forget her tearful eyes on the other side of the glass door, after I had said No to her entreaties and closed the door behind me. About one year after her death, these tearful eyes are still haunting me. Whenever I am not doing anything, which had often been the case in the first two months or so after her death, and now whenever at the day's end I have gone to bed but am still awake, the memory of our last unhappy days, especially Maria's unhappy days in the care home, causes tears to swell up in my eyes.

I do not know how long I still have to live. I only know I cannot myself put an end to my life, although this world is, as a whole, a horrible place. I cannot continue to mourn Maria's absence all the time. I must have something sensible to do, in order that I forget my mourning.

Writing My Last Books

During the politically active period of my life, apart from my four full-length books, I have also been writing political-theoretical essays and articles, and trying to publish them in serious journals and magazines. In most cases, I succeeded. But there were also some which could not be published. I then photocopied them and sent them by post, free of charge, to people whom I regarded as relevant for the question I had dealt with in my said articles. That was the general practice among all political authors in the pre-computer- pre-e-mail era.

But then, when I too bought a computer and got an e-mail connection, these difficulties vanished. Previously, I used to write mostly in German, because sending articles to English-speaking or -reading countries was a costly affair. But in the computer era, it became easy. I started writing most of my essays and articles in English, and mailed them to the relevant people all over the world. Soon, I learnt the blog-technique and got two personal blogsites created for me – one each in German and English. Sometime later, I was writing only in English.

That was approximately also the time when Maria started getting her epileptic fits and required more care and attention from me. So, I had to postpone, if not give up entirely, my latest idea of writing something serious on the question of conflict and peace. But writing relatively short essays and articles was still possible, and I continued to do that. Ever since I had a computer, I published them all first in my own blogsites.

Around the end of 2022, a young Viennese friend of mine, Ernst Schriefl, so to speak, rediscovered me after about 20 years. That time, he and his friends had formed a roughly Green or ecological group within ATTAC Austria. They had invited me to Vienna to give a lecture on the renewable energies question (resp. on the relation between economic growth and ecological issues). In 2022, I had long since lost contact with him because he had changed his e-mail address and had not communicated it to me. Anyway, I received a book written by him. It was entitled *Öko-Bilanz*[*].

---

[*] Schriefl, Ernst (2021): Öko-Bilanz – Wo wir stehen, was zu tun wäre, wohin wir steuern. Norderstedt, Books on Demand.

So I was interested. I read the book immediately, at least the more important parts of it and conveyed my opinion to him.

After we had revived our contact, Ernst told me I should also publish all my English blog-articles in the same Books-on-Demand (self-publishing) system, in which he too had published his book. I found the system attractive, but also expressed my technical inabilities and unwillingness to learn a new high-tech at my old age.

To make the story a little shorter, Ernst offered his technical know-how and labor to bring out a *Collected Writings of Saral Sarkar*, and I offered some money for the wages of a helping hand with the necessary technical abilities (a friend of Ernst helped with layouting).

The two volumes of my Collected Works came out in August resp. in September 2023[*]. The publication with the help of my much younger friend gave me, frankly speaking, an enormous boost to my will to live – at a time, when I was in a very depressed mood due to Maria's death about two months earlier.

This boost, together with the psychological merit of doing something useful in the time of mourning, prompted me to revive the idea of writing something on the question of conflict and peace. The idea had not been dead, but only postponed. Originally, the idea was to write a substantially thorough book. But in view of my advanced age and my doubts about my remaining life-time, I decided to reduce my ambition and cut the idea to the size of an essay, which it might be possible to complete by the end of 2023. This projected essay was completed in time, and Ernst is presently working hard on it[†].

Now it is April 2024 and I am still living. After hearing that I had already completed the manuscript on *Factors of Conflict and Conditons of Peace* in December 2023, some of my friends asked me what I was now planning to write. Actually, at that time, I did not have any plans to write

---

[*] Note from the layouter and editor (Ernst Schriefl): A selection of articles from Saral's Collected Writings was translated into German by Bruno Kern and published by Metropolis under the title *Was ist Ökosozialismus?*. Bruno is a very good friend of both of us (Saral and Ernst), working and living in Mainz as translator and author.

[†] Sarkar, Saral (2024): Factors of Conflict and Conditions of Peace, Books on Demand (published in June 2024)

anything more. It was they, three friends (one of them was Ernst), who suggested that I should start writing my autobiography.

I had never toyed with this idea before. An autobiography was, I thought, for famous people. Even though I had written and published some theoretical and political books and many essays and articles, that would not suffice, I thought, to regard me as famous. But my friends argued that I have had a very interesting life: I spent 46 years of my life in India, in those days one of the poorest Third World countries, and thereafter, till now, 42 years in Germany, one of the richest countries of the rich West. That is, I have spent about half of my life in the Third World and the next half in the First World. In both worlds, I have made rich experiences. I have been a keen observer as well as an activist in both worlds. That has been rare, they argued.

I felt flattered as well as convinced that I should do it. I started writing, I guess around mid-January. The first draft might be ready in another two weeks. Then I will send it to Ernst, my friend and my publisher.

This is the present state of my life.

German Translation of the Bangla song (done by Saral Sarkar)

Vor uns liegt der Ozean von Frieden,
Du Steuermann, lass die Leinen los,
Du wirst sein der ewige Begleiter,
Nimm, nimm mich auf den Schoss.
Auf dem Weg zum Unendlichen
Wird für immer scheinen
Der Polarstern.

Vor uns liegt der Ozean von Frieden,
Lass los, du Steuermann, die Leinen!

Befreier, Deine Vergebung, deine Gnade
Wird der Proviant sein für die ewige Reise.

Möge die Fesseln dieser Erde brechen,
Die große Welt wartet mit offenen Armen,
Möge die Seele das große Unbekannte
Lernen furchtlos kennen.

Vor uns liegt der Ozean von Frieden,
Lass los, du Steuermann, die Leinen!
(*Rabindranath Thakur*)

Literature

Bahro, Rudolf (1977): Die Alternative. Zur Kritik des real existierenden Sozialismus, Europäische Verlagsanstalt (engl.: The Alternative in Eastern Europe NLB, London 1978)

Chattopadhyaya, Debiprasad (1992): Lokayata – A Study in Ancient Indian Materialism, People's Publishing House

Daly, Herman (1977): Steady State Economics, Island Press, Washington, DC

Gruhl, Herbert (1975): Ein Planet wird geplündert. Die Schreckensbilanz unserer Politik, S. Fischer

Kovel, Joel (2002): The Enemy of Nature. The End of Capitalism or the End of the World?, Zed Books, London

Meadows, Donella, Meadows, Dennis, Randers, Jorgen, Behrens, Willam W. III (1972): The Limits to Growth. A Report for the Club of Rome's Project in the Predicament of Mankind, Potomac Associates – Universe Books

Mies, Maria (1982): Lace Makers of Narsapur. Indian Housewives Produce for the World Market, Zed Books, London

Mies, Maria (2009): Das Dorf und die Welt. Lebensgeschichten – Zeitgeschichten, PapyRossa Verlag

Sarkar, Saral (1993): Green-Alternative Politics in West Germany. Vol. 1: The New Social Movements, United Nations University Press, Tokyo & New Delhi

Sarkar, Saral (1994): Green-Alternative Politics in West Germany. Vol. 2: The Greens, United Nations University Press, Tokyo & New Delhi

Sarkar, Saral (1999): Eco-Socialism or Eco-Capitalism? Zed Books, London

Sarkar, Saral (2010): Die Krisen des Kapitalismus. Eine andere Studie der politischen Ökonomie, AG SPAK Bücher, Neu-Ulm

Sarkar, Saral (2012): The Crises of Capitalism. A Different Study of Political Economy, Counterpoint, Berkeley

Sarkar, Saral (2023a): Eco-Socialism or "Green" Capitalism? Collected Writings of Saral Sarkar, Volume I & II, Books on Demand, Norderstedt

Sarkar, Saral (2023b): From Marxist Socialism to Eco-Socialism – Turning Points of A Personal Journey Through a Theory of Socialism. In: Eco-Socialism or "Green" Capitalism?: in: Collected Writings of Saral Sarkar, Volume 1, Books on Demand, Norderstedt

Sarkar, Saral (2024): Was ist Ökosozialismus?, Metropolis, Marburg

Sarkar, Saral (2024): Factors of Conflict and Conditions of Peace. An Essay, Books on Demand, Norderstedt

Schriefl, Ernst (2021): Öko-Bilanz. Wo wir stehen, was zu tun wäre, wohin wir steuern, Books on Demand, Norderstedt

Traube, Klaus (1979): Wachstum oder Askese? Über die Industrialisierung der Bedürfnisse, Rowohlt, Reinbek bei Hamburg

Ullrich, Otto (1979): Weltniveau – In der Sackgasse des Industriesystems, Rotbuch Verlag

v. Weizsäcker, Ernst Ulrich (1989): Erdpolitik, Wissenschaftliche Buchgesellschaft, Darmstadt